Love Is for the Living

Albion Rising: Book One

Nicholas Kinsley

I0686839

ForbiddenFiction
www.forbiddenfiction.com

an imprint of

Fantastic Fiction Publishing
www.fantasticfictionpublishing.com

LOVE IS FOR THE LIVING
A Forbidden Fiction book

Fantastic Fiction Publishing
Hayward, California

© Nicholas Kinsley, 2015

CREDITS
Editor: Lon Sarver
Cover Design: Siolnatine
Cover Art: Cover creation by Nola Bee. Adapted from photos © Stryjek and Andrei Vishnyakov at Dreamstime.com
Production Editor: Erika L Firanc
Proofreading: Nola Bee and Jae Knight

SKU: NK1-000217-02 FFP
ISBN: 978-1-62234-258-7

Published in the United States of America

Blaine looked in through the window and his stomach dropped.

The keys were still on the driver's seat.

The sound of dragging feet was definitely closer. Blaine threw a look over his shoulder and trembled when he saw how close she was, near enough that Blaine could see the muted blue colour of her clouded eyes.

Distraught, he turned back to the car and started pounding on the window. He was too scared to think, and his hands ached from how hard he beat the glass.

It was useless, of course. The infected woman was right behind him; he could see her reflection in the glass. He was about to turn around and kick her, shove her, *anything*, when a shot rang out.

Blaine screamed and went to his knees with his arms over his head. He squeezed his eyes shut, chanting, "Please don't kill me, please don't kill me, please don't kill me..."

Also recommended...

You may also enjoy these other ForbiddenFiction works:

Lovers in Arms by Osiris and Brackhaus
In 1946, after World War II, US Army Captain Frank Hawthorne is returning to Germany to testify in Nuremberg trials in the military tribunal of former Nazi Officer Johann von Biehn. Despite explicit orders to the contrary, Frank is trying to save Johann's life. Three years ago, at the height of the war, Frank had been sent to kill the very man he is now defending. With his own government forbidding Frank to reveal anything political that happened during the war, and society forcing him to conceal their personal relationship, Frank will have to find something truly unexpected to prevent Johann's all-but-certain death sentence. (M/M)
http://forbiddenfiction.com/story/OB1-1.000053

Broken Ink by Jack L. Pyke
Carrying a tattoo on your skin no longer just comes with a risk of infection. Get the composition right, you have the latest mind-control drug on the market. It's the sex-traders' dream, or worst nightmare, depending on the concentrated dose of the ink—and just who's wearing it. For Kiyen, the ink means he's able to strip raw the minds of the best and worst of society. For Falen, the ink has ensured he's spent his early years as a willing sex slave and low-grade empath. But the ink itself has a mind of its own; when Kiyen is forced into Fal's small world, prejudice battles a pure need to touch. (M/M)
http://forbiddenfiction.com/story/JP2-1.000111

ii

DISCLAIMER

For Alby, who likes zombies and sex
(not necessarily in that order), and whose artwork
inspired the original story.

Contents

Chapter 1

With a Bang

London, England
DAY 1
11:21

It was the moment just before the perfect photo. It was one of those days when the sun came out for brief periods of time, randomly and sporadically so that each occurrence seemed to reveal something of new importance, something to be cherished.

Blaine held his camera up, ready to capture just such a moment. He could sense the impending magnificence in the air, in the way the breeze pushed the clouds across the sky. He could sense it in the peaceful shift of the trees and the rustling noise of the leaves brushing against each other.

Holding himself absolutely still, Blaine watched a quiet girl sitting on a bench through his viewfinder. He brought into focus the dark waves of hair that fell over her face, spilling onto the pages of the book in her lap.

He counted seconds. *Ten, nine, eight...*

He pushed his eye more firmly against the black device in his hands, like a scientist pressing his skull to a microscope for an impossibly closer view of bacteria. He squinted and just barely made out the glint of sunshine off the corner of the girl's eyeglasses.

Seven, six, five...

It was the moment before the perfect photo, before the clouds would part and the sun would reveal fully the beauty of the quiet, unassuming girl reading a book in the park. The moment before Blaine

1

pressed down on the shutter button and captured forever a moment that would never happen again.

Four, three, two...

Overhead, the clouds were parting, moved by the same breeze that was blowing through Blaine's hair and across his skin. The shadows were shifting to the soundtrack of the leaves, the moment was nearly upon him, she was turning the page, everything was falling perfectly into place...

"Blaine! Get up!"

...and he was jolted into the waking world, where the pale, freckled face of his friend Paul hovered above, russet eyes wide with urgency.

It took a moment for Blaine to remember when and where he was — in a London flat, on a Sunday in July 2020, the summer before his second year at university. He blinked and opened his mouth to ask what Paul was interrupting his sleep for when Paul yanked his arm, pulling him roughly out of bed.

"Hey!" Blaine yelped.

"No time. Get up, come on!"

Blaine stumbled onto his feet, feeling dizzy from the sudden rush of blood that left his head. "What the hell, Paul?"

He was opening Blaine's closet and pulling clothes out. His curly hair was even more unkempt this morning, the back of his head seeming like a birds' nest. "Get as many clothes as you can stuff in a bag, get socks, get pants, get whatever you love most," he was saying.

"What?"

"Just—" Paul abruptly stopped and spun around before looking Blaine up and down hopelessly. "Just pack like it's the end of the world, okay?"

Blaine waited a moment to see if Paul was serious, if he wouldn't crack a smile in the next second and say it was all a big joke. He held Paul's gaze long, searching his friend's eyes for any trace of humour.

There was none.

Half of Blaine's mind didn't want to believe it, the other half couldn't deny that there'd been warning signs. There'd been curfews in some areas of the city, news reports that he'd barely paid attention to; things going on in distant parts of the world that he never

2

would've thought would have any importance here, in the safety of his home.

He ran from the room, needing to see for himself. He ignored Paul's shouts and hurried through the flat to look out the window, onto the street below.

Instantly, terror gripped his heart. The same neighbourhood he'd walked through a thousand times, the graffitied wall across the street, the broken bicycle that never got repaired — it was all there underneath graphic scenes that seemed to come straight out of a horror film.

One woman, clutching a child to her chest, was being followed by what Blaine assumed used to be a young man but was now a contorted monster. He was scampering about on all fours at an alarming speed, and the woman and her child barely made it into the tower block. When they did manage to close the door and shut out their attacker, it wasn't long before it gave way under the force of the creature's pounding.

Further down, an elderly woman was attacking an unsuspecting couple; businessmen shuffled along wearing tattered, bloodstained suits; two teenage girls crouched over the crushed remains of someone's skull, where brains spilled onto the pavement.

Stepping back, Blaine saw his reflection in the glass, a translucent image over the chaos on the other side. He saw his usually wavy brown hair still sticking up from sleep, streaks of blond visible underneath. He saw his brown eyes, illuminated nearly bronze by the sun. His honey complexion seemed paler than usual, and his thick eyebrows (which he took pains to shave, as they naturally formed a monobrow) were drawn together in an expression of bewilderment and fright.

In short, he saw his young, inexperienced face in the window and was suddenly even more terrified than before. He couldn't imagine himself, that boy he saw reflected back at him, walking outside into what lay beyond and surviving. He'd only just managed to leave home and go to uni — now he was meant to go into *that*?

A hand fell on Blaine's shoulder, and suddenly Paul's voice was in his ear.

"Blaine. We have to go. There'll be time to sort this shit out when we're somewhere safe."

3

Paul was right. As much as Blaine wanted to lock the doors and hide in the closet, they'd be sitting ducks here. They had to run.

"I need to make sure Emily is okay," Paul murmured.

Of course. Emily. Where was their friend amongst all this? Was she alright, was she dead, or was she whatever the creatures on the street were now?

"Right." Blaine turned from the window and started back for his bedroom. "Have you got your things together? Can you tell me what's going on while we pack?"

"I... No, sorry."

Blaine grabbed his suitcase from under his bed. "Why not?"

He looked over his shoulder when there was no answer, just in time to see Paul retreating to his own room.

Blaine went to his closet and took out an armful of clothes to shove into his suitcase. He took his rucksack to the bathroom and threw in medicine, his toothbrush, his comb, and as much loo roll as he could, just in case. When he returned to his room to get his mobile and charger, he heard the muffled tone of Paul's voice through the thin wall.

"Stay there, alright? We're coming to get you... Emily? Emily!... Board up the windows! Slide the sofa in front of the door, and don't let anyone in unless they sound like me or Blaine... I know, I love you, too..."

A scream cut through the rest of their conversation, and the danger that had been looming before, now seemed upon them. Blaine froze in the middle of zipping his rucksack and listened to the sounds of stomping feet and yelling going on in the corridor. There was the heavy thudding of frantic footsteps, and the softer, more menacing sound of something being dragged.

Suddenly Paul was in the doorway, his face flushed. "Ready to go? Good. We're getting out of here."

Blaine finished zipping his bag and slung it over his shoulder. Paul only had one bag while Blaine had a whole additional suitcase to carry around, but hopefully it wouldn't slow him down. There was no time to second-guess anything now. He'd take it as far as he could and if he ended up needing to abandon it, he supposed that would be that.

As they hurried to the door, Blaine asked, "Is Emily alright?"

"You know our Em. She's a tough one."

Blaine supposed that was the best he'd get out of Paul. Perhaps it was better not to ask too much, considering Paul's hand shook as he reached out for the doorknob.

There was a moment when each of them took a deep breath. Another when Paul looked over his shoulder into Blaine's eyes and nodded.

"All those times we said we'd go to the gym," Paul said suddenly, grinning a little. "Would've been useful now, eh?"

Blaine chuckled for his friend's benefit. He knew that's what Paul did, made light of things to get through them, but Blaine couldn't always follow, and now was one of those times. He looked between them, at their equally thin frames and fragile bones, their bony elbows and knees. He didn't feel the slightest bit able to joke about their chance of survival the way Paul did.

"We'll be fine," Blaine said. A second later, something banged on the other side of the door before sliding across the wall, making both of them jump.

"Right. Guess we've got speed on our side. Just don't trip," Paul said.

Blaine nodded, swallowing his fear. His heart was still racing, he was still sweating through his shirt, and he still had no idea what he'd woken up to, but he could also feel some sort of awareness surfacing within. It was almost as though, bouncing on the balls of his feet as he waited for Paul to open the door, he could feel some part of his natural survival instincts kicking in.

He hoped it'd be enough to get him to safety, so he could figure out what the hell was going on.

"Let's go," he said, anxious to get it over with.

After another deep breath, Paul twisted the knob, pulled the door open, and bolted out.

"C'mon, c'mon, c'mon!"

Blaine barely spared a glance at the body slumped across the corridor in the corner. He had to focus on keeping Paul in his sight, on telling the difference between monster and man, on carrying the small suitcase which was already proving a burden. When Paul suddenly turned on his heel, shouting something about the lift being no good and they had to take the stairs, Blaine tried not to fall over the discarded luggage across the floor.

At the end of the corridor was a woman backed against the wall, beating a creature back and screaming loud enough to make Blaine's ears ring. At the top of the stair was another one of the monsters bent over the sprawled body of a man, intently peeling off flesh and bringing it to his mouth. Blaine nearly *did* trip when he saw that, his suitcase threatening to throw him off balance. He gripped the railing and tore his gaze away, focusing again on the frizzy mess of Paul's head.

It was like a house of horrors, the sort of place kids went on Halloween for a fright. The stairwell reeked of corpses, sweat, and urine, and screams echoed off the walls, adding to the feeling of suffocation. It seemed to Blaine to be one never-ending tower of clawing, biting obstacles, and the only thing keeping him alive as far as he could tell was the force with which he pushed through anything that got in his way.

That, and the creatures seemed to be otherwise distracted by most of the people who'd come through before them.

Bursting out into daylight was like coming up from underwater. Blaine breathed in lungfuls of fresh air as his eyes adjusted, but even then he couldn't pause for long. Over the sound of Paul yelling his name, telling him not to fall behind, was the louder sound of a gurgling groan over his shoulder.

Turning around, the first thing Blaine noticed was the eyes. They were clouded over, the blue irises nearly entirely white, even fading into a sickly yellow around the edges. The only definite feature was the small black pupil in the centre, and the hollow effect was only worsened by the way the eyeballs were sunken into the woman's skull.

Blaine's gaze passed over the hole where the nose was meant to be, down planes of wrinkled skin to the mouth. The lips were torn away, revealing two rows of rotten teeth, and something—Blaine didn't want to ponder too hard what—dripped from the corner of her jaw.

Then, of course, were the hands, the bony claws with withered fingernails that were reaching out for him, getting closer with every passing second.

He couldn't swallow. He couldn't move. All he could do was stand there in terror as this *thing* leaned closer in, overwhelming him with its rancid smell.

"BLAINE, RUN!"

The sound of Paul shouting his name unfroze him and he spun around just as the skeletal fingers brushed his shirt. There was another one of them in front of him, just off to his right, and he only barely made it past by shimmying along the wall to his left. Paul grabbed hold of his sleeve the instant he was within reach.

"Stay close, mate," he said, pushing Blaine forward before taking off into a run himself.

Blaine grit his teeth and kept on. Emily didn't live too far. He hadn't eaten anything and his body was starting to complain, but he pushed himself onward, telling himself that they'd all be together soon, that they'd find somewhere to go and work through it. They'd survive.

Most of the run to Emily's was a blur. It was all shapes and sounds, mainly focusing on not slowing down no matter how tired his limbs felt, and keeping up with Paul. But, occasionally, certain sights and sounds pierced through the fog of determination.

Like the little girl in a white dress cowering in front of a shop. She had red bows in her hair, contrasting enough to catch Blaine's attention amongst everything else. She was crying into her knees, arms above her head in a futile attempt to hide from the monster looming over her. Blaine told himself not to slow down, not to lose focus, but as he passed he couldn't close his ears to the sound of her sobs.

"Mummy! Mummy, help me!"

Blaine ignored the urge to stop, even as he heard her continue screaming behind him. What could he do anyway? He didn't have a weapon and he couldn't save her when he barely had a plan to save himself.

Keep going, don't think about it, just keep going.

When they finally made it to Emily's building, Blaine felt like his arms were going to fall off. He wanted to collapse on the ground right then. Carrying the suitcase around, forcing his heart to work harder than it had in ages — he was reaching his limit.

Paul looked worse off than him. His usually frizzy curls were damp with sweat, a few strands plastered to his forehead. He was dripping in perspiration, each breath a laboured huff that seemed as desperate for oxygen as the last, but still he kept going.

"We're nearly there, Blaine, c'mon," he said as he grabbed Blaine's hand to keep close.

Inside, it was just as bad as the building they'd left. The walls exaggerated everything—the screams, the blood, the filth. It'd been completely different before, as clean and sterile as a hospital. The state of the place now, crawling with what seemed to be walking corpses and overrun with panicked people, just made terror grip Blaine's heart once more.

How were they meant to get through all of this to Emily?

The same way they got out of their building, apparently. Like here, the lifts seemed to be in working order, but were too crowded to be of any use. One of them was even blaring an alarm because the detached bottom half of a corpse wouldn't allow the doors to close.

No, they'd have to take the stairs, to go against the flow of onrushing people and brave the unthinkable.

This is madness, Blaine thought as Paul pulled him along. Dodging blows on the way up, they passed more crying children, more bodies sprawled over steps, and more men and women who were trying in vain to beat back the dead. Realising he would eventually need to do *something* similar to what these others were doing, Blaine went as far as swinging his suitcase a few times. It seemed the creatures had terrible balance, and went falling down the stairs with the slightest misstep.

Blaine was even gaining confidence, starting to think they really would survive. Then he saw something of the same spider-like build as the creature who'd chased the woman from before. It leapt onto the wall of the stairwell and skittered along the vertical surface.

"Paul!"

Paul was currently trying not to be barrelled over by a giant of a man wearing nothing but a bathrobe. He looked over his shoulder at Blaine, clutching the railing.

"What?"

It was on the ceiling now, latched on, right above their heads. From this close, Blaine could make out a face from under the long black hair—high, sharp cheekbones, close-set, curved eyes, and a long pointed nose over a mouth that was now stretching wide open to let out a piercing screech.

Blaine raised a shaking finger. "Up there."

Paul only glanced at it a second. He darted his eyes up, darted them back down as he swore under his breath, then grabbed Blaine's hand again.

"Go, go, go!"

Once more, they were off, putting more and more distance between them and the lurking creature above.

Emily lived on the seventh floor. Even over the screaming, groaning, and yelling, Blaine could hear Paul's sigh of relief when they reached it.

"Told ya we'd make it," Paul said, shooting Blaine a smile over his shoulder.

"Yeah. Let's not jinx it when we're so close. That thing from the ceiling is still out and about."

Paul nodded. Emily's flat was just around the corner, not four doors down. Blaine worried when he saw that a few of the other doors were splintered open or gone altogether, but luckily Emily's wasn't one of them.

"Em?" Paul called, banging on the door. "Em, it's me and Blaine, let us in."

Emily's muffled voice answered through the layer of reinforced wood. "Paul?"

"Yeah, open up before we get mauled to death!"

A few seconds later, after the sound of something heavy being dragged away, the door opened. Blaine let out a sigh of relief when he saw Emily unharmed. Her short, pink hair looked about as brushed as his—which was to say, not at all—and she, too, had shadows of exhaustion under her eyes, but was otherwise the same as ever.

Paul hurried inside, and Blaine followed. Emily shut the door as soon as they cleared the doorway, then returned the armchair in front of it.

After that, Paul was all over her.

"Are you okay? You sounded upset on the phone. Have you heard from your dad?"

9

Emily put her hands on Paul's shoulders and smiled. "I'm fine. Better now you're here."

"And your dad? Did he answer your call?"

Blaine made his way toward the kitchen, hoping it was as spared from disaster as the rest of the flat so he could finally eat something. He dropped his suitcase and rucksack by the sofa, then froze under the single light in the corridor when he saw what lay on the kitchen floor.

To his left, Emily was telling Paul what Blaine was seeing for himself. "My dad's fine for now, but there's something you should know..."

Blaine backed away until he hit the wall. He suddenly felt ill, and put his hand over his mouth just in case.

"...burst in just after I got off the phone with you. It's in the kitchen."

Slumped against the cupboard was one of those *things*, a kitchen knife sticking out of its skull. Its clouded eyes seemed to be staring right at Blaine, and rivulets of thick, black blood poured out of the wound in its head, streaming down its rotted face.

There was a person under there, Blaine saw that now. It'd been easy enough to see them as monsters when they were active and chasing after him, but now, unmoving and seemingly harmless, this one just looked sad. The lank brown hair draped over the shoulders, the sunken in chest barely covered by a torn yellow shirt... Everything about it gave Blaine the impression of a corpse desecrated after death. It wasn't right.

Paul was suddenly at Blaine's side. "Oh my God."

"Got its blood all over my clothes," Emily said. "Had to shower and change and everything."

Paul took a deep breath. "Okay. So we know head wounds kill them, or at least get them to stop moving. That's something, yeah?" He nudged Blaine. "Blaine?"

It's staring at me, oh God it's staring at me.

"Blaine!"

"Close the eyes," Blaine said, turning away. "Or cover them. Something. Just make it stop staring."

Emily walked forward, but Blaine couldn't see much else in his peripheral vision. He saw the shape of her arm reach out, then shut his eyes against the sight.

He could still hear screams out in the corridor, the sound of that scampering mutation on the walls. Everything felt wrong. Blaine's skin prickled with unease and he itched all over.

How could Emily be so calm about this? He'd never have been able to simply clean himself up and go about things as normal after dealing with the thing in the kitchen.

"Let's sit down, mate," Paul said, taking Blaine's arm. "Come on."

Sitting on the sofa back in the living room, Blaine did feel a bit better. But he also felt somewhat like he was in a dream. After all the running and shoving, after the exhausting trip to get here, Blaine almost couldn't believe it was all happening. Flashes of the journey shot across his mind—the frantic escape down the stairwell, the crying girl in the white dress, the creature on the ceiling—and he almost couldn't convince himself that it had really happened.

One look at his surroundings should've been convincing enough. The hordes of people in the corridor, desperately trying to save themselves, should've been enough. But it all passed through Blaine's senses as though he were hallucinating, as though none of it were real.

He put his elbows on his knees, sunk his fingers into the thick mess of his hair, and tried to breathe. His heart was still pounding too fast, his stomach was still all clenched up from hunger, and he was still shaking uncontrollably.

"I forgot my camera," he said, to no one in particular.

"That's alright," Paul said. "I forgot my video games."

11

Chapter 2

Infection

Portsmouth
THE DAY BEFORE
16:37

In Andrew's daydream, he wasn't stuck on land. Though his eyes were closed, and sunlight shone through his eyelids, colouring his vision orange and pink, he saw past it to the ocean. He saw the clear blue of the surface deepening into indigo. He saw the spray of white where water splashed against the boat, the momentary rainbow, then the azure sky above. He inhaled and smelled the salt so acutely he could almost taste it.

But Andrew wasn't at sea. The scent of the water wasn't quite the same. Close to shore, the pure scent he knew so well was always polluted with land smells. And he could hear the sounds of others on the dock around him, footsteps thudding as they hurried to and fro, carrying out some urgent order.

"Lieutenant Peterson."

Andrew snapped his eyes open and turned on his heel, away from the water. He didn't know the young man who'd addressed him, a brown-eyed lad with far too much enthusiasm, but saw from the insignia on the collar that he was a Midshipman.

"What is it?" Andrew demanded.

"Commander Green sent me to—"

"Where is he?"

"He said you'd know. Sir."

Andrew suppressed a smile. Yes, when that was the answer to his question, he did know where Commander Green was, and that they would have the utmost privacy.

"Of course," Andrew, said. "Thank you."

He left the midshipman on the dock. He knew his way to where Green was waiting.

16:44

Commander Luke Green was leaning over a desk of documents when Andrew walked in. He didn't look to be particularly interested in them, as was evident in the slump of his shoulders and the frustrated furrow in his brow.

Luke was the sort of man who didn't look like he should be as highly ranked as he was, considering his slender build and naturally meek expression. Andrew had thought his friend would always rank lower than him until the end of their service. He'd been as surprised as Luke when he'd heard the news of the promotion to Lieutenant Commander. The second time, to Commander, had been even more of a shock.

Luke Green, a commander at twenty-seven. Andrew was more than a little jealous, but so far it hadn't spoilt their friendship. Luke was in Comms & Info anyway, a submariner, while Andrew was a Marine. The circumstances were entirely different. Sort of.

Andrew wasn't an overly tactile person. He didn't touch anyone if he could help it, and even felt awkward hugging his own sister. Things weren't like that with Luke, though of course they had been at the start. Luke was warm and friendly, and usually made Andrew feel comfortable no matter the situation. It seemed to be the normal progression of things that quick touches start to linger a bit, quiet moments of comfort turning into something more heated.

They weren't involved. They weren't in love in the slightest, though they did love each other, Andrew supposed. Perhaps the best way Andrew could put it was "close friends with benefits."

Luke brightened the instant he noticed Andrew's presence. A wide smile stretched across his long face, making his green eyes twinkle with delight.

"Peterson!"

Andrew finally let himself grin fully, and relaxed his practiced attentive stance. "Green."

He knew how he must've looked to Luke — two years older, freshly shaved, standing with the confidence of a man who'd successfully endured Hell for his country again. His hair — which when he wasn't required to keep short, he liked wearing much longer, with a fringe hiding his high forehead — was cut close on the sides, and was no doubt sticking up a bit on top from being blown by the wind on the dock. Though the natural tone of his skin was almost a creamy milk colour, it was more often than not a bronzed butterscotch from being out in the sun.

Based on the amused glint in Luke's eyes, Andrew knew also that his old friend was eyeing his ears. They were large ordinarily, when he let his straight blond hair grow out to cover the tips, but with the sides of his head shaved, he knew they had to appear larger than normal, something about which Luke never tired of teasing him.

"I had to hear from someone else you've been back three days. Why didn't you ring?" Luke asked.

"Why didn't you? What's all this sending a middie to come fetch me?"

Luke waved it off. "It's good for them. Keeps them on their toes and all that."

"So how're things on land?" Andrew asked, nodding at the important-looking documents between them. "I take it you've been back longer than me. Enjoying it?"

Luke walked around the desk as Andrew stepped forward to return the embrace before the thought even crossed his mind. Though they were nearly the same height, the top of Luke's dark-haired head nearly level with Andrew's blond one, Andrew was broader and more muscular, while Luke was more lean. Andrew always felt he had to be gentle when hugging his friend.

"Would be enjoying it more if I had my best mate with me," Luke said into Andrew's ear. He gave one final squeeze then stepped back enough to plant a kiss on Andrew's lips.

Andrew kissed back, glad to feel his friend again after so long away. "Unlike some people, I joined the Navy to be out at sea. You know I can't stand being landlocked for long."

Luke sighed, caressing Andrew's plump lower lip with a finger before thumbing the dimple in his chin. Andrew had long since gotten used to such tender gestures, though there'd been a time when he would've protested being treated so gently. He knew now it was just part of Luke's personality, and though he wasn't a man for sentiment, he could allow Luke to be.

"You've been staring at it again. Your eyes are as blue as the water, like they've been soaking up the colour," Luke remarked.

"And you're a bit pale from being inside all the time. What else is new?"

Luke chuckled and turned to walk back around the desk. By the time he'd taken up his old place, Andrew could tell they were to return to business. He'd wondered if this wasn't meant to be solely a social visit. They were once again Commander and Lieutenant.

"About being landlocked," Luke began. "I'm afraid I have some troubling news."

"I didn't expect to be sent out again right away, of course."

Luke shook his head. "That's not it. While you were gone, we've had a few incidents. It's why we had to bring you home early."

"I'm aware there've been quarantines in some of the larger cities. I did wish to ask but wasn't sure I had the clearance."

"We haven't had much of an issue here, but London especially has been worrisome."

"May I ask why?"

Luke sighed again, and dropped his gaze to the papers on the desk. "In the simplest of terms, I suppose you could say there's been an infection."

The words echoed in Andrew's head over and over. *An infection, an infection, an infection.*

If there were quarantines going into effect, it had to be something serious.

"It's expected to spread rapidly," Luke continued.

"What symptoms?" Andrew dared to ask. He was too frightened to ask if there was a treatment or if it was fatal. He had a feeling he wouldn't like the answer.

Luke frowned, fingers drumming over the wooden desk, but finally plucked up a page decisively. He held it out to Andrew, offering it silently, but with a meaningful look.

Andrew wasn't meant to be seeing this. It was classified top secret, above his clearance. The only reason Luke was showing him was because of their relationship.

Not wasting time, Andrew took it. He scanned the contents of the page as quickly as he could, taking advantage of the opportunity.

16 July 2020

National Institute for Communicable Diseases

After 37 days of testing, the following results have been concluded:

A. Subjects begin to show adverse symptoms between 6 and 10 hours after initial infection.
B. Stages of infection can be summarised as follows:
   1. Intense pain at the site of injury, lasts approximately 1 hour.
   2. Fever. Generally begins during hour-long first stage and persists through Stage 3.
   3. Numbness, deterioration of brain capacity, loss of function. Subjects report feeling listless, lethargic, and apathetic.
   4. Aggressive, violent behaviour. Subjects exhibit cannibalistic tendencies.
      a. Several subjects afflicted with Stage 4 infection began to show signs of physiological mutations, such as:
         a. Extended limbs
         ii. Increased mobility of joints
         iii. Increased speed of movement
         iv. Lengthened teeth
         v. Lengthened nails
      b. Mutations are suspected to be result of

variation in virus. No tests have been completed as of yet.
  c. Further physiological changes as a result of decreased brain function include:
    i.   Failure to repair skin tissue
    ii. Decreased rate of postmortem bodily decay
    iii. Failure to send and receive pain signals
    iv. Loss of speech capability
C. Spread of infection (for now) limited to exposure of infected saliva and blood to healthy bloodstream. Researchers scratched by violent subjects have not as of yet shown signs of infection.
D. Due to permanent damage done to critical regions of the brain, the virus is currently irreversible and incurable.

What the hell? he thought. *Cannibalistic tendencies?*

"Where's the National Institute for—"

"South Africa," Luke answered. "The date on that was two days ago. The place is destroyed now."

"Destroyed? Entirely?"

"Entirely." Luke reached across the desk and Andrew handed back the page. "We've been trying to keep it quiet. Minimise panic while the scientists worked on some form of treatment or cure, and all that."

Andrew nodded. "Of course."

"With the destruction of the research facility, that doesn't appear to be an option anymore. The quarantines and curfews were meant to keep an eye on the status of the public health and neutralise any threats—"

"Neutralise?"

Luke gave him an even look. "A few people were showing symptoms. They had to be dealt with before they reached Stage Four and posed a threat to the public."

Neutralised. Dealt with. If those weren't enough to give Andrew an idea of what had been done, the look in Luke's eye was.

"How long has this been going on? The report says thirty-seven days of testing."

"About two months," Luke replied. "The first reported instance was in early May, not far from the west coast of Africa."

Andrew blanched. "*I* was on the west coast of Africa!"

"Another reason why we brought you home early. We need everyone at our disposal here."

"Just tell me what's going on, Luke."

Luke was back at Andrew's side in three long strides, gripping Andrew's elbow hard enough to hurt.

"A national state of emergency, Andrew, that's what's going on. There's going to be VIP boarding on armed cruise ships and they'll need every man available to keep unauthorised people from trying to get on."

"They," Luke had said. No longer "we." Because Luke knew Andrew wouldn't do it. Andrew was loyal to the Royal Navy as much as anyone else, but he'd kill himself before killing an innocent.

"What do *you* want me to do?"

Luke looked as torn between duties as Andrew was. "It's not for me to say."

"Say it anyway."

Luke's touch turned gentle, his clutching hold softening. His lips were nearly against Andrew's when he said, "I want you to spend one more night with me. Then I want you to find Madison and get on one of those ships."

"Here is the safest place for me."

"Here is where they want you to kill ordinary citizens who are only trying to survive. Your sister deserves a chance, and you can protect her."

"Protect her from what?" Andrew asked, pulling away a bit to meet Luke's eyes. "What are these infected subjects? What exactly are we fighting?"

Luke raised a hand to hold Andrew's face and stared at him earnestly. "I need you to stay calm, Andrew."

Andrew clenched his jaw and yanked Luke's hand down by the wrist. "Stop touching me and tell me. You know everything between us stays between us. You can trust me, so just give it to me straight and I won't tell a soul."

Luke's expression turned serious and he retreated, once more taking up his official role. Andrew waited as patiently as he could, but his patience was wearing thin.

"Cannibalistic tendencies?" Andrew prompted, quoting the report. "What's that about?"

Again, Luke sighed. He leaned against the wall beside his desk, crossing his arms.

"In colloquial terms," he said. "Zombies."

Andrew barked out a laugh. "You're mad."

"Do you need to read the file again?" Luke quipped angrily, pushing off the wall. "Because I've read it five times already. 'Decreased rate of postmortem bodily decay,' 'spread of infection limited to exposure to infected saliva.' What else does it sound like?"

Andrew shook his head. "No."

"There are video recordings as well. The day of the laboratory's destruction was caught on security cameras. Those *things* broke free and overran the place. Now the virus is gaining a foothold here and we have no idea how to stop it. The world governments have known for *weeks*, Andrew, it's just a matter of crowd control now."

"You want me to go, then?" Andrew nearly shouted. "You want me to abandon my men to save my sister from the zombies? Maybe that's the sort of cowardly thing you would do, but—"

"Do you *want* me to order you to kill civilians? Is that it?" Luke asked, stepping into Andrew's face again. "I'm giving you a choice, Andrew. Do the cowardly thing and run, save your sister, or stay here and be the murderer they want you to be. It's as simple as that."

As simple as that. Luke always made things simple for himself, probably, Andrew suspected, because it made things easier on his conscience. Not to mention the RN liked simple. They liked decisive leaders. Andrew was capable of it, for how else would he have made it to Lieutenant? But he didn't like making things simple. Not everything was black and white in the world, and the Navy tended to frown upon people who questioned authority too much.

"You don't have to decide right this minute," Luke said, softening once again. "You have until tomorrow. But even now, the clock is ticking."

"I know."

Luke placed a hand on the small of Andrew's back. "Are you staying at your usual place?"

18:37

It was rare that Andrew offer himself to be the one receiving, but he wanted it tonight. He felt particularly empty after two years away, and wanted Luke to fill the void.

And if what Luke claimed was true, if the end was nigh, Andrew had better make this the fuck of a lifetime.

"Want you to fuck me tonight," Andrew panted. He ended with a low moan that had everything to do with the way Luke was tonguing the tip of his cock.

Luke pulled off with a loud smack and grinned up at Andrew from between his legs. "Alright. Turn over."

Andrew slid back and turned on his stomach. He spread his knees and pillowed his head on his folded arms as he waited.

The initial breach of a finger, slick with lube, made him wince. It had been a while, even considering the time before he left. When the finger retreated, leaving a dull ache, Andrew began to relax.

"You've tanned, you know," Luke said over the sound of ripping foil. "Skin's a bit orange. Hair's more blond."

"African sun'll do that," Andrew muttered.

"You ready?"

Andrew curved his spine a bit more, raising his arse. "Yeah."

It hurt sliding in, more than Andrew remembered. He curled his fingers in the sheets and bit his lip until he couldn't take any more.

"Slower," he managed.

"Almost there."

Luke retreated a bit before pushing back in. Andrew exhaled as slow as he could, forcing himself to relax.

Then it was there. Luke's thighs pressed flush against the back of Andrew's, and Andrew felt his hole swallowing every glorious inch of the cock lodged inside him. He felt stretched. He felt full.

"God, I missed you," Luke sighed as he ran a hand up Andrew's back, the other squeezing one of Andrew's buttocks. "And your *arse*. Christ, it's like sliding into a glove."

Andrew let himself be caressed for a moment, but then pushed back, rolling his hips.

"Come on, then."

Luke chuckled, then pulled Andrew up by his shoulders into a kneeling position. Andrew had to bend his back even more to keep himself at the most pleasing angle.

"You know the game," Luke purred as he slung an arm around Andrew's neck. "The one doing the fucking makes the rules."

Andrew clenched his arse and rolled his hips again. The pain was nearly gone now, and he was done with the games, was ready to take it in earnest.

"So make the rules," he challenged.

Luke gave a good thrust forward, expelling a sudden gasp from Andrew's mouth. Andrew had to reach back and grab hold of Luke's hip to keep from falling forward.

"Rule number one. Always respect your commanding officer."

Andrew laughed breathlessly, even as Luke started plunging in and out more forcefully. "Oh, I'm gonna shoot you."

"Rule number two," Luke continued, and now Andrew could feel the smile against his left ear. "Stop getting more gorgeous every time I see you. Those lips'll be the death of me."

"Suppose I'll have to invest in a—*nngh*—in a mask."

"Fuck yeah you will."

Faster, faster, and now Andrew's heart was pumping, almost in time to the slap of flesh. He wrapped a hand around his cock and let his head fall back as he began stroking, which was just perfect given the way Luke's arm was tightening around his throat. The feeling of Luke thrusting in and out, firm and penetrating, was just what Andrew needed.

"And finally, rule number three. Stay alive."

The last rule was followed abruptly by a wet kiss to Andrew's neck. Andrew pushed down the feelings that rushed to the surface in favour of focusing on the present pleasure. He wouldn't let two little words ruin the moment when the next day was sure to bring enough pain.

Instead, he closed his eyes and lost himself to the sensation of Luke's hands on him, fingertips roaming over his skin. He broke the first rule and started rocking back, taking Luke's cock as deep as it would go and moaning when Luke's hand wrapped around his own.

"You never were one for following rules, were you?"

Andrew meant to reply, but his mouth only made it as far as opening. The only sound that came out was a choked off gasp when Luke gave another forceful thrust, jerking Andrew out of his rhythm. After that, Andrew thought maybe giving in and letting Luke fuck him at his own pace wasn't a bad idea.

It was a good pace, after all.

It got better when Luke unwound his arm from around Andrew's neck and bent him forward, pushing him once again onto hands and knees. Andrew grunted at the new position but immediately felt the benefits. Luke widened his legs and slammed into him, shoving in deeper. Andrew put his forehead over his arms and braced himself to do nothing but take what was being given.

Fuck, Luke.

Luke was rarely ever so rough, and when he was, Andrew suspected it was some form of overcompensation. Andrew's muscles bulged impressively whereas Luke's were more toned and lean. Luke was slim where Andrew was built. Of course whenever Andrew wanted to switch up the roles Luke tried to make up for the difference.

Andrew didn't mind. Some part of him was even smug that Luke felt the need to prove his strength.

Andrew could tell it was nearly over when Luke's hand returned, slender fingers curling around his dick. He could tell when Luke picked up speed and started panting in his ear. He could tell even more when Luke started grunting and groaning.

"Back up," Luke said hoarsely, pulling Andrew by the shoulders again. Andrew followed, just as eager to finish as Luke. He planted his knees on either sides of Luke's and started doing the very thing Luke had forbade in the first place—he leaned back and started fucking himself on Luke's cock, taking his pleasure his own way with subtle rolls of his hips and quick strokes of his hand.

"Oh fuck," Andrew whined, throwing his head back. His balls were drawn up, he could feel the heat coiling in his thighs, and any second he was going to explode.

God, that's so good, oh Jesus

Pulsing heat rushed out of him, a stripe of it painting his chest, and he clenched around Luke to anchor himself. He exhaled as the rest ran over his hand, and held himself as steady as he could while Luke fucked into him a few more times, chasing his own release.

With a final moan, Luke went still as well, before at last collapsing and going boneless. Andrew pushed himself up and off, then fell onto his back on the bed.

"Think we both needed that," Luke remarked with a breathy chuckle.

Andrew sighed and stared at the blank hotel ceiling. He felt good. He felt great. But he could also feel duty and responsibility looming over his head. It was the same nearly every time he and Luke did this, but so much worse now.

"What are we doing, Luke?"

By that time, Luke had gone to the bathroom and returned with a towel for Andrew, tossing it over his stomach.

"What d'you mean?" Luke plopped on the bed next to Andrew and put his hands behind his head. "Isn't it obvious?"

"Not the fucking, idiot." Andrew wiped himself off, folded the towel, then wiped his forehead as well. "Earlier today you told me it's the end of the world, that zombies are headed our way, and now here we are messing around."

Luke shrugged. "What would you rather do? Panic?"

"Could be preparing."

"What good would that do? How do you prepare for something like this?" Luke cut Andrew off before he could even reply. "There's mental cases who spend half their lives preparing for some sort of apocalypse and chances are they die along with everyone else. Then there's people who don't have a clue and manage to survive anyway. Don't stress about it, Andrew. It could happen in two minutes, to-morrow, a week from now, and everyone would still be in the same boat."

"Honestly, it's a wonder you're a commander. Sometimes I get it, and sometimes I just have to ask myself how in the hell—"

"Yeah, yeah, yeah, shut up already. I know you hate it, but c'mere, we're having a cuddle."

Andrew groaned, but he only half-heartedly tried to slide away.

"And in the morning you'll phone your sister," Luke continued once he'd got Andrew where he wanted him. "Check up on her and all."

"Yeah." A few seconds passed in which Andrew simply let Luke handle him the way he pleased, but then he had to ask. "Do you really think it could happen at any moment? Shouldn't the public be notified?"

Luke grunted in Andrew's shoulder. Andrew knew it was the only answer he'd get out of him.

Chapter 3

The Dead Land

London
DAY 1
18:49

"Do not leave your homes. Repeat, do not leave your homes. Contact with the virus spreads infection. Exposed citizens reportedly show symptoms within only a few hours. Please take every precaution and stay indoors. Do not leave your homes."

"Turn it off," Blaine snapped.

Paul pressed a button, but it wasn't to shut the telly off. It was to change the channel.

" – are saying it came from the Russians, others from the Chinese. What do you think, Niall?"

"To be honest, David, I'm with those who say the Americans brought it. About what time did all this start happening? One o'clock this morning. What time did that cruise ship dock? About midnight. I don't know what experiments they're up to over there, but have you taken a look at some of their news headlines? The president himself has released a statement urging people to leave the midwest region as they consider impromptu cleansing – "

"I said turn it off!"

Blaine snatched the remote out of Paul's hand and clicked off the screen. He'd had enough of it all for one day. If he wanted to see the world falling to pieces, he'd look out the window. If he wanted to see more of those walking corpses, he'd go ten yards to the kitchen.

It had finally got quiet out in the corridor and now he wanted to sit here and pretend everything was normal, at least while he still could.

Paul was of another mind. "We need to stay informed!"

"Right now, we need to stay safe."

"Which we'd be able to do if we were knew what we were up against." When Blaine didn't acknowledge Paul with a response, Paul looked to Emily sitting in the chair on his left. "Tell him, Em. Your dad was in the Army or RAF, one of those. He'd say to keep informed, wouldn't he?"

Emily didn't say anything either. She blinked once, slowly lifted her hand to scratch absentmindedly at her shoulder, then let her hand fall back down to her lap.

"Em."

Blaine eyed her more closely. A sheen of sweat had formed over her skin, and she looked sickly. Her usually tawny complexion had yellowed into some sort of strange ginger colour.

Her eyes were even worse. On top of being listless and dull, her unblinking eyes made it seem like the lights in her head had gone out entirely.

"You alright, Emily?" Blaine asked hesitantly.

Paul waved a hand before her eyes, and that finally got a reaction out of her. She blinked and slid her gaze to Paul.

"Huh?"

"Everything okay?" Paul asked.

"Oh. Sorry. Yeah. Just tired, I guess."

"Tell Blaine we need to stay informed. So we know how to deal with those things when we need to make a run for food and all."

Her eyes slid over Paul to Blaine, and Blaine got that prickly feeling again. She seemed to have thinned remarkably in only a matter of hours, skin stretching taut over her cheekbones and temples. Staring blankly at Blaine, she looked worse than sickly, and her shock of pink hair was now more incongruously vibrant than ever. She looked near death.

Blaine couldn't believe she was still capable of thought, let alone speech. "We need to stay informed," she said, reaching up to scratch her shoulder again. "I'm sure that's what my dad's doing. Probably arming himself, even."

"Told ya," Paul said, then held his hand out for the remote.

Emily got to her feet, pushing herself up off the armrests. "I'm gonna lie down for a bit. I'm more tired than I thought."

Paul seemed to forget the remote entirely as he suddenly stood with her. "Are you sure everything's alright?"

"Yeah. Fine."

Paul raised a hand to her forehead, brushing back her pink fringe, and frowned. "You're sweating. I think you've got a fever."

"I'm fine," she insisted. "Just feel a bit off. I'm gonna lie down a bit."

"I'll come with you."

"No, you should stay here." She glanced at Blaine, and Blaine couldn't help but tighten his grip on the remote. He hardly recognised his friend. "Blaine needs you. You know how he is," she finished.

Anger flared, and before Blaine knew what he was doing, he'd snapped, "I'm sorry we can't all be as bad-ass as you. My father was a musician, not a killer."

Paul shot him a warning look, but it proved unnecessary when all Emily did was turn and walk to her bedroom without another word. Blaine huffed and crossed his arms. He'd thought he was doing rather well considering the circumstances.

"Oh, stop pouting, you know your monobrow always freaks me out when you do that," Paul said, flicking Blaine's ear.

Blaine resisted the urge to rub between his eyes, because he knew Paul was just being a twat. He'd shaved only two days ago, so there was no way the hair that usually bridged the gap had grown back yet.

"Fuck off."

Paul plopped back down on the sofa next to him, running a hand through his wild curls. "Seriously, though. You gonna be okay?"

Blaine shrugged. "Too soon to tell. Yesterday everything was normal, and now it's all..." He sighed and brought his legs up to wrap his arms around his calves. "I haven't even phoned my mum. I'm sure she's worried sick."

"Benefits of being an orphan, eh," Paul muttered.

"At least you're with Emily."

"Yeah, at least there's that."

Blaine put his forehead on his knees, and for a few moments there

27

was silence. That was almost worse than the television, because any second Blaine expected the calm to be disrupted. He expected the screaming to start again or one of those crawling monsters to skitter across the ceiling. He thought perhaps the dead thing in the kitchen wasn't completely dead after all, and half believed himself to be feeling bony fingers clutching his shoulder from behind.

"Here," he said, tossing Paul the remote. "Turn the stupid thing back on if you want."

Paul grinned in victory and switched the TV on. The glow of the screen lit up the room, replacing the fading light from the window and throwing shadows over the walls.

" – *can now confirm that it is, in fact, contagious. What we seem to be facing here is a bloodborne virus, though the origin is still unknown,*" a woman was narrating.

The camera flew over the top of high-rise buildings where people had barricaded the roof exits and had now settled down for the night. Candles and torches lit pockets of survivors, though below, electric lights hadn't gone out just yet.

"*Just seven, almost eight hours after the initial event authorities are calling the Outbreak, many people have now taken shelter on the roofs of their homes, while others choose to stay in – perhaps the safer location – personal residences.*"

"Fucking idiots," Paul scoffed.

"Which ones?"

"All of them."

Now the screen showed the streets of what Blaine figured used to be Hackney. Glass of broken shop windows was scattered across the pavement, cars were on fire, ordinary men who'd happened to have guns were shooting the mindless hordes. The camera panned over to a row of houses where windows and doors had been covered in red tape.

"*Some believe this to be the work of a higher power, and, as in the Bible, mark their homes with what they believe will keep out the plague. Sights such as this one, among others, have become common in many neighbourhoods, as people desperately strive to be spared from the effects of this tragic event. Still others follow the path of the more conventionally religious, and make their way to the house of God.*"

Now it showed St Paul's Cathedral, which was just as lit up with lights and candles as the high-rise buildings. The doors were shut, and it seemed both monster and man alike were pounding on them, demanding entry. Blaine wondered how many people had managed to get inside while they'd had the chance.

Abruptly, the narrator herself appeared, her image superimposed on the background of the church. The first thing Blaine noticed was her striking red lipstick, then the curled ends of her almost equally red hair and how they swept up dramatically, flaring off to the side. It was amazing how even at the end of the world some people took pains to do their hair.

"Earlier some of our reporters contacted Jane Welling, Chief of the Defence Staff, and asked her if today's events were somehow linked to the series of quarantines that have been occurring over the past two months. Until now there's been no response, but it seems we've just received confirmation that the quarantines and today's Outbreak are, in fact, in no way related – "

A shot rang out and suddenly she was falling left, out of the frame. The background view of more people stretching red tape over windows faded, until the screen showed the empty field where she and the remote-controlled reporter camera had apparently been filming before the camera jerked to the right and showed a bloody-faced man holding a pistol.

His hair was sticking up in tufts, and though he was large in the stomach and had fat hanging from his upraised arm, he seemed healthy enough to have survived so far. The up and down heaving of his shoulders suggested he'd been running.

"Fucking liars, the lot of you!" he screamed, waving the gun around. *"You cunts knew all about this, didn't you? Didn't you?!"*

Blaine gaped. "Oh my God."

Onscreen, the man pointed his gun at the camera, and for a moment Blaine felt it was pointing right at him. The man had a crazed look in his dark, beady eyes, and Blaine almost believed he would crawl through the TV.

The reporter camera didn't stick around for long. Whoever was controlling the device moved it far in the air, out of danger, and the last thing it showed before switching off was the large man on the grass surrounded by others, some of them shooting infected and some aiming at the camera.

The screen went black. There was nothing but the hum of the television for a few seconds, as if the channel had stopped broadcasting entirely. Then, suddenly, there was another woman, this one with long blond hair and glistening pink lippy across her thin lips.

How she was smiling so brightly while the world was falling to pieces, Blaine would never know. It seemed disrespectful.

"World leaders around the globe have boarded helicopters and other private aircraft this afternoon, reportedly flying to a secure, undisclosed location," she said. *"Among them includes British Prime Minister Philip Houghton, US President Adam Goldberg, and of course, Pope Paul VII. Other representatives of NATO – "*

"Can you fucking believe that!" Paul exclaimed. "Of course all the first class VIPs get a ticket out of here. While here we are, huddled in a doomed arse-hole of a flat hoping to see the light of tomorrow."

"Ever the optimist, Paul."

"Well it's true!" Paul jumped to his feet angrily. "I'm gonna go check on Em. You keep watching in case something of actual importance happens."

What? No! Paul couldn't leave him alone, not with the terrible things being shown on TV, not with that corpse still rotting in the kitchen. The last thing Blaine wanted was to be separated from his friends, even if they were just in different rooms.

"But – "

"I'll just be a second, okay? You'll be fine, won't you?"

Blaine frowned and glanced behind Paul down the dark corridor leading to the kitchen and beyond. Everything seemed alright now, but everything had been alright yesterday as well, and today the world was ending. Blaine didn't know if he could trust anything anymore.

"Just a second?"

Paul nodded. "Just a second. I've seen Emily with a broken wrist saying she's fine, and with a hangover saying she's dying. Can never be too careful with her, you know."

"Yeah, okay. Now's a pretty shit time to get sick, though."

"No kidding. I'll be right back."

Paul disappeared into the shadow of the corridor, and Blaine turned back to the television. He recalled Emily's haunted eyes, the emaciated look of her usually healthy body, and hunched his shoulders, lowering deeper into the sofa. He thought again of his mum and wondered how she was doing. Was she still alive? Had she, too, left home in search of more reliable shelter, or had she bolted the windows and doors?

He should've called right away. Most of the phone lines were still functional, or at least they were the last time Blaine had checked. He wasn't sure how long it would take for things like electricity to go out, but the time had to be short. Yes, as soon as Paul got back they'd switch—he'd use Paul's mobile to ring his mother and Paul would take over watching the telly for any new developments.

Speaking of developments, they were now showing boats on the screen, large ships that seemed to be cruise liners.

"First on board will be priority passengers, with cabins starting at approximately twenty thousand pounds. Following priority boarding will be those on the lower decks, with cabins at approximately fifteen thousand pounds."

Blaine snorted. "Of course."

"Passengers are allowed a maximum of three family members, excluding persons over sixty years of age. Boarding begins at six tomorrow morning—"

"Ahh!"

Blaine shot up and spun to face the direction of the scream. It was a male scream, no doubt Paul's, but Blaine was too frightened, too unprepared to go down the dark corridor to the bedroom and investigate the source of the outburst.

"Paul?" Blaine called out weakly. "Everything okay?"

Paul's form emerged from the shadows, his grey tee-shirt coming into view before his pale, freckled face. He was staring incredulously at his forearm, which Blaine saw had a rather nasty bite mark in the flesh.

"She fucking bit me!"

Blaine gaped. "Why the hell would she—"

"Fucked if I know! I put my hand on her forehead again and the next thing I know she's groaning and trying to take a bite out of me."

"Is she okay now?"

31

"I think so. I pushed her off and she just fell back to the bed like she'd fallen to sleep or something. I dunno what the hell got into her, she's never bitten me before. Well, not like *that*."

Paul hissed at the pain, and in the glow of the television Blaine could just barely make out how bad the bite was. It was deep, deep enough for blood to seep from the wound down Paul's wrist to the tips of his fingers.

"Come on, let's get it cleaned up," Blaine said. He took Paul's elbow and led him to the bathroom, much more comfortable traversing the hallway with his friend at his side. He flicked the light on and their two haggard reflections appeared in the mirror. The stark lighting made every fatigued shadow of their faces seem even worse.

"Jesus, it's throbbing," Paul said. "Something's not right with this, I don't think it's supposed to feel this way."

Blaine wet a flannel under the tap and wrung out the excess water. "Ever been bitten that hard by someone before?"

"No."

"So you don't know what it's supposed to feel like."

Frowning, Paul winced as Blaine wiped the blood away. "What if..." He stopped, shook his head, then started over. "What if those things are like, zombies or something?"

Blaine froze. "Paul."

But Paul was more insistent now. "What if the one in the kitchen bit her before she killed it? What if she's—"

"Would you listen to yourself? You sound mad."

"This whole situation is mad! Look at where we are, Blaine. Look at what's happened, what's going on outside. People are *eating* other people. What does that sound like to you?"

Blaine shook his head. He could too clearly see the creature from before, the contorted limbs as it clung to the ceiling, its hollow eyes staring down at him from between the curtains of its hair. He could feel the brush of skeletal fingers across his sleeve and hear the anguished screams echoing in the stairwell. He saw the teenage girls crouched over a lifeless body, gnawing on bones, and the man at the top of the stairs peeling flesh from a corpse before bringing it to his rotten mouth.

The trip here, which had seemed before like a dream, was starting to feel all too real again. A tightness was swelling up in Blaine's chest that he couldn't quite manage to push down, and his fingers once more began to tremble.

"Blaine." With his good hand, Paul stilled Blaine's fingers, then looked him in the eye. "Let's at least check to see if she's been bitten. There's no harm in checking."

Blaine still didn't like it. He didn't want to think about what it would mean for Emily if Paul's theory was right. But it had to be worse for Paul, who was in love with her.

"Yeah, alright."

He finished bandaging Paul's wound, then together they left the bathroom. As soon as they turned the corner to the bedroom, they saw Emily standing in the centre, slouching in front of the bed.

"Em?" Paul said. "You feeling any better?"

It was dark in the room, so dark that only Emily's shadowy figure was visible against the lighter shade of her surroundings. She said nothing in response to Paul, simply ambled slowly forward.

Fear seeped into Blaine again. His pulse quickened and he stepped back, instinctively stood on the balls of his feet, ready to bolt if necessary. Emily didn't move like that, didn't walk with her arms limp on either side and her feet dragging with each step forward. Emily would've said something if her boyfriend had addressed her.

That wasn't Emily.

As though in confirmation to Blaine's thoughts, the thing before him groaned. That, too, wasn't a sound their Emily would've made, nothing so deep and guttural. As she neared, she started moving quicker, as if she'd all of a sudden decided on a course of action. Her arms raised and she lunged right for them.

"Get back!" Blaine yelled. He grabbed Paul's collar and yanked him back, immensely grateful that Paul's hand was still on the doorknob and he'd had the sense to close the door in their retreat.

Unfortunately, there was no way to lock it, not from this side.

"Shit," Paul exhaled. "Oh shit, *shit*. I knew it. I fucking knew it."

Paul was breaking, Blaine could see it. He'd been barely holding it together before they left their flat to come here, and now, with the loss of Emily, he had nothing to keep him together anymore.

It was perhaps more terrifying to see than anything else. If Blaine lost Paul, if Paul couldn't keep his head now, when he needed him, Blaine didn't know what he'd do. He'd be alone, with no plan, no way to survive—nothing.

On the other side of the door, what used to be Emily was pounding on the wood, splintering the frame. It would only hold for so long, but what troubled Blaine more was the way Paul was cracking. When tears began to fall, running in twin streams down Paul's cheeks, Blaine reached out and clutched his shirt desperately.

"Paul. *Paul.*"

He could see the effort it took Paul to swallow. He could see the wheels turning in Paul's eyes as together they held the doorknob, keeping the door firmly in place. He knew Paul well enough to know when he was thinking, when he was committing himself to a decision he didn't like but had no choice but to go with.

"Paul, what are we going to do now?" Blaine asked. He needed Paul to tell him, he needed Paul to say *something*.

Suddenly Paul's face twisted in pain and he grunted again, curling his wounded arm around his stomach. His brows remained drawn together, but most of his expression smoothed out a moment later.

"My rucksack's bigger than yours," he said.

Blaine was at a loss. "What?"

"You can't carry that suitcase and bag with you everywhere," he continued, raising his eyes to meet Blaine's. "It'll slow you down, you'll die for sure, and that's a shit way to go. Take all your things and put them in my rucksack."

"What the hell are you talking about?"

A screeching crack of wood sounded, and sure enough there was a long, thin slice in the door. Emily was breaking through.

"Blaine, *listen* to me," Paul hissed. He grabbed Blaine's arm, hard enough for pain to throb under the pressure of the grip. "Emily was bitten, and now she's one of them. Emily bit me. It's only a matter of time—"

"We don't know that for sure!"

"Take Emily's car and go find your mum. The keys are in the kitchen."

"Stop talking like I'm going anywhere without you!"

"You *are*! I'm doomed, mate, we both know it. And even if I wasn't... Emily was all I had left. You know I can't kill her, even with her being what she is now. You've still got a chance."

Now Blaine was crying, not just because he was certain to lose both his friends but because he could already see the fate he was sure to meet as soon as he walked out the door. He was a weak, bony, uncoordinated twig of a thing, and it was a wonder he'd made it this far. What Paul was suggesting he do was about as wise as telling him to jump out the window.

"I don't," Blaine croaked. "Paul, I haven't even got a sliver of a chance on my own. Even if you are infected we could just...You could come with me until you start feeling ill, yeah? We don't have to split up right now, you could at least help me find—"

The door cracked again, this time a whole piece splintering off. Emily's bleeding fist blocked Blaine's view of Paul's face, and poking out from beneath the papery layer of skin, Blaine could see the ivory white of bone.

"Blaine, *go!*"

Three seconds passed, during which Emily's hand slowly retreated, and Paul's face once more slid into view. He looked desperate, more desperate than Blaine had ever seen him, and though the last thing Blaine wanted to do was leave his friend to meet a fate worse than death, he didn't see any other option.

"Go!"

When faced with the decision of fight or flight, Blaine's position was easy—flight. He was a coward, he knew it and usually wasn't ashamed to admit it. So even though he had no idea how he'd survive or what he'd do when he managed to get out of danger, when the door cracked again under the weight of Emily's fist, he followed his cowardly instincts.

He ran.

Chapter 4

Promotion

Portsmouth
THE DAY BEFORE
21:13

The second Andrew realised Luke's breathing had evened out, he slid forward out of Luke's arms and off the bed. Without another's body heat to keep him warm, the room was colder. He would've put on his clothes, but he didn't expect to be out of bed for long. He just needed to phone Madison, then he'd slide back under the duvet and go to sleep properly.

It wasn't too late, especially for a Saturday. Andrew didn't doubt for a second that his sister was still awake, and wasn't surprised when she answered on only the third ring.

"Hello?"

Andrew felt better already just hearing her voice. In his mind's eye, her exuberant face and broad smile was as clear as if she was right in front of him.

"Hey, Maddie?"

"Andrew, how's it going? Are you back from Africa, then?"

"Yeah, I've been back a few days."

"Why didn't you ring right away, idiot?"

Andrew lied. "I thought you might be busy. It was the middle of the week and I figured you had lectures."

"It's *summer*, Andrew, I don't take courses in the summer. And you could've messaged, at least."

"Slipped my mind, sorry. There was a lot to be done here as well.

I had to... get things sorted."

"Right. Can you video call?"

Andrew looked over his shoulder at where Luke lay sleeping. His mouth was open and he was drooling on the pillow. Lovely.

"Now's not a good time," Andrew said.

"Oh? I take it that means you got back together with your friend?"

"Shut up."

"That's a yes."

Andrew could hear the knowing grin in her voice and sighed, but couldn't help smiling.

"I've met someone too," Madison sang.

Of course you have, Andrew thought. Madison always had someone, ever since she'd reached puberty and sprouted breasts. As much as Andrew hated to admit it, his sister wasn't unattractive. It probably had something to do with the blond hair and blue eyes that ran in their family.

Not that either of them had any other family left. Their mother had died when Andrew was eleven, mugged and fatally stabbed one night in London. Their father had gone more recently, hit by a car back when Andrew was a midshipman.

"Does he know you have a brother in the Navy?" Andrew asked.

"He does, and he says he could probably take you."

"I'd like to see him try. How old is he, same age as you?"

"A year older. He's graduating next year."

Now was about the time Andrew could picture her twirling a long lock of blond hair around her finger. Maddie was full of odd contradictions, twirling her hair like one of those air-headed tarts but being utterly brilliant and strong beneath the surface. She was probably smarter than Andrew, if he was being honest.

Andrew smiled, and might've sounded more fond than usual when he said, "He doesn't stand a chance."

"*I* know that, but it'd still be fun to see him have a go, wouldn't it?"

Laughing, Andrew said, "Anyway, where are you staying for the summer?"

"What d'you mean where am I staying? I have a flat here in Oxford, don't you remember?"

"No."

Madison groaned dramatically. "You're hopeless."

"You can't expect me to remember little details like that."

"Yet you can remember coordinates and little pieces of weapons and—"

"Would you just answer the question?"

Madison sighed again. "Twelve Littlegate Street. Looks out on Albion Place. It's not too bad, even *you* would probably approve. Flatmate's a bit messy, though."

Andrew hesitated before asking his next question, but he had to know. "And do you still have the pistol I gave you?"

"Yes, Andrew, *and* the taser. And no, nobody knows I have them."

"Do you—"

"Yes, I remember how to use them. I'm not an idiot. Idiots don't get into Oxford."

"Right. Listen, there's something else."

Movement behind him made Andrew pause. Looking over his shoulder, he was just in time to see Luke sitting up, rubbing his eyes. Luke propped himself up on his elbow and blinked a few times before raising a questioning eyebrow. Suddenly Andrew was all too aware of the fact that he was still naked, standing beside the bed.

"Andrew?" Madison said through the phone. "What is it? Is something wrong?"

Andrew turned back around and wrapped an arm around himself to fight the chill. "Sorry. Can you come here?"

"To Portsmouth?"

"Yeah."

"I guess so, yeah. Why?"

"I wanna see you but I can't leave yet. They need me here," Andrew said. It was as much of the truth he could say. "The sofa in my hotel room pulls out into a bed. You could sleep there."

"Alright, I can drive down Monday."

"No, Maddie, you need to come tomorrow."

"Can't. I've already got plans with—"

"You're coming tomorrow."

He hadn't meant to snap. It had been an honest mistake, the way he'd demanded it like an order. He hadn't forgotten to whom he was speaking, that it was his little sister on the other end, but for a moment, just a brief moment, he'd felt the same irritation he always felt when someone didn't obey him. His orders were always meant to be carried out as soon as he issued them, he thought that went without saying.

But then the irritation passed, and he felt mortified for having forgotten that normal people — civilians — didn't operate that way.

"Maddie, I'm —"

"Fine. I'll leave at twelve hundred hours, how's that sound, Lieutenant?"

The line went dead before Andrew could respond. He lowered the phone and looked at the blinking screen miserably.

"I see that went well," Luke remarked dryly from the bed.

"Shut up."

"Happens to the best of us, Big-Ears. Come back to bed."

Andrew curled his hand around his mobile. He suddenly had the urge to shoot something.

Luke sighed. "Did she say she was coming tomorrow?"

"Yes."

"So you'll make up with her then. Don't stress over it. There are bigger things to be stressing over."

Slowly unclenching his hand, Andrew figured Luke was right. He placed his mobile on the bedside table and tried not to let Madison's parting tone get to him. He had other issues to focus on, other decisions that would soon require his attention. For now, all he could do was go back to bed and try to relax.

Luke helped, settling his nerves by lying atop his body, entangling their legs, and passionately kissing him into a state of peace and contentment.

DAY 1
07:33

By the time they arrived at the naval base the next morning, a perimeter of fences had been set up inside the surrounding wall. Andrew could tell from the wiring that one touch would give someone a nasty shock.

From the passenger seat of Luke's car, Andrew asked, "What's all this?"

Luke looked grave as he peered over the steering wheel and squinted into the rearview mirror. "They're quarantining the area."

"This early?"

Luke nodded.

"Aren't quarantines meant to keep *in* the infection?" Andrew asked.

"Not in this case." Luke reduced his speed to a crawl. "Something's going on and I've got a bad feeling about it. I need to know now if you've made up your mind, Andrew. Stay here or—"

"Madison'll be here later today. I planned to get her on one of those ships you say will be here."

"And you?" Luke turned to look at him. "Was part of your plan to go with her?"

Andrew hadn't made it that far yet. He was still working on it.

Luke put a hand on his shoulder. "Andrew, you've had enough combat. Go with your sister. You'll be at sea and you'll be safe."

That made up Andrew's mind, but not in the way Luke had meant it to. Yes, Andrew would be at sea if he ran, he'd be safe with his sister, but what about everyone else here? What about the men and women who looked up to him?

Few others had the knowledge Luke had given him, warning enough to provide a head start. The majority was blind to the danger coming their way, and it was because of that that Andrew finally refused to leave. He had a duty here, perhaps not to the Navy which expected him to fire on innocents, but to the people he'd originally sworn to protect. After the VIPs departed for safety, who would be left to help those who couldn't fend for themselves against what was coming? To leave now, when he was needed most, would be wrong.

"I'm staying here."

Luke sighed and increased speed again. "You're a fool, Peterson."

08:00

Andrew took a quick glance around at the other officers before redirecting his attention forward. He could tell right away that none of them had any idea what they were doing here, why they were lined up outside like this, rising sun shining into their eyes, outfitted in combat-wear and equipped with weapons as though about to go into battle.

A few people Andrew recognised. Hawthorne was a familiar face. He was a good man, perhaps too soft on those under his command, with a tendency to suck up to his superiors, but nothing Andrew would criticise too harshly. He was a pudgy little ginger, with freckles all over and a nose that turned up like a pig's, but he was friendly and amicable. That was probably the only reason anyone listened to him, because he was just so likable.

Stelling was more like Andrew himself, and maybe that was why Andrew liked him so much. He only spoke when something needed to be said and had a general look of boredom on his face at all times. His face was thin and red, all hard angles and lines, which only made him more unapproachable. He was a good Marine, a good officer, and Andrew had a deep respect for him.

Witbeck, however, was a pansy, and not in the way Andrew was a pansy. Witbeck shouldn't have ever been an officer, full stop. He hardly had any backbone, and it was a wonder anyone followed his orders at all, given the jokes everyone told about him. He wasn't small — he was more like Luke, in the way that he had a slender build made of mostly bone and muscle and not much else — but his voice was. The way he spoke, raspy and too low and a bit rough, made Andrew think he was constantly covering up his natural tone. He had a feeling Witbeck actually had a thin, reedy voice and was only playing at being tough, especially since it was always Witbeck who started arguments before suddenly backing out of them.

In front of them, Commodore Paulson looked around, then demanded, "Where's Lieutenant Commander Firth?"

Silence.

Behind the commodore, Captain Wymore stepped forward and whispered into Paulson's ear. The commodore's wizened face pinched

41

up in disapproval and disgust as he received the message.

"Peterson!"

Andrew stiffened at the sound of his name, suddenly alert, and held Paulson's stern gaze. "Sir?"

"I'm promoting you. Get up here."

Andrew stepped out of line and walked forward. He was full of conflicting feelings — shame, pride, exhilaration. Shame, because just hours ago he'd been contemplating abandoning his post altogether. Pride, because despite his momentary wavering loyalty, he deserved this. Exhilaration, because out of all the others, *he* had been chosen to take the missing Lt Commander's place.

He could already hear Luke's voice in his head. *Congratulations, Big-Ears, you've been promoted.*

As soon as Andrew turned on his heel to face the men and women he'd only just left, his stomach sank and all his conflicted feelings turned to one: dread.

Commodore Paulson raised an arm to point behind the officers, over their heads. "You all see those new fences?"

A few of them twisted their necks to look behind them, at the new barbed, electric fence outlining the inside of the naval base. Most remained staring forward, squinting against the sunlight that reflected off the water.

"One unit will be posted at each entrance, changing at six hour intervals. One more will patrol the perimeter, changing at six hour intervals. Anything tries to get past that border without authorisation, you shoot on sight."

Having just been stood on the other side, Andrew knew how they looked standing along the edge of the water. With the sun rising over their heads, it was hard to make them out. The sun was blinding in its intensity, even this early in the morning. To the officers on the other side, Andrew and the rest of them were only shadows giving out orders.

From this side, Andrew could see every face in clear detail. He could see the clench of Stelling's jaw. The man didn't know what the order meant — Shoot any*thing* that tries to get past them? Not any*one*? — but because he was a good Marine, he'd follow without question.

Witbeck's fingers twitched, and Andrew imagined for a moment that he could make out the bob of his Adam's apple as he swallowed his uncertainty.

Hawthorne's brow furrowed in confusion. He, too, didn't like it, thought the whole situation was in a grey area, but wouldn't say anything.

Andrew could see the bewilderment and hesitation in all of their faces. With his new rank came the heavy burden of being asked to send these people to kill innocent civilians. It was worse than Luke had said it would be. Andrew wasn't doing the murdering himself, no. He was stepping back and having others do it for him. He couldn't even consider disobeying any orders given to him when he was just promoted, the weight of responsibility thrust upon him.

"Remaining units will patrol the city," Paulson continued. "Kill anything that poses a threat." A clipboard hit Andrew in the chest as Paulson's hand slammed it against him. "Lieutenant Commander Peterson will read off your assignments."

Just like that, Andrew's superiors cleaned their hands of the job. Commodore Paulson and Captain Wymore left without another word, leaving Andrew to stare blankly at the list of officers and their corresponding units. Units that would kill civilian and infected alike, not fighting alongside the people they'd promised to protect as Andrew had hoped.

Andrew cleared his throat and swallowed. He glanced up at the men and women now looking to him for orders before returning his gaze to the words in front of him, laid out as easily as a script for any actor to read aloud. He forced authority into his voice as he had so many times before, as though he believed with as much conviction as the commodore that this was the best course of action.

"Outbreak is expected to reach Portsmouth at or around ten hundred hours. You're to kill any life form threatening the integrity of the base's perimeter. Assignments are as follows: Lieutenant Reynolds, first patrol along eastern border. Lieutenant Stelling, second patrol along eastern border..."

He was halfway through the list before his first statement finally registered. *Outbreak expected to reach Portsmouth around ten.* Two hours before Madison said she would leave.

Chapter 5

Departure

London
DAY 2
04:13

Blaine couldn't sleep. At first it was because of the crying. Running from Emily's flat through the corridors of wandering infected, clutching his newly acquired rucksack to his chest, Blaine had had tears steadily streaming down his face. He'd been crying as he hastily unlocked the white Jeep Grand Cherokee waiting for him in the building's garage, and he'd been crying as he huddled between the rows of seats, making himself small and invisible. The tears hadn't stopped once.

Then, what felt like hours later, after he dared to climb into the seats to curl up on his side, he couldn't sleep because of the noises.

He could hear everything.

His breathing was too loud. It sounded harsh in the quiet of the car, like the wet, laboured breathing of a dying grandmother. But he could hear things even over that. He could hear the crunch of bones and ripping of flesh as the monsters just outside fed from the corpses littering the ground. He could hear the slow, methodical dragging of feet as they walked aimlessly to and fro.

On two occasions, he heard running. He heard the desperate sound of people trying to escape — a fall — a scream — more crunching — then silence. Once, there was even the piercing cry of an infant echoing in the concrete garage after the initial scream of what was almost certainly its mother. Both times Blaine had had to bite his forearm to muffle his sobs.

He'd thought about starting the car. He'd thought about driving out of here, heading straight to Bristol to find his mother. But then he thought about the streets and the people on it. What if there were more like that madman from the telly? What if he was shot at, what if someone killed him just as point blank as they'd killed that reporter, all so they could take his car?

He didn't know what to do, so he stayed curled up on the backseat, unable to sleep because of the noises outside and unable to move from fear of being murdered.

11:22

He must've managed to doze off at some point, because when he opened his eyes again, his limbs ached from the awkward position and his mouth was cottony from sleep. For a second, he forgot what had happened and why he was sleeping in Emily's car, until the memory came crashing back with staggering force.

A few more tears escaped, but now Blaine simply felt empty. He was cut off from his friends, hollow, alone. Though his eyes were open, staring unblinkingly at a small tear in the leather seats, he saw nothing. For a few peaceful moments, he was numb.

"You're a smart boy, Blaine, you'll do well, I know you will."

It was his mother's voice Blaine heard from some place deep in his skull, the same words she'd said the day he left for university. Frowning at the break in silence, he closed his eyes and there was his mother's smiling face, kind and bright.

"Luck runs in the family, you know," she continued. "You'll be just fine."

Her brows were just as dark and bushy as Blaine's, though not nearly as close together, and the eyes over which they sat were a soft, serene blue, not liquid brown. Her brown hair wasn't thick like his, with natural streaks of blond, but dark and curly, which always made her look young for her age.

Mum...

The vision of his mother tugged at his heart, and he longed not for just an image, but the real thing he could throw his arms around and hold close. He realised that though he might have lost his closest friends, he wasn't alone. Paul's wish had been for him to get to her, and even if the thought of trying and failing frightened him to no end, he had to try. For Paul, for his mum, for himself.

First was the matter of getting out of the city. The streets were sure to be congested, and Blaine still wasn't over the underlying fear of running into other survivors. Then there were the infected still roaming around just outside.

Blaine only saw one solution, the solution that so far hadn't failed him — speed.

M4 Motorway
12:03

Blaine gripped the wheel, shifted gears, and put more weight on the pedal, pushing the Jeep faster. "Fuck, fuck, fuck," he muttered under his breath. Another glance to the rearview mirror told him the skittering monster behind him was still close enough to be a danger.

At least he was past the worst of it, the city. He'd closed his eyes more than a few times as he drove through people he wasn't sure were alive or dead, but now he was on open road for the most part, heading out of London toward Bristol.

Another quick look backward, and Blaine saw the crawler finally falling behind. For the first time in twenty-four hours, Blaine felt a sliver of hope.

The road wasn't as crowded here. The landscape wasn't too changed either, not the way the city was, with its broken windows and buildings spotted with bullet holes. Out here, the scenery was mostly the same, though there was the occasional pack of infected wandering the fields. Sometimes Blaine saw other cars, some going his way, some going the way from which he'd come, but mostly it was a lonely trip. He found himself drifting into a daze as he sped along the long, empty motorway.

Fifteen minutes after losing the crawler, Blaine glanced down at the dashboard in despair. He'd been desperate to make his escape, had been so focused on maintaining speed before he lost his nerve that he hadn't thought of how much petrol the Jeep had. He was nearly out of fuel, and if he didn't stop within the next few miles, he wouldn't stand a chance of making it to Bristol.

Taking the exit to the nearest petrol station, Blaine thought maybe he'd get lucky. Maybe nobody would be infected on this particular stretch of road. Maybe he could get in, grab what he needed, and get out in a matter of minutes.

His palms started to sweat at the thought of leaving the safety of the car, of stopping his forward momentum, but it was something that had to be done. Paul would've said as much. Paul would've said to stop being an idiot and just get petrol so he could keep going, that it really wasn't that big of a deal.

Blaine nodded to himself, mind made up. Then, remembering he didn't have even a kitchen knife with which to defend himself, his courage wavered.

Speed, he thought to reassure himself. *Just keep running.*

There was only a Ford Focus at the station, otherwise deserted. Blaine parked by the pump closest to the convenience store, and pushed the button to open the lid on the fuel tank. He looked around quickly before jumping out and slamming the door of the Jeep shut behind him. Not a soul, clean or infected, in sight, not by the Costa Coffee across the road or in the car park with empty buses. It was almost *too* deserted.

Walking hesitantly around the Ford across from him, he saw the reason for his unease on the ground. There was one of those red petrol cans near the back tyre, underneath the open fuel tank. Picking it up, he found it nearly full, the fumes wafting up to meet his nose.

The car was here, the fuel was here, ready to be poured in, but where was the owner?

It was possible they were in the convenience store, looting the place for food. It was also possible they were dead, which, judging by the spattering of blood on the ground, Blaine figured was probably more likely. Looking around again, he took the can back to his Jeep and hurried to pour it into the tank, his blood rushing with a sense of urgency.

He emptied the whole can and set the empty container down to open the car door. He was feeling his pockets for the keys when he heard the sound of feet dragging across the ground, a grating, sliding noise.

A noise he'd become acquainted with in the wee hours of the morning while clutching his legs to his chest and weeping.

Blaine spun around. He knew what to expect, but his body tensed up all the same. At the sight of a dirty, suntanned, young blonde woman, blood dripping from her mouth with the remnants of her last meal, Blaine started patting himself all over, feeling desperately for the keys.

The Jeep was locked, no getting around it. He panicked when he didn't feel them and wasted another few precious seconds refusing to believe it.

He *knew* he had them. He had driven up to the pump, taken the keys out of the ignition, opened the door, got out...

Blaine looked in through the window and his stomach dropped. The keys were still on the driver's seat.

The sound of dragging feet was definitely closer. Blaine threw a look over his shoulder and trembled when he saw how close she was, near enough that Blaine could see the muted blue colour of her clouded eyes.

Distraught, he turned back to the car and started pounding on the window. He was too scared to think, and his hands ached from how hard he beat the glass.

It was useless, of course. The infected woman was right behind him; he could see her reflection in the glass. He was about to turn around and kick her, shove her, *anything*, when a shot rang out.

Blaine screamed and went to his knees with his arms over his head. He squeezed his eyes shut, chanting, "Please don't kill me, please don't kill me, please don't kill me..."

After about a minute, he realised he was still alive. He slowly looked up and saw the woman motionless on the ground before him. Raising his eyes a little more, he saw a man standing above him with a contemptuous look on his wrinkled, drooping face.

As far as first impressions went, Blaine's impression of the old man was that he was rather surly and generally unpleasant. He had a rifle slung across his broad shoulders and his cut, spiked hair was a mix of grey and white. He also seemed to have never grown into his nose, which was large and bulbous at the end with thick, grey hairs sprouting out of cavernous nostrils.

Blaine couldn't even make out the man's eyes. The skin there was so wizened and pinched that he seemed to be constantly squinting. More than anything else, the lack of ability to meet the man's eyes unsettled Blaine the most.

"Well, are you going to get up?" the old man said in a raspy voice. Blaine suspected he smoked quite a bit or had in his younger days. It was easy to imagine a fag perched between those stretched thin lips.

Blaine lowered his arms and stood with as much dignity as he could, which wasn't much. "I'm, uh, nineteen," he said, as if that would explain everything. What he meant to convey was, *I'm just a kid, don't think any less of me for screaming like that.*

The man just snorted and nodded in the direction of the convenience store. "Hungry?"

Blaine realised yes, he was quite hungry. He hadn't eaten anything since yesterday afternoon, and had been running mainly on adrenaline and fear. His stomach answered for him and the old man chuckled.

"Come on, I'll fix you something."

Hesitantly, Blaine followed. He kept looking around nervously just in case there were any more infected lurking nearby.

"Is this your place?" Blaine asked as they walked past a Staff Only sign.

"Yes."

"And, er, you are...?"

"James Merrick. Just call me Merrick."

"Thanks for killing that thing, Merrick. And, uh, sorry that woman stole your petrol."

Merrick shrugged. "It was bound to happen. I doubt our little pieces of paper and coin mean much now anyway."

It seemed Blaine had been right about him being surly, but surly fit Blaine just fine if it meant getting a meal. So far, Merrick hadn't tried to shoot him, and was being nothing but helpful.

Luck runs in the family, he thought wryly. He heard it in his mother's voice, and once again felt his spirits lift despite the earlier fright. He'd have something to eat and he'd be back on his way to Bristol in no time.

Merrick led Blaine back through a room that seemed part office and part bedroom, and into a small kitchen area. He opened a fridge in the corner, pulled out a container of some brown stew, slopped some into a couple bowls, and put them in a microwave.

Looking around, Blaine found a chair to sit in while he waited for the food to heat. He picked at the dirt under his fingernails and sighed, trying not to let his thoughts wander. When the microwave beeped, Blaine was glad for something else to keep his hands and mouth busy.

"Where are you headed?" Merrick asked as he handed Blaine a bowl of stew along with a spoon.

"Bristol." Blaine took a wary mouthful, found the broth to his liking, and dared to try the other ingredients mixed in.

"Family?"

"My mum."

Merrick hummed and nodded, slipping a spoonful between his own chapped lips.

"Don't suppose you could help get my keys out of my car?" Blaine asked.

Merrick pursed his mouth with thought. "How soon are you trying to get to Bristol?"

"As soon as possible."

"And once you get there? Once you find your mother, if she's even still alive?"

Blaine stirred his stew. He knew that part of the plan was important, but he hadn't got around to figuring it out yet. He'd only just managed to kick himself into action an hour ago. He'd seen his whole city transformed into a nightmare, lost his friends, and had all his dreams taken away from him. He thought he was doing rather well for himself considering the circumstances.

"I don't know," he said. "But I'd rather be with her than not. I'd rather get *there* and die instead of dying out here. At least she'll know where I am, and I'll know where she is. And if she is dead or turned into one of them, at least I won't be left guessing."

Blaine tried not to sound like a little boy that just wanted his mum, but the words sort of seemed to come out that way. Merrick made a noise of acknowledgement, though Blaine couldn't tell if it was accepting or patronising.

He didn't have to wonder which it was for long. Merrick only took a few bites before saying, "I'm not sure there are words to express how ridiculous I find that plan."

"Excuse me?"

"You walk and talk like a fairy, so you either are one or just happen to be incredibly effeminate—"

"I do *not* walk like—"

"You're limp-wristed. You're skin and bones and the wind could blow you over. You haven't got a chance out there."

Blaine futilely grasped for words, but didn't have any. Merrick was right, after all.

"You'll stay here until you have the skills you need to survive," Merrick continued.

Blaine wasn't sure if Merrick was serious or not. Who was this mental old man? How did Blaine know he even really owned this place?

"You've got to be kidding me."

"I don't usually make jokes."

"You—Help me get my keys *now*! Help me!" Blaine demanded.

Merrick, damn him, just chuckled and ate another spoonful.

Blaine gripped the bowl with equal parts rage and despair. He risked everything if he stayed here. What if his mum... No, he couldn't even bear to think it. Those glazed blue eyes of the blonde woman haunted him. He wouldn't let such a thing happen to his mother.

And Merrick had no right to decide what would become of Blaine's life. Like hell would he let this insignificant little station owner stand between him and his only chance at happiness in this nightmare of a world. Like *hell*.

"Fine," Blaine snapped and set his bowl down on the small table beside him. "I'll just get something to...to smash in the window. I don't need your—"

"Sit down."

51

"No."

A pistol appeared from nowhere, the barrel suddenly pointed at Blaine's forehead. Blaine felt the colour drain from his face.

"Sit. Down."

Blaine sat.

"Now finish that," he nodded to Blaine's bowl. "You'll need your energy."

Blaine glared at him but wasn't about to disobey the man with a gun.

Chapter 6

Cactus Land

Near Chieveley
DAY 2
12:56

Blaine followed Merrick through the shop and into the garage, feeling like he should have been miles away. He snapped his fingers, bounced on the balls of his feet, and looked around anxiously. He planned to wait until the dead of night when Merrick was asleep, lock him in, steal a heavy tool to smash his window open, and drive off.

That plan fell apart when Merrick opened a trunk full of guns.

"Glock 17, takes nine millimetre rounds, standard individual weapon for close range," he said, raising the gun he'd pointed at Blaine earlier. "There's seventeen rounds in one mag, which means you won't want to be using this unless you have to, and count your shots when you do. I can already tell you're the type to try and shoot something only to find you've run out of bullets."

"I'm not the type to shoot at all."

Merrick ignored him and put the gun on a wooden table near the trunk before pulling out a larger one. "This is the L129A1, a semi-automatic rifle with four sights, as well as this image intensifier here, which can identify targets up to thirteen hundred metres."

Two others. "Here we have the SA80 Light Support Weapon and the Individual Weapon, both of which take 5.56 millimetre rounds—"

"Stop, stop," Blaine cut him off, shaking his head. "Firstly, I don't understand a word of what you're saying. Secondly, why the hell do

53

you have all these stowed away in the back of a BP? That's got to be illegal."

"I was in the British Army," Merrick explained. "I was, and still am, the best sniper there is. And I liked to be prepared."

"You're mental."

"I'm alive." He put away the weapons he'd pulled out, removed a smaller pistol with a thinner barrel, and closed the trunk. "We'll start out simple and work our way up. Like I said, I'm the best. I'm sure even you have the potential to get there eventually."

Blaine rolled his eyes and crossed his arms over his chest, feigning nonchalance. Merrick was probably talented, given the way he seemed to pick off that infected woman with ease, but there was no way he was the best, not when he barely had eyes to see with.

Merrick grabbed Blaine's collar so roughly Blaine yelped. "Do not. Take. Me lightly," Merrick bit out.

He was so close into Blaine's personal space that Blaine could see the pores in his face. Swallowing hard, Blaine nodded. When Merrick all but dropped him, Blaine only had another reason to hate him. Sure, he could acknowledge the fact that he was a coward, but it was something else entirely when someone he didn't even know could seem to smell it on him.

"Got a name?" Merrick asked as he retrieved some things from behind the trunk.

"No," Blaine said petulantly. He was still angry about being manhandled, and by a dodgy old man at that.

Merrick shrugged and held a pistol out to Blaine, who just stared at it.

"Come on, John, we don't have all day," Merrick said impatiently.

Blaine's brow furrowed. "What?"

"Take the gun."

"No, what did you call me?"

"It doesn't matter. You don't have a name." Merrick shoved the gun to Blaine's chest and Blaine held it there automatically. "Let's go."

"Where are we going?" Blaine forgot about being irritated for a moment because he was *holding a fucking gun* and it could *potentially*

54

kill someone.

"Outside."

"But there are infected outside."

"Not as dumb as you look, are you?"

Blaine glared at the back of his head.

Outside, the only thing that detracted from the nice weather and general summer serenity was the infected corpse by Blaine's car. Blaine's skin prickled when the wind blew and his nerves were shot to hell. It didn't help that he was holding a gun. He didn't like holding a gun *at all*.

Merrick took him around the back. They passed a skip and a fenced off area, and after crossing the street, they walked through a sparse line of trees into an open field. Blaine looked around. As far as he could see, they were alone. The sun was high, the breeze was cool, and it seemed an ordinary day.

Except for the fact that each of them were holding firearms.

Merrick turned around on his feet a couple times. He pulled something out of the bag Blaine hadn't noticed before and held his hand out. Blaine was only too glad to be rid of the gun, but Merrick twisted on a cylinder and handed it right back to him. It was even heavier now, much to Blaine's dismay.

"Shoot it."

Blaine had figured those words would come eventually. He'd been dreading it ever since Merrick had said he'd teach him how to survive.

"Do I—"

"Shoot it, John."

Blaine sighed and wrapped his fingers loosely around the grip. It seemed to weigh less the more he tightened his hold on it, but grew suddenly heavier when he tried to raise it. Even the pistol knew he shouldn't have been trying to wield it.

He suddenly remembered a night a couple weeks ago, when he and Paul had been looking at something on television—some stupid programme Blaine hadn't even wanted to watch—when Paul commented on how the strong, muscular types always got girls. Paul had elbowed him and said, "Maybe we ought to go to the gym, yeah? I'll work on these biceps and you'll get to see blokes all sweaty."

Blaine had laughed because Paul always said that, he always joked about working out and then neither of them ever did. Looking at the gun now, feeling as though he could barely lift it, Blaine ached to have his friend back. He felt the void more than ever. He couldn't face something like this without Paul's endless light-heartedness.

He was familiar with the feeling of inadequacy. When he'd passed some of the other students that were doing law or business while he was only going for photography, he'd felt incredibly foolish. When he'd told his mum he wasn't interested in women, he had felt like he'd let her down somehow, until she told him otherwise. Now he felt Merrick's old, sharp eyes watching, waiting for him to act, and he hated how much this man seemed to have taken control of his life in so short a time.

Perhaps anger wasn't the best motivator, but it made up Blaine's mind. Yes, he was weak, yes, he was young and all kinds of naïve, but he wasn't going to be looked at with pity anymore. He wasn't going to tolerate underhanded statements like Emily's "You know how he is." He had never been ashamed of loving photography, or loving men for that matter, and he wasn't going to start being ashamed of his inability to protect himself.

He raised the gun and pulled the trigger.

There was a *click* noise. Nothing happened.

Merrick nodded. "Good. Now, let's take the safety off and do it for real."

Blaine exploded. "What? You mean you—What?!"

Merrick took the gun from him and flicked something on the side before handing it back to Blaine. "I wanted to be certain you could do it. You can. Do it again."

You can, Merrick's words echoed in his mind. Blaine wet his lips, took a deep breath, and raised the gun again, pointing straight ahead. This time when he pulled the trigger, he felt it as the bullet shot forward. He wavered on his feet but managed to stay upright.

"That...wasn't as loud as I thought it would be," Blaine said.

Merrick put a heavy hand on Blaine's shoulder. Even though the old man's expression hadn't changed, Blaine felt approval in the gesture.

"I put a silencer on it, and it's only a pistol. Rifles are completely different." He stepped away and looked around again, probably just as worried as Blaine that the sound, however soft, attracted the infected.

Merrick looked at the sky briefly. "Shoot it a few more times just to get the feel of it. Then we've got to start boarding up the windows."

DAYS 2 – 35

Blaine soon learnt that whenever Merrick said "we," what he meant was "you." He also still didn't know Blaine's real name, so it changed from day to day. The first day it was John. The second day it was Oliver. The third day it was Stanley.

Blaine finished boarding up the front windows of the station on his second day. He himself would have preferred to work during the night, because he would have felt a hell of a lot safer when he slept, but Merrick said the infected would be drawn to the light like moths. So locked doors and half-boarded windows it was.

Merrick wasn't one for talking much, which suited Blaine fine, because when he wasn't trying to learn what he could about surviving, he was worrying about his mum. Merrick kept saying he owed him his life every time Blaine was particularly moody, but Blaine thought it was only a matter of time before that excuse got old.

He got his first kill on day three with the Glock. Merrick had made him practise the day before on still targets, and would have preferred more of that until Blaine was comfortable, but they only had so much ammunition to work with. Merrick sounded a loud emergency siren that attracted infected from the area and stood on the roof of the station shooting them in the knees, reducing them to a crawl. Blaine perched on the roof of his Jeep and finished them off as they came slowly for him.

It was a lot like photography, actually. Point and shoot. Blaine had always been good at that.

"Excellent work, Stanley!" Merrick called down from the station roof after Blaine's tenth victory. "Let's head inside. I'm starving."

For the first two weeks, it was just killing what Merrick had named 'walkers' with a simple pistol. Blaine was a quick learner, and apparently a natural when it came to shooting, but he had to give credit where credit was due, and Merrick wasn't too bad of a teacher. There was only one minor incident, when an infected boy who looked to be about nine appeared and Blaine couldn't bring himself to fire. Merrick had rained down commands from the roof and all Blaine had done was stare wide-eyed, the Glock pointed at the boy's head. Eventually Merrick killed it himself and Blaine had received a terrible lecture that night.

Blaine's third week consisted of rifle training, assault weapons, and assembly. Rifles were completely different from pistols and seemed to have all sorts of complicated names—L129A1, SA80. The one Merrick expected Blaine to master and "love more than he loved his right hand" was the L115A3. The long range sniper rifle.

Blaine had to stand with the gun raised until his arms ached, not even shooting it, just holding it. Merrick quizzed Blaine over meals, made him recite which guns used which calibre bullets, which had the furthest range, and the number of rounds in each magazine. He did it as he washed their clothes by hand, as he checked the boards in the windows for wear, as he cooked food, and the number of times Blaine had to dis- and reassemble each gun should have been illegal. It got to the point where Blaine was seeing diagrams and mumbling things in his dreams.

To be fair, it was so much work it took his mind off of his mother. There were still moments when he'd look out at the road, or push food around on his plate, and wonder what she was doing, if she was safe. When the electric grid had gone down during the third week, and Merrick had Blaine start up a generator, he'd wondered if his mum was doing the same thing and if she had anyone to help her.

Around the start of week five, Merrick had cycled through his short list of names back to John and Blaine could now shoot things that were moving relatively faster, most of the time using the SA80 IW. Merrick still watched from the roof just in case, but Blaine picked off infected one by one from the top of his car usually without his help. Then one of the mutations Merrick, like Blaine, called "crawlers" showed up and Blaine panicked.

"Merrick!" he yelled. "Merrick!"

He saw Merrick take aim from the corner of his eye but no shot went off.

"Kill it, kill it, kill it!" Blaine screamed.

"Waiting for you, John."

"I—I can't—"

"You can."

The human beneath seemed to have been a middle-aged woman. No doubt her hair had been greying but Blaine couldn't tell behind the scraggly mess and matted blood. She scampered off the main road on bony limbs, her floral dress ripped and hanging from her thin frame. The closer she came, the more dead her eyes looked. Blaine knew all too well how horrific the infected looked up close.

Blaine took a few breaths to steady the shaking in his arms and raised the gun to look through the sight. She was so fast! And she was scurrying all over the place, not in a straight line like the slow ones did.

Blaine couldn't keep up, and he heard the drag of footsteps on either side of him as more walkers approached where he stood on the car, the sound grating on his concentration. He knew he only had so many rounds left and had to make each shot count, and he felt himself losing control of his composure with every passing second.

He saw flashes of the first time he'd been so close to a crawler, heard the screams echoing in the cramped stairwell, and felt stiff, unable to act. The walkers on his side were nearing the car, their skeletal arms reaching up to try and claw at him.

"Do it, Blaine, do it *now!*" Merrick shouted from above.

Blaine shifted his weight on his feet and locked his limbs. He could do this. What if it was Paul and Emily behind him, unarmed and helpless? What if his mother's life depended on him?

Blaine traced its movements with the sight and pulled the trigger. He kept his finger tight, kept firing until the magazine was empty.

She was still twitching, but only every few seconds. Blaine was acutely aware of the fact that there were still walkers around him, clawing at his car, but he'd poured the last of his ammo into the crawler. Finally, Merrick finished her off with a single well-placed shot.

"Get inside, John," he said.

Blaine thought he heard a twinge of disappointment in his voice.

Not looking forward to the conversation sure to follow, Blaine kicked a walker off the bonnet, jumped through the resulting gap, and ran inside. It was just like the little boy all over again.

Blaine yanked open their small fridge and pulled out a bottle of water. He twisted the cap off angrily and started chugging it, not caring that he was wasting it because he was in for a lecture anyway. He heard bodies hitting the ground outside as Merrick picked them off.

He knew trying to explain for the millionth time that he was just a student would lead to nowhere. Merrick was always saying that nobody was *just* anything, that everyone had the potential to be something great if they strived for it. That everyone had a destiny.

Blaine thought the old man was full of it. It was enough that Blaine knew how to shoot. Why did he have to know what a stock was or how to place his hand just right? It was point and shoot, simple as that.

Blaine sighed and sat against the wall next to the pile of blankets that passed for his bed. He once again tried to run a hand through his overgrown brown-blond hair to no avail. It wasn't that simple at all, not really. Nothing in life was simple.

He heard Merrick's efficient footsteps on the roof walking toward the ladder. How anyone made footsteps sound efficient, Blaine would never know, but that's exactly how Merrick walked. Efficiently.

Soon enough, the old wrinkled face appeared through the doorway. As expected, he wore a frown so pronounced it was bordering on a scowl. His voice wasn't sharp and quick, but slow and measured. That made it worse.

"One day, John, I will put you out there and I will tell you to shoot. I will be expecting you to defend yourself. And if you tell me you can't, I will simply look at you and say 'Too bad.'"

Blaine tensed. Merrick didn't lie. He may have sometimes omitted things, but he never spoke anything but the truth. If Blaine didn't do as he said, he would leave him to die.

Merrick sat down and laid his rifle across his lap, fixing Blaine with a calculating stare. A short while ago, Blaine might have looked away. Now he stared back just as stoically, silently waiting for what Merrick had to say next.

Blaine spoke first when a sudden realisation hit him.

"You called me Blaine."

"What?" Merrick looked at him like he'd just said the sun was green.

"Outside. You didn't call me John. You called me Blaine."

Merrick shook his head, deeming the matter irrelevant. "You have to learn to act on your instincts. You can't panic each time you see a crawler. Act first, think later. That's how you'll survive."

"I don't *have* instincts. If I did, they'd be to run and hide. I've only been at this for a month. Give me a little credit, yeah?"

"When the time comes, I will. For now, we make the most of what little time we have to instil some instincts into you."

Blaine groaned. It sounded like more training.

Chapter 7

Desertion

Portsmouth
DAY 2
08:49

"Please, my mother—"

"You can't do this!"

"I *need* to get on, you don't under—"

"My baby, at least let my baby onboard, *please*!"

After only three hours, Andrew had heard it all—*My relative is handicapped, my son deserves a chance to live, it's against my religion that I die this way, how dare you let those corrupt wealthy pigs live while the rest of us suffer...*

Commodore Paulson wasn't out here with them. The Admiral surely wasn't, Captain Wymore, Paulson's bitch, wasn't either, and Andrew hadn't even seen Luke since the previous morning.

They'd been abandoned. Their superiors gave orders from the comfort of a nearby docked ship, and knowing Luke, he'd returned to his cosy submarine.

In the span of one day of Outbreak, Andrew had been promoted again following the death of Commander Bristow. Under any other circumstances, Andrew would've been thrilled.

Andrew Peterson, a commander at twenty-five.

It had such a nice ring to it—Commander Peterson. It rolled off the tongue. But it was as heavy a burden as the rank preceding it. More so, in fact.

"Those cabins could fit a whole family! How can you live with yourself knowing—"

"God punishes those who go against his design, you Satanists, you—"

"Please, I'm pregnant, you can't let those monsters have me!"

One man made a run for the wall. A few had driven cars up to it and tried to climb over, so no one had made it to the fence on the other side yet. No one knew it was electrified.

But Andrew had orders. They all had orders.

Andrew raised a hand, pointing a straight finger at the man running toward the perimeter. "Stop him." Though there was shouting going on all around him, he didn't need to say it too loudly.

He didn't know who fired. He saw someone turn, saw the rifle take aim, and heard the shot. The man fell.

They didn't have orders to do anything with the dead. When a shrieking wail pierced the general uproar and a woman darted forward to clutch the man's body to her chest, Andrew realised it wasn't a man at all. It was a boy, just a teenage boy.

He didn't give the order, but someone shot the woman mourning her son anyway.

DAY 59
17:44

It took nearly two months for Andrew to realise that his sister wasn't going to make it.

He'd done all he could those first few days of the Outbreak. He'd phoned her the second he had a moment to himself, he'd left a message telling her to come right away, to fight her way to Portsmouth if she had to. She was strong, he'd taught her enough to survive something like this surely, and she *could* make it. Andrew believed with all his heart that she could make it.

He'd said he would meet her at the gate. Before the phone lines went down, he'd messaged her every day telling her where he'd be on patrol and what not to do if she wanted to avoid being killed on sight.

He commanded his unit. He oversaw assignments, routes, schedules. He went on patrols. He made himself into the numb, brutal Marine he often needed to be overseas, and killed whomever, *what*ever, was required of him.

It took nearly two months. Then Luke died.

The people of Portsmouth had stopped trying to get into the naval base by the end of the first week of the Outbreak, and the boats taking away the VIP passengers were only docked for three days anyway. They could only try to break through the militarised line of defence for so long before having to turn around and defend themselves against the infected. At first, once the healthy were no longer the immediate threat, Andrew had given the order to shoot infected first. To prioritise and conserve ammo for the real enemy.

Once the civilians started getting as murderous as the monsters, Andrew had had to change his orders a bit.

"For the love of God, if it's a threat and it's close to you, just fucking kill it," he'd growled.

Too many people had questions and he didn't have answers. He'd already lost half a unit in a riot and another half to some purple-skinned beast the civilians called a hunter. His resources were spread thin, and the people who'd left him in charge didn't seem to care one bit.

It was as though he'd been made the local authority over everything, a small army at his command that would do whatever he said. While there was no one to stop him from doing whatever he wanted, there was also no one to tell him just what to do.

The base was in a constant state of waiting, indefinitely on the defence to keep the outside at bay for apparently no other reason than that it had been ordered so. While Andrew waited for further instructions from above, there were certain choices he had to make, rules of his own he'd had to set.

Rule number one: If you get bit, you get a bullet.

It was the fifteenth of September now. Andrew was on patrol with Stelling, who he'd made his second in command. They were by the Cascades Shopping Centre, walking on Commercial Road when they suddenly came upon Witbeck.

He was as twitchy as ever, aiming his SA80 jerkily as he attempted to follow an enemy above him. The sun was setting, but Andrew could make out the shape of what Witbeck was trying to pin down, scampering along the front of the buildings on their left.

The civilians had taken to calling them crawlers. The official term was Type II Mutation.

Several subjects afflicted with Stage 4 infection began to show signs of physiological mutations such as: extended limbs, increased mobility of joints, increased speed, Andrew's memory supplied.

The T2s liked to pounce. They were like spiders that way, circling their prey and getting into position before leaping and pinning them down. The hunters, T3s, liked to pounce too, but theirs was more of a charge-and-tackle method before ripping their prey limb from limb. It was lucky that so far they'd only seen one in the city, but that one had given them enough trouble.

Witbeck was alone, which meant his partner had either died or left him to slack off. Andrew sighed, and beside him he heard Stelling's throaty chuckle. Witbeck was spinning in circles, looking like he was doing some odd ritualistic dance. Andrew and Stelling were only about fifty or so yards away, and Andrew was just about to call out to ask Witbeck where his partner had gone when the crawler finally made its move.

In the quiet of the evening, there was a sudden burst of shots as Witbeck fired. Andrew halted. Maybe half of the bullets hit the crawler, none of them piercing the skull. In all of two seconds, it had Witbeck flat on his back, with Witbeck screaming at the top of his lungs underneath it.

Stelling raised his rifle and took aim. Andrew put a hand on the barrel of Stelling's gun and slowly lowered it for him.

"Wait."

Too late for him, Andrew thought. *He was bitten as soon as it landed on him. Wouldn't do to waste ammo when he's dead already.*

The good thing about having Stelling along was that he didn't ask questions. Anyone else would've looked at Andrew like he'd gone mad, but Stelling, because they were so alike, knew what Andrew was thinking without him having to spell it out for him.

It didn't take long for Witbeck to stop moving. One moment his legs were flailing around, heels skidding over the ground, and the next they'd gone limp. Andrew heard the splitting sound of bone as the crawler cracked open the skull and went straight for the brain.

"Now," Andrew said.

Stelling raised his rifle again. One shot, and the crawler collapsed over what used to be Lieutenant Witbeck.

DAY 61
06:58

Andrew was patrolling alone. It wasn't something he did often, but it'd been quiet lately, and this early in the morning there were generally no disturbances with civilians.

People had tried to assassinate him a few times. Perhaps at first it was the way he walked or the insignia on his uniform, but now most of the rebels knew his face. He was Commander Andrew Peterson, the one playing God in Portsmouth, the tyrant, the man who wasn't letting them into the safety of the naval base.

They didn't know anything about him. Andrew had orders. He had *orders*.

He wasn't worried about being assassinated now, at seven in the morning walking along Queen Street. He wasn't really worried about anything. In his daydream, he wasn't stuck on land. In the theatre of his mind, the waves swayed back and forth, splashing in the bowl of his skull as he walked without a care. He was close enough to the sea that he could smell it if he inhaled deeply.

"Peterson!"

Andrew stopped. He knew that voice. He'd know it anywhere. But he hadn't heard it in weeks. He'd thought it—and its owner—had left long ago.

"Andrew."

Andrew turned. Standing in the alley to the right of the George Hotel, leaning up against the wall, was none other than Commander Luke Green.

He was in civilian clothes, dirty blue jeans and a tattered grey flannel shirt. His beard had grown out, making his skin look even more pale, and his green eyes no longer twinkled with their usual mischief. They were dimmed somehow, older and more resigned. He still looked meek in the expression, but now he also looked exhausted.

"Luke?"

Luke smiled, but it was a shadow of its usual brilliance. Just like his eyes, it too was resigned.

"C'mere," Luke beckoned, waving Andrew over.

Andrew crossed the street in a daze. He'd thought Luke had abandoned his post, ducked into a submarine somewhere. He'd thought Luke had fled, left the city entirely. He hadn't known what to think. He'd lost all hope of hearing from both his sister and his best friend ever again.

Luke's arms were strange when they brought Andrew in for the customary embrace. They felt foreign somehow, but no less welcoming.

"I thought you'd left," Andrew said.

"I only left the Navy."

"You could've told me."

A sound behind Luke made them separate. Looking over Luke's shoulder, Andrew saw it was a T1, a walker, making its way down the narrow alley in which they stood.

"Let's talk inside," Luke said. He took Andrew's arm and led him into the George, through the restaurant and toward the back. With it still being early, it was quiet, though Andrew could tell from the personal items and low-burning candles scattered about that there were other people staying here, probably sleeping upstairs.

"Gun down," Luke said, taking Andrew's rifle and laying it on a table. Andrew felt uneasy already.

"Have you been here the entire time?" Andrew asked.

Luke didn't answer. Instead, he put his hands on Andrew's shoulders and pushed him back a step so he could look him up and down. When he'd finally seemed to have looked his fill, Andrew spread his hands, palms out.

"What?"

Luke sighed and let Andrew go. "You're a fool, Peterson."

"What the hell are you talking about?"

"You should've left. I told you to leave."

"It was too late!"

"Bullshit. They promoted you and *that's* why you didn't leave."

"I was waiting for my sister," Andrew explained. An edge of desperation had slipped into his voice, which he now tried to stamp out. "I left her dozens of messages, I begged her to come. What if she'd tried to make her way here and I wasn't waiting for her? This was the safest place."

Luke shook his head and chuckled bitterly. "Fool, just like I said."

"What would you have had me do? Leave after being promoted? I'm telling you it was too late!" he finished angrily.

Luke's eyes widened and he stepped toward Andrew, shushing and putting a finger to his lips. "You have to keep your voice down."

Andrew swatted the hand away. "Why?"

"You're not supposed to be in here. If they wake up, they'll kill you."

"Let them try."

Luke's face contorted in dismay and it was then that Andrew could see his friend again. The hand Andrew had pushed away raised once more, this time to cup Andrew's face as it had many times before. Andrew tightened his jaw but didn't step back.

"This isn't you, Andrew," Luke murmured. "You know it isn't."

Something in the statement made Andrew's stomach turn, but he reflexively pushed the feeling down. "I am who I need to be."

"Do you know what they say about you?"

"I've heard a few things."

"They say you're worse than the infected. That you and all the rest are a greater threat than—"

"They don't know anything. I'm just a man following orders, nothing more."

Another hand came up as Luke gripped Andrew's face firmly. They were so close that their noses brushed and Andrew could see nothing but Luke's eyes. He felt his vision blurring as his eyes crossed, and tried to bring the green irises into focus.

"What?" Andrew asked at last. He didn't know what this intense staring was, but it was making him uncomfortable. He could only endure so much of Luke's touchiness at a time, and he was nearing his limit.

"Look at me, Andrew. Just look at me."

Luke's hair had grown longer. He had a fringe of dark hair that fell to his eyebrows now, and as Luke pressed their foreheads together, Andrew could feel the sweat-damp strands.

Andrew's hair had grown as well. Not quite as long as Luke's, as it had started the Outbreak a bit shorter, but enough that his high forehead had been fortunately covered. As they stood there, holding each other's gaze, Andrew imagined the blond and sable strands intermixing, tangling together.

Finally he just closed his eyes and shifted his head side to side a bit, rubbing his forehead against Luke's to entangle them even further.

Andrew wasn't surprised when Luke kissed him. He'd wanted to, but it was always Luke who kissed first. He'd missed the way their lips melded together, how their tongues swirled passionately in sync. He'd missed the soft moans of pleasure Luke always made sure to make just loud enough to reach Andrew's ears and vibrate through his jaw.

He'd missed Luke *so fucking much.*

Luke tugged on Andrew's ears. "There you are, Big-Ears."

"I'm still gonna shoot you," Andrew chuckled.

"Hey." Luke tilted Andrew's chin up to look at him again. "In all seriousness. You should leave."

Andrew sighed. "I can't."

"You *can.* Andrew, look around. Look outside. It's the end of the world, okay?"

"That's not true," Andrew said, shaking his head. "There's been an outbreak. A virus, a plague, whatever you want to call it. It'll be over eventually and things will be rebuilt. The higher-ups are just waiting—"

"Exactly. They're no better than the people who boarded the ships. You think they're just bunkered in the subs, living on MREs and waiting until it's safe to come back? Maybe in the beginning, when they thought there was a chance, but they're long gone now, trust me. You haven't gotten any more orders since the first day, have you? Have you?"

Andrew frowned, not wanting to believe he and everyone under him had been left for dead. "They wouldn't just let the structure collapse. Don't be ridiculous."

"You're the one being ridiculous!" Luke grabbed hold of Andrew's shoulders and shook him. "Andrew, you don't have any obligations anymore. Don't you get it? It's a free for all now. Nothing's stopping you from just walking away. There won't be any consequences."

"There are people depending on me."

"I'm going to shoot *you* in a minute if you don't see sense!" Luke growled. "Take off your uniform, go to Oxford, and find your fucking sister."

Footsteps upstairs cut short Andrew's reply. Luke's eyes went wide again and he swore under his breath before picking up Andrew's rifle and pushing him toward the door.

"You have to go. Do what I said."

"Luke—"

"*Go!*"

"What's all this yelling going on down here?" a female voice called from the stairs. "There's people trying to—Oh my God."

Luke spun on his heels and stood right in front of Andrew. There was a woman in black jeans and a faded black jumper about two sizes too big standing across the room, her bright red hair frizzy from sleep.

"Amanda," Luke began. "I told you, Andrew's a friend."

Amanda produced a pistol from behind her back and the barrel was suddenly pointed right at them. Her expression had gone from tired and confused to alert and venomous in a matter of seconds.

"I know what he is," she spat. "That's the commander. You know how many people are dead because of him? How many people are worse than dead?"

"Amanda—"

"Step aside, Luke."

Andrew's brain kicked back into combat mode like a reflex. He had his rifle in his hands and the safety was off; all he'd have to do was aim and pull the trigger. She was still slow, half-awake—Andrew could use that. He was quicker than her, there was no doubt about it.

"He was just leaving," Luke said.

"So he can kill more of us? I don't think so."

Andrew's heartbeat didn't even speed up. He didn't start to sweat. He was that confident.

Still, as was usually the case in such situations, it all happened so fast.

Andrew only knew three things for sure: He'd raised his gun. He'd heard Luke yell for him to stop. He'd heard a shot, but he hadn't fired.

Before he could process it all into something coherent, Luke was falling forward to his knees, looking down at his chest.

"Luke!"

Andrew dropped his gun and knelt before Luke could hit the floor. He didn't see Amanda, he didn't see the little girl poking her head from behind the wall, or the old man who'd hobbled to join the others and see what was going on. He was half-aware of their presence, but all of his attention was on Luke, his best friend and lover, the mate he'd thought he'd lost once already and would now probably lose for good.

Luke smiling in his office, kissing Andrew after two years apart. Luke inside him, running hands up his back and saying how much he missed him. Luke leaning against the wall, two months later, looking completely different.

Luke here, in Andrew's arms, a bullet too close to his heart, dying. Andrew breaking.

it's my fault, it's all my fault, he's dying, he'll never be warm again, he'll never smile again or call me Big-Ears and it's all my fault

"Shh," Luke hushed him. He raised a finger to Andrew's lips, and for a moment Andrew was confused about why everything was going blurry. "Don't cry."

Andrew squeezed his eyes shut. The sob that escaped hurt him deeper than he thought anything could hurt. He felt the heaviness in his heart, his arms, his fingers. He clutched Luke to his chest as though he could pull him away from death. As long as he held him, he'd continue to live.

"I'm sorry," he managed. "I'm so sorry."

It was the first and last time he kissed Luke first. Luke's lips were chapped and dry, but still warm. For now.

"You're... a fool, Peterson."

One more caress of a finger across Andrew's cheek, and then the hand fell.

Andrew picked up his gun and pointed it at Amanda. She was still standing there, gaping and motionless. It was years of training from which Andrew pulled to force some firmness into his voice.

"Bring me his things. Now."

08:10

Using the jeep he usually ran longer patrols in, he got as far as where the M4 crossed over the A34, just about near Chieveley. There was an accident under the bridge, two lorries and a huge pile-up stretched across every lane. There was no getting past it.

Andrew considered his options. He could backtrack and get off at the petrol station he'd passed. He was fairly certain there was also a Costa Coffee and maybe an hotel in the area, which would help his food situation, of which there was none as he'd taken the jeep and Luke's rucksack of things along with his gun and just left. Not to mention he would need petrol soon anyway.

Sighing, Andrew turned off the car. He'd walk up the hill, see what the other side of the bridge was like, and maybe try to clear his head in the process. There was a duffel bag full of weapons in the back of the jeep, leftover from running patrols, and he figured he might as well take that, too. He didn't feel right just leaving it for any other wanderer to take.

It wasn't a terrible day outside. Wispy clouds scattered the skies, the sun was shining low in the horizon, the temperature was maybe 18° and climbing, and every so often a light breeze would blow across the grass. If it weren't for the bodies strewn along the road and the cars turned on their sides, Andrew could've believed it was an ordinary day.

Andrew threw the duffel bag over the fence at the top of the hill before climbing over himself. The M4 had more cars but fewer accidents, and one lane was completely free. Andrew slung the duffel bag over his shoulder and readied his rifle as he walked forward, scanning the area for infected.

By the time he reached the other side of the motorway, he hadn't seen anything. Then a noise behind him made him spin around.

It was a kid, a little boy trapped under a blue car. The first thing Andrew noticed was that he didn't have eyes. Or rather, he did, but somehow, perhaps in the crash, his eyeglasses had broken and pierced his eyeballs. Shards of glass poked out of his sockets and dried blood ran down his face like black tears.

The next thing was the arms. They reached out like living tree branches, clawing blindly for Andrew as the boy growled and tried in vain to move forward from beneath the car.

Andrew stared and stared and stared, not sure what he was feeling or if he was feeling at all. He didn't know how long he stared, only that there was something oddly mesmerising about watching the infected boy walker try to get at him and make absolutely no progress.

The weight of the duffel bag was starting to dig into his skin when he finally realised what made it so hypnotising to watch. He didn't feel like he was making any progress either. He'd been promoted in Portsmouth, but he'd been labelled a murderer, a demon. He'd tried to contact Madison, but hadn't heard a word. He'd found Luke, but only minutes later Luke had died in his arms.

One step forward, two steps back.

Madison probably wasn't even alive anymore. He didn't have anybody. So why was he still trying to pull his way from under his own burden?

Andrew nearly didn't believe it when he heard the sound of a car coming up the road. He turned and saw the front of a white Jeep getting steadily closer, maybe two hundred yards away.

He didn't know what he was doing anymore. He could've been hallucinating and there was no car coming his way at all. Maybe that's why he ran out in front of it.

Chapter 8

Graduation

Near Chieveley
DAY 36
11:46

Merrick sounded the alarm for only one minute before cutting it. Blaine sat on the roof with him, watching the mindless infected walk aimlessly around through binoculars, while Merrick looked through the scope of the sniper rifle. It was almost comical to see the walkers trip over fallen corpses and pick themselves up to keep going.

"Why are we just watching them?" Blaine asked.

"To learn their movements. Sniping is all about predicting movements, Oliver."

Blaine sighed. "Alright. So the girl in the green hoodie and ripped jeans. Where's she going?"

The girl in the green hoodie and ripped jeans was at that moment not going anywhere considering she was trying to walk through rather than around pump number seven.

"Watch. It's not where, it's when," Merrick said cryptically. "When will she get bored and turn around to go somewhere else? Perhaps she'll realise that she's not making progress and will turn in a few seconds. What factors in the environment will affect her future actions?"

"How am I supposed to know?"

"Observe."

Blaine huffed. "Why can't you just tell me?"

"What would you do if I were not here to tell you?"

"But you *are*, so just tell me so I'll know for the next time."

"That's not how we learn, Oliver."

Blaine grit his teeth and raised the binoculars again. He looked around the immediate radius surrounding the girl. He felt like he was doing one of those puzzles where he had to find what was out of place. He had always been good at visual games and things like that, but try as he might, he couldn't figure out what clue he was looking for. He hadn't the faintest idea.

"Would you please just tell me?" Blaine gave up with a sigh.

Merrick raised a single finger to point at her. "Look." Blaine looked. "She'll turn and walk forward in three...two...one."

The girl ceased walking in place and fell into step behind a man with a t-shirt half falling off his emaciated torso. Blaine was amazed.

"How did you—"

"They're predators, Oliver. She is searching for food. When a fellow predator walks by, she follows, thinking maybe he has seen something. She has no reason to change her pattern of behaviour unless acted upon by an outside force."

"But..." It made a ridiculous amount of sense when Merrick explained it like that. "How was I supposed to know that?"

Merrick shrugged a single shoulder, since the gun rested against the other. "We are also predators. The smartest on the planet. Use that human brain of yours for something other than taking pretty photos."

Blaine wanted to snap back that it wasn't just taking "pretty photos." There was subject and light and framing and apertures and focus. Merrick wouldn't understand the first thing about capturing a moment.

Then he thought about it. Instead of a subject, it was a target. Instead of light and framing, it was observation and prediction. The aperture was just a scope, and the shutter button was a trigger. In the end, Blaine supposed Merrick was a photographer in his own right. He framed the subject, waited for the perfect moment, and acted on it.

"Can I look through the scope?" Blaine asked, feeling the old excitement of playing with a new camera. He knew how to handle the weapon, had had to hold it for what seemed like hours at a time and assemble it over three dozen at least, but had never actually shot it. He'd never used a scope as large as the one Merrick currently had equipped. It was like changing lenses for a more powerful resolution.

Merrick wordlessly shifted the rifle over to Blaine. Blaine knew now why he needed to know all the parts; he had to adjust where the stock rested against his shoulder when he looked through the scope. He lay on his stomach and held it the way Merrick had taught him to.

"Wow," Blaine said appreciatively. He could see every gory detail of all of the targets below. He could make out the old blood from the fresh blood, see the wispy strands of hair blowing in the wind around their skulls, and even the yellow in their eyeballs when they turned toward him. He could see it all from this safe distance away.

"Can I—"

"Watch a little longer," Merrick instructed. "You can start shooting after lunch."

Blaine nodded and continued watching. He picked a target and followed it, mentally predicting its movements, paying attention to the force and direction of the wind. It was like people-watching, wondering what they'd do next. Only now the end goal was to put a bullet in them. Blaine idly wondered if all forms of hunting were really just games taken to the extreme.

After lunch, Merrick brought up the rifle again.

"This is yours now, Oliver," Merrick said, placing it in Blaine's hands. "It is your best friend. It is your lover. It is your god. As it takes care of you, you must take care of it."

"The bond between a man and his rifle is sacred," Blaine quoted his mentor with a wry smile.

Merrick nodded in approval. "Let's begin."

"Once you take the first shot, they'll go into a frenzy," Merrick said when they were in position. "They'll recognise the presence of a threat, but they won't know where from. Remember what I said about walkers?"

"Strong as a group, weak individually," Blaine recited.

"Exactly, and they know it as well. They have a pack mentality, and move in groups. They won't scatter, they'll clump. We use that knowledge to predict their movements."

"They'll move towards the sound," Blaine said. "Low wind, closest walker is about four metres away, so he'll hear it, even with the silencer on. He'll look up, the one next to him will follow, and they'll all fall behind trying to get at us."

Blaine heard Merrick make a noise that clearly conveyed he was impressed. He smiled and decided he would give away his secret.

"I've seen how they react from below. Happens nearly every time you get their attention."

Merrick snorted but Blaine didn't miss the little chuckle that followed it.

"Alright, smartarse." Without warning, Merrick shot one near the road and they all awoke. "I expect you to kill one every ten seconds. Go."

DAYS 50 – 60
15:55

By the end of two weeks, Blaine could kill one every five seconds, sometimes more depending on their proximity to each other. The front of the station became so crowded with bodies that they had to drag them on a tarp around back and burn them, which of course only attracted more.

It had been almost two months since Blaine came to Merrick. He could snipe in a crouch, prone, standing, cross-legged—Merrick had made sure to cover it all and drill him relentlessly. He'd made Blaine run from one edge of the roof to the other, turn around, run back, and shoot to kill without pausing for more than two seconds. Blaine wouldn't always be in a position to sit and take his time aiming, he said.

And more than just Blaine's rifle skills changed over time. He'd lost the battle against the natural growth pattern of his eyebrows and they'd finally connected over the top of his long, pointed nose, and there wasn't much he could do about it. Nor could he do anything about the beard that annoyed him to no end, making him itch to shave it off.

He wasn't quite as pale now either, his normally honey complexion tanned to more of a burnt marigold, though some of that was due to the thin layer of dirt he'd acquired over time. Looking in the mirror these days, he seemed to find more and more streaks of blond in his unkempt hair. His elbows and knees were still as bony as ever, but he was no longer tall and lanky, moving about clumsily and gracelessly. He was instead more tall and wiry, his arms and legs firm with muscle.

If only he could've looked this good before the end of the world.

The middle of week seven after the world ended, a new kind of infected showed up. It moved faster than all the rest, sniffed the air like some sort of animal, and made loud shrieking noises when it saw them up on the roof. Its skin was a maroon colour, its shape a dark blur in Blaine's scope. It was like an undead werewolf.

"The hell," Merrick gasped, shocked. He watched as it stampeded through walkers, coming directly for them.

Blaine held his breath and kept the crosshairs on the part of the blur he hoped was the head. He quickly realised its movements were a combination of walker and crawler—determined and straight-forward, but also fast. Like a bull, it had only one objective.

Blaine made an instinctual adjustment to account for the high winds and pulled the trigger. It dropped ten metres in front of them.

When the rest had been disposed of and he and Merrick went down to look at it, Blaine turned to him and asked, "What do you call these?"

Merrick lifted its upper lip with the muzzle of his gun, got a look at the dagger-sharp teeth, and said, "Hunters."

21:02

"You're ready," Merrick said that night.

Blaine looked up from his tin of beans. "What?"

"You can leave tomorrow." Merrick stood, opened the safe in the corner and got out Blaine's keys. He put them on the table in front of him. "You're ready."

Images of Blaine's mother flooded his mind and he fought the urge to get up and drive off right then. But it was dark and the light would draw infected.

"What about you?" he asked Merrick. "When the food and ammo runs out, what will you do?"

"I'll kill myself."

Blaine felt like he'd been punched in the gut. "What?"

"I'm old, Sam. I haven't got much longer left. And I'm not going to let myself become one of those things. Best to just put a gun in my mouth and pull the trigger."

Blaine ached for the old man for the first time. He knew Merrick was old, but he'd never known how old. Sometimes Merrick would cough early in the morning or late at night, so long and forceful Blaine worried he would fall over and die right then. Most of the time Merrick seemed as healthy as a man half his age.

"Then why did you... why did you make me stay here and train so hard?" Blaine never had understood the reason.

"You should have seen yourself that first day. Truly pathetic."

Blaine rolled his eyes but couldn't exactly argue with him. He'd often remembered the first day of the Outbreak with shame and embarrassment as time had passed. For the most part, he'd stopped recalling Paul and Emily and feeling a twist of grief in his stomach; he'd instead started feeling warmth bloom in his chest, because he knew they'd be proud of him.

He wasn't a coward anymore. Underneath the new strength and ability, he was still—according to Merrick—flamboyant as all hell, and he still had plenty of fear, but it was no longer a paralysing fear.

"I knew you'd never make it to Bristol. It wasn't food and petrol you needed, but knowledge. I knew if I taught you, you'd live to teach someone else. I wasn't going to give up and die before passing on my skills. Now that I have, there's nothing left for me."

Blaine didn't know how to respond. He wasn't going to try and convince Merrick to fight for a life that might not have been worth living. It was the end of the world and Merrick was old. The least Blaine could do was allow the man some control over his own demise.

"Thank you for giving me a chance to live," Blaine said. He put his keys in his pocket and finished his meal.

DAY 61
08:20

He woke early the next day to take advantage of daylight. Merrick gave him all the ammo he could spare, along with a pistol and a shotgun. Blaine packed the boot with water, the backseat with snacks to hold him until Bristol, and the passenger side was reserved for his rifle and rucksack. Merrick had added extra painkillers in case he came across someone that needed it.

And, of course, petrol.

Merrick didn't want a heartfelt goodbye. He simply held out his arm and looked at Blaine firmly, as an equal. Blaine reached through the open window of his car and shook the arm offered him.

"Goodbye, old friend."

"You've done well. It has been a pleasure to know you, Blaine."

Blaine smiled. "You looked through my wallet, didn't you?"

Merrick returned the smile and stepped back. Laughing, Blaine started the engine and drove off.

About five minutes later he braked so hard that the tyres squealed. The most beautiful man in the world had run right in front his car.

Chapter 9

In This Last of Meeting Places

M4/A34 Junction
DAY 61
08:25

Andrew didn't close his eyes like someone else might have. He kept them firmly open the entire time, watching as the Jeep neared.

The car didn't hit him. The driver seemed to have noticed him just in time to apply the brakes, and swerved out of the way before screeching to a halt. A few seconds passed, perhaps half a minute, during which Andrew felt like he was in a daze and simply looked around stupidly, but then he heard the sound of a car door open and slam shut.

His first thought when he saw the driver walk around the bonnet, pointing a pistol at him, was, *This is how it ends, Big-Ears. Some Hispanic bloke with a monobrow kills you.*

"What the fuck is your problem?" the man demanded. His single brow was drawn in a low V above where amber eyes stared at Andrew angrily. "If you wanted to off yourself, there's better ways than running in front of my car."

Andrew opened his mouth but couldn't find words. He hadn't been trying to off himself, had he?

The man came closer, eyeing Andrew up and down. "You infected?"

That Andrew did have an answer to. "No."

"Were you bitten?"

"No."

"You're acting really... Like how they act before they go mad."

Subjects report feeling listless, lethargic, and apathetic.

"I wasn't bitten," Andrew said.

The infected boy under the car was still growling. The man in front of Andrew shifted his aim and put it out of its misery before pointing the gun back at him.

"Prove it," he said.

"What?"

"Take off your shirt. Show me."

Andrew looked down at his shirt, at the grey flannel with a red stain spread across the chest. It was too small for him and the top of his arms threatened to burst it if he wasn't careful.

It was Luke's.

Andrew dropped the duffel bag and rucksack from his shoulders, then went at the buttons, undoing them slowly. He tried in vain to avoid thinking too much about the hole in the fabric near the left pocket, and how it'd been only an hour before that he'd undid the buttons to take the garment from Luke's body.

He pulled his arms out of the sleeves and held them out. "Nothing."

"T-Trousers."

"I wasn't bitten," Andrew snapped. *And like hell am I about to undress in the middle of the motorway.* "Even if I was, what's it to you anyway?"

"Why were you trying to kill yourself?"

Andrew lowered his eyes and started putting his shirt back on. "If you have to ask, you must've been living under a rock the past couple months," he muttered.

"Look, I don't know you, but don't kill yourself, okay? I've lost people too, but I'm not—"

"Mind your own fucking business."

Andrew didn't need this. He could already feel the ache in his chest threatening to overwhelm his body with heaviness again, and he definitely did not need it.

The man sighed and lowered his gun. "You can come with me, if you want."

Andrew didn't say anything.

"Unless there's food in either one of those bags, I'd say you're fucked. I have ammo, too. That's an SA80, right?"

"Yeah."

"Looks a bit beat up if you don't mind my saying so."

Andrew snorted. "It does what it's supposed to, though it is a bit loud."

The bloke smiled, and for a moment it took Andrew off guard. It had a cocky sort of air to it, and he looked even younger despite the scruffy beard over his jaw. Andrew had thought before that he was about twenty but now he guessed seventeen or eighteen.

He looks so naïve.

"What's your name?"

"Peterson." Andrew winced. "I mean Andrew."

"I'm Blaine."

Blaine walked forward and extended his arm. Andrew stared at the hand offered him and hesitated. The last person he'd touched was Luke.

The hand dropped when Andrew didn't move.

"Besides trying to off yourself, did you have a destination in mind?" Blaine asked.

Take off your uniform, go to Oxford, and find your fucking sister.

"Oxford. I have a sister in Oxford."

A34 Motorway, near Drayton
08:52

They'd been driving almost thirty minutes and Andrew still hadn't said a word since getting in the car. Blaine didn't know what had possessed him to offer him a lift in the first place—it was probably a combination of factors, like the bloke was fit and looked depressed and Blaine didn't really fancy travelling alone—but now he was thinking he might've made a mistake. Oxford wasn't on his way at all, and he just knew Merrick wouldn't have approved of the action. "It's every man for himself," the old man would've said.

Blaine slid his gaze to the left, chancing a look. Andrew was still staring blankly out the window.

"So..." He already had a feeling he'd regret asking. "What's your sister like?"

Andrew sighed in reply.

"Is she blond too?" Blaine asked.

"Yes," Andrew muttered.

"How old is she?"

"Twenty."

"Oh. She in Oxford for uni, then? She must be smart."

Nothing.

Blaine sighed. "Okay, sitting in silence isn't really my thing. I like talking."

"That much was obvious."

"And you'll have to tell me where I'm going when we reach the city anyway, so you might as well try to be friendly."

Andrew's head lifted from the window, and for a second Blaine thought he would turn to actually face him. Instead Andrew tilted his head back in a bored manner, Adam's apple jutting forward.

Blaine tried again. "What are your parents like?"

"They're dead."

Blaine deflated. "Oh. Sorry."

"Not recently. They've been dead for years."

"So it's just you and your sister?"

Andrew's head rolled to stare out the window again. "Yeah."

End of that conversation, obviously. Blaine slumped in his seat and focused on navigating the road. With the sun rising higher, it was getting hotter, so eventually he lowered the window.

Four minutes seemed to stretch on forever, then Andrew said, "If you like talking so much, talk about yourself. What's your last name?"

Blaine fought back a pleased smile. "Edwards."

"Yeah? That doesn't sound Hispanic. Or Latino or whatever you prefer to be called."

Blaine furrowed his brow in confusion but then laughed. It seemed even with the world gone to shit some things never changed. People still looked at his skin and thought he was some flavour of Spanish.

"I'm not Hispanic, you idiot."

"Then what are you?"

"Romanian. Well, half Romanian."

"Explains all the hair."

Blaine rubbed between his eyes before he realised what he was doing, then promptly dropped his hand back to the wheel.

"Shut up."

A whole minute of silence passed. Blaine awkwardly cleared his throat.

"I didn't actually mean you had to shut up," he said.

Andrew sighed. "Talk about your parents, then. Assuming they're not dead like mine."

Blaine shot him a look. *Real piece of work he is, even if he is built like bloody Adonis,* he thought wryly.

"Just my dad's dead, actually," Blaine said. "Died when I was nine. He was a musician before that, a drummer in a band. My mum works at a pub and she's great."

Blaine cringed. *Past tense, not present.*

"She did work at a pub, I mean. I dunno what... If she's — "

"Were you going to university before?"

Blaine was grateful for the interruption. "Yeah. I was going to Middlesex in London and staying with my mate Paul for the summer when the Outbreak happened. I was studying to be a photographer."

"Hmm."

"I know, Emily always said I was an idealist, thinking I'd make a career out of it. But I wanted to try first. I've always thought I should try to make money doing what I love before giving in, you know?"

"Emily your girlfriend?" Andrew asked.

"Paul's girlfriend. But... not anymore."

"Sorry."

Blaine shrugged, trying to shake it off. He even managed to half-convince himself it didn't really bother him. "It's okay. We've all lost someone, I suppose."

Andrew said nothing.

"Is that why you were trying to... you know... kill yourself earlier?"

Blaine regretted it the moment it left his mouth. Not surprisingly, Andrew didn't reply to that either.

Blaine supposed it was for the best.
So much for conversation.

Oxford
09:34

It was only about thirty minutes later that they entered Oxford. It wasn't quite as tightly packed as a city like London, but the streets were less crowded than Andrew had anticipated. There were *maybe* twenty walkers on every stretch of road, and Blaine drove by so fast they paid little attention. Where was everyone?

Blaine seemed confused and put off by it as well. He sat ramrod straight, his rifle in his lap, sweeping his gaze across the path ahead, as though expecting the worst to come at any second. Andrew wished the kid wouldn't be so tightly wound, because he had a feeling if he so much as coughed Blaine would pull the trigger and blow his head off.

The city certainly did not look promising. Andrew had been hoping for a sign, maybe a piece of cardboard or wall with some graffiti advertising where survivors should go. Portsmouth had been much more active than this. So far, there was nothing, just the consistent sight of smashed windows, overturned cars, and bullet holes. And, of course, the walking dead.

"It's at twelve Littlegate Street," Andrew said. "I've never been there before. I don't know the building."

"I think I can get to Littlegate Street, but—"

"She said it looks out on Albion Place."

"That helps."

Finally, they approached where Albion Place met Littlegate Street, and after considering the state the building was in, Blaine shot him a concerned look that Andrew ignored. Madison was resourceful; there was a chance she'd gone somewhere else, maybe taken refuge on the roof. She probably hadn't stayed in her flat, but this was as good a place as any to start the search. She might have even left a note saying where she'd be.

There had to be something. Andrew had left too many messages for there to not be something. She'd had plenty of warning, so there was every chance that she was holed up just like those people Luke had been with.

In front of the building, the nearby walkers had begun making for them. Andrew grabbed the bag of weaponry from the back and brought it up front, opening it wide as the walkers starting pounding the windows.

"Oh, nice!" Blaine exclaimed. "What are we taking?" He slung his rifle over his shoulder and his hands danced restlessly over the open bag.

Andrew reloaded his rifle. Blaine had seemed to know enough before when he'd correctly guessed the model of his gun, but being able to identify and knowing how to use were two completely different things.

"You ever fire an SA80 before?"

Blaine picked up the SA80 A2 and inspected it closely. "Not with this kind of sight. And it wasn't this new, that's for sure."

"But you can use it? It's my life on the line here, I need to know if you can cover me."

Blaine nodded. "Definitely."

"CQB isn't like fighting outside. They'll be packed in an enclosed space and if you get backed into a corner, you're dead."

"Don't you think I know that? I've survived this long, I'm sure I can—"

Blaine's reply was cut short by a particularly hard thud on one of the back windows that ended up cracking the glass, drawing a spiderweb of lines across the clear pane. The walker responsible left a face-shaped bloodstain, which smudged when they bashed their head against the glass again.

"Come on." Andrew zipped the bag. "Just follow me, pick off what I don't kill."

Blaine nodded again, and Andrew could see him mentally preparing himself. He had a strong feeling Blaine wouldn't let him die, but he wasn't too sure about Blaine getting himself killed. He'd seen selfless kids like that before, looking to be a hero or prove themselves. He'd *been* a selfless kid like that before. With a final deep breath, Andrew opened the door, shooting the throat of the walker just outside it.

There was a quick moment of unease when Blaine wasn't right at his side, but soon enough Blaine had run around the bonnet and joined him again. Andrew raised his rifle firmly, aiming for the general area of the head, and the ones that didn't instantly fall, Blaine picked off one by one. Andrew felt the familiar mixed feeling of adrenaline, disgust, and excitement.

He could kill as many of these as he wanted and feel absolutely no guilt. Nobody would hate him for these deaths.

They cleared the walkers on the street easily. It was the mass sure to be waiting in the stairwell that Andrew dreaded. Clenching his jaw, Andrew stepped through the shattered entryway, glass crunching beneath his feet.

It didn't look like anyone living was still here, but Andrew quickly pushed down any other dangerous trains of thought.

Blaine shot first, taking out a walker that lurked just down a side corridor with a single well-placed bullet. Andrew was grateful, but he'd also felt the whizz of the bullet as it shot past his ear, and Blaine had *not* followed the plan.

"I said to finish off anything I don't!" Andrew snapped over his shoulder. He would have spun around and given Blaine a proper glare if he hadn't been otherwise occupied with the infected in front of him.

"It was already so close, it was practically kissing you," Blaine countered. "On your left, on your left!"

Andrew groaned and turned left, shooting the walker that was coming out of an open doorway before returning right.

"I didn't need that image in my head," he muttered as he continued onward and upward.

Andrew navigated through the stairwell, trying to save ammunition by targeting the head. There were only so many flats in the building, only so many floors, and Madison had to be on one of them.

"Madison!" Andrew called out.

She hadn't been in Flat 1 or Flat 2, she wasn't in Flat 8 or Flat 9... Andrew was starting to find it hard to think properly with how desperately he began searching.

"Is your family rich or something?" Blaine was mumbling behind him. "Seriously, what uni student can afford these?"

Infected poured in from the corridors, crashing through the already battered doors, and it often got to the point when Blaine and he walked on bodies. It seemed the majority of Oxford wasn't to be seen on the streets, but inside, where they'd been told to lock themselves for safety.

"Jesus, Andrew, does she live on the bloody roof?" Blaine asked from three steps behind him.

"There's only a few more flats left she could be. We're almost—"

"Stop!"

Blaine's hand yanked Andrew back by the collar of his shirt, sending them both tumbling into the wall of the previous storey. Andrew quickly saw the reason for Blaine's outcry when it dropped from the ceiling and landed neatly, scampering towards them.

A crawler. Her shirt was ripped, baring one of her breasts, and the lower half of her jaw was gone. She was also missing a leg, making her one of the more deformed crawlers they'd seen. For being so handicapped, she was certainly making good speed.

Blaine was still semi-crushed between Andrew and the wall, so Andrew raised his rifle and fired, pulling the trigger until a clicking sound signalled depletion. The crawler lay sprawled on the steps, her body so full of holes that she was almost entirely drenched in black blood.

Andrew took a step forward, breathing heavily. It was eerily quiet in the stairwell, and maybe that's why Blaine didn't immediately continue their journey upwards, because he too was puzzled by the sudden calm. Andrew didn't move for a different reason.

There, on the crawler's wrist, was a flash of silver, a bracelet so wide it could almost be considered a bracer. It was an accessory Andrew knew well, had been handed down through generations and worn at all times, ever since his mother had died, even though the style was so old it looked almost medieval. Andrew took one step closer, then another, not wanting to check and see if the inlaid gold pattern would look familiar, but knowing in his gut that it would.

"Andrew?"

Andrew couldn't breathe. His throat felt tight, preventing him from swallowing, and his blood pounded in his head, right behind his eyes. He dropped to his knees just at the bottom of the steps and picked up the contorted hand, outstretching the arm.

Not her, too, please not her, too.

He couldn't lose the only person he had left in the world, not only hours after having lost Luke. He felt the full-body aching sense of despair seeping back into his bones, only this was a thousand times worse, because at least Luke hadn't been so completely altered and reduced to *this*. At least he hadn't shot Luke like some rabid animal.

You know how many people are dead because of you? How many people are worse than dead?

Andrew distantly heard the sound of gunfire behind him, and the growling of undead as they dragged themselves up the stairs. He ought to snap himself out of his daze, stop his mourning and leave it for a more appropriate time. It was what he'd done with Luke. It was what Blaine needed him to do, judging by the sound of hasty reloading.

Andrew pried the bracelet from Madison's twisted corpse and forced himself to swallow. He held it to his chest and took large, deep breaths before finally pushing up his sleeve and sliding it over his own wrist.

When Andrew got to his feet and began shooting, Blaine's sigh of relief was audible even over the gunfire, and his guilty cringe was poorly masked as well. Andrew pushed down the swell of feelings once more and met Blaine's eyes when they glanced his way.

"Let's go," he said stoically. "There's nothing here for us."

Chapter 10

Helen's Boy

A420 Motorway
10:48

Blaine wanted to say something. When they'd got back to the car, he'd wanted to apologise, but he feared Andrew snapping at him. When he had driven past the final buildings and they were back into mostly countryside, he'd wanted to say they should stop so Blaine could refill the tank with petrol, but he feared sounding unsympathetic. In the end, he stayed silent and tried not to think about what he would do if he found his mum the same way.

Then Blaine had to stop, right in the middle of the road. He knew what it had been like when he'd lost Emily and Paul, and he could only imagine what it would've been like if they'd been his siblings, the only people he had left in the world. He didn't know who Andrew was or where he was from, but it wasn't right that a man didn't show some kind of emotion after seeing that happen to his sister.

Blaine stopped, applied the brake, and waited.

Andrew didn't seem to notice or care about the fact that they'd stopped. He was staring ahead, as he had been the past forty or so minutes, his face turning an angry shade of red from the effort he must surely have been exerting not to cry. Blaine had never seen such raw emotion held back in anyone, and it was making him tear up just witnessing it, remembering the feeling.

Finally, after what seemed an endless, painful silence, Andrew fell apart. Blaine had expected maybe a gush of tears and broken inhalations of breath, or the quiet whimpering kind of crying that usually

91

went hand in hand with hopeless situations. He hadn't at all expected full body sobbing with wails so loud they penetrated his ribcage and pierced his heart.

Blaine couldn't help but be pulled into it. His eyes overfilled and hot tears ran down his cheeks. He didn't think he could speak, his throat was so restricted, but he reached a hand out to Andrew's shoulder and tried anyways, just to say *something*, even if it was only one word.

"Andrew."

Andrew reacted the instant Blaine's hand touched him. He completely turned to the side and buried his face in Blaine's chest. The sobbing was muffled, and Blaine's ears were grateful, but the rest of Blaine's body thrummed with electric energy. Andrew's arms wrapped around him, clutching him tight enough to border on painful, while Blaine could do nothing but stroke the back of Andrew's head as he cried along with him.

Blaine briefly wondered if he should say something again, but somehow knew that no words would be able to help. He wanted to let Andrew know that he was here for him, but that might remind him of the person who *wasn't* here, and Blaine didn't want that. Eventually he just whispered, "She's free now, Andrew. You freed her," and hoped that was enough, whether Andrew heard him or not.

He didn't know who Andrew was or where he was from, but he knew they'd both lost people close to them. For the moment, it seemed to be enough.

It had to have been at least fifteen minutes. The sobbing faded to whimpering, which gave way to sniffling, and Andrew's grip around Blaine's chest relaxed into a simple hold. Blaine's shirt was damp, and his body still felt lit up with emotion. At some point, one of his hands had started rubbing Andrew's back, and he abruptly stopped the second he realised it. It felt too much like feeling Andrew up in his time of mourning.

When Andrew pulled away, his arms seeming hesitant to let go, Blaine quickly spoke to brush away any awkwardness. He could *not* do awkwardness, not if they were going to be stuck in a car together.

"You can still come with me, if you like," he said. "I'm headed to Bristol to find my mum. I just need to put petrol in the tank and then we can be off again."

Andrew rubbed his eyes and nodded. His voice came out raw and hoarse. "Yeah. Yeah, I want to stay with you."

Blaine felt horrible for how good the words made him feel in that moment. "Alright. Why don't you, um. Lie in the back? We'll be moving shortly."

Blaine didn't wait for a response. He turned off the engine then got out to open the boot, where the extra petrol was stored. He heard Andrew moving around and very blatantly paid him no mind.

Blaine poured almost half the container into the tank, then put it back. He paused on the way back to the driver's seat, watching Andrew through the window for a few seconds as Andrew held the silver bracelet in his lap.

Then he thought of his mother and sprang back into action, getting in the car and starting the engine. A few minutes later, he heard the sound of Andrew shifting around, followed by Andrew's voice.

"I don't usually... do things like that. Sorry."

Blaine shrugged. "It's alright. Anyone would've done the same."

Bristol
11:41

Bristol looked the way that Blaine had thought Oxford would look—fetid, infected corpses littering the streets, signs like NEED WATER in front of boarded up houses, shop-fronts exposing the scavenged shelves inside. The people of Bristol seemed to stand on firmer ground. Even the weather had started to turn rainy, as if making its own contribution to help wash away the smell of plague.

Blaine drained the last of his water a little guiltily, and he heard Andrew in the backseat crumbling an empty bag of crisps. It felt like the windows were watching them pass by, with their perfectly decent Jeep full of petrol and their fully loaded guns. For the first time in weeks, Blaine worried more about the living than the infected.

Looking down some side-streets, Blaine noticed cars that completely blocked the way, and had to adjust his route. He hoped blocked paths were the least of his problems.

After a series of twists, turns, and roundabout navigation, Blaine made it to Milsom Street. The road was just as strewn with bodies as the rest, and therefore just as bumpy, but luckily the cars that were usually parked on either side had gone. Blaine drove up to the cream vanilla house with a blue door — his childhood home.

It looked better than the building they'd found Andrew's sister in. Both the door and the windows were boarded up, and overall the street was quiet. There was a chance nobody was inside, but Blaine held onto the hope that at least one person was.

Blaine turned off the engine, made sure the keys were in his bag, and picked up his two pistols. He didn't wait for Andrew. He jumped out and ran up to the door.

He hesitated two seconds, because his heart was hammering in his chest and he didn't know what he would do if no one answered, but then he finally knocked. He gave four hard raps of his knuckles against the wood.

Besides Andrew getting out of the car behind him, Blaine heard nothing. He waited ten seconds, knocked again, harder this time and more insistent, and thought for sure he may have possibly heard whispers and shuffling feet.

"Hello?" he said into the cracks of wood.

Please be home, oh please please be home, it's me, your son, I just want to know you're alive.

Part of the boarded door slid open to reveal a pair of blue eyes. Female, *healthy*, blue eyes that were not at all the same shade as his mum's.

"What do you want?" the woman asked curtly. Her eyes darted to the pistols in Blaine's hands, then over Blaine's shoulder where Blaine felt Andrew edging closer.

"I'm looking for my mother," Blaine said. "Helen? This is her house."

The eyes widened and lit up in surprise. "Oh, you're Helen's boy!" she exclaimed, pleased. Blaine smiled, relieved, and nodded his head vigorously. "I'm Elizabeth. I'll let you in."

The wood slid back into place and the door swung open. Elizabeth was a tall blonde with loads of freckles across her face and what seemed to be thin everything—thin arms, thin legs, thin lips, even a thin nose. She wore a rather impractical hot pink dress that came to just below her knees and clung to the curves of her skeletal body. The cleavage of her breasts (the only large thing about her) were on display due to the diving v-neck, and she wasn't wearing a bra, which made Blaine blush and avert his eyes.

"Honestly, I should have recognised you immediately from the photos, but the beard changes your face so much. I've been sleeping on the floor of your bedroom, if that's alright," she said, smiling amicably as she ran fingers through her stringy blonde hair.

Blaine stepped inside and nodded that it was quite alright. He waited for Andrew's reassuring presence to follow him in, but found it missing. Furrowing his brow, he spun around.

Andrew was walking back to the Jeep, and it didn't take long for Blaine to piece together what he was doing. He turned back to Elizabeth.

"We've got supplies in the car. Can you help us bring them in?" he asked.

"Of course. I'll go get Tim—"

"I'm here," a gruff voice said. A tanned man a few centimetres shorter than Blaine walked in from the living room, his body mostly muscular with a bit of fat around the waist. His black hair was thick and unruly, his eyes grey as storm clouds, and his demeanour reminded Blaine of one. "Don't want the delicate little princess to get dirt under her nails, do we?"

Blaine noticed he spoke with an American accent, and wondered where his mother had picked him up. How many more of them were there? Elizabeth glared at Tim before giving Blaine an apologetic smile.

"Just try to be quick about it, okay?" she said. She disappeared from the hallway into the living room Tim had emerged from.

Tim whistled when he saw the duffel bag Andrew was carrying towards the house. "Who'd y'all have to kill to get all that?"

Andrew halted in his tracks, quirked a brow at Tim before eyeing him up and down with obvious contempt, then snorted in amusement and brushed past him into the house. Blaine, even though he had less than friendly thoughts about Tim himself, didn't think it was fair of

Andrew to antagonise him right away, and tried to make amends.

"He's just in a mood," Blaine said quietly. "It's not you."

Tim grunted and made for the Jeep. Blaine opened the boot, and it only took them two trips each to get all the petrol, food, water, and ammunition inside.

They carried it to the kitchen and placed it all on the table. The house was mostly dark and lit with numerous candles, so when Blaine turned to Elizabeth, who was leaning against the worktop with her arms crossed under her breasts, she was half in shadow.

"My mum...?"

Elizabeth smiled. "Upstairs. The kid got in a bit of a scrape and she's seeing to him."

"Thanks."

Blaine left the kitchen just as he heard Elizabeth turn to Andrew and ask, "So what's your name?"

He tried not to bolt up the stairs. He was hungry and really didn't have the energy to expend, but his pulse was racing already so he compromised and went two steps at a time. He had to see his mum alive and well, he just had to.

Blaine burst through the open doorway of his mother's room and the first thing he saw in the candlelight was the outline of his mother's brown curls on top of her head. She was kneeling by the bed, cleaning the chest wound of a young man that looked about Blaine's age.

"Mum?" Blaine said breathlessly.

Helen whipped her head around so fast that her hair swung with the motion, and the curls bounced as perkily as Blaine had remembered them always having done.

There she was, pointed nose, soft blue eyes, bushy brows and all. In contrast to Blaine's tanned complexion, her usually rosy tone had apparently paled to more of a pastel shade, but she, too, seemed to have acquired a layer of dirt. Either way, she looked to be in the bloom of health.

"Blaine?"

Blaine broke out into a grin at the sound of her voice and the warmth he felt just from that.

"Blaine!"

He had taken two steps forward before she had got to her feet and assaulted him with a crushing hug. He buried his face in her hair and squeezed her just as tightly as she did him, having to bend down because she was nearly two heads shorter.

"I was so worried," she said.

"I know, I know, I was, too."

"I heard the most terrible things about London."

"I got out as soon as I could. I was delayed a bit, but I promise my first thought was to come straight here."

She finally let go a little and Blaine pulled back as well, smiling as he looked down into her blue eyes. "Tell me all about it later. I want to know what you've been doing these past two months."

Blaine nodded. "And I want to know who all these people are."

"Oh!" Helen spun around and returned to the young man laying on the bed. "Darren, this is my son, Blaine."

The incredibly handsome dark-haired boy that raised his arm to shake Blaine's hand was shirtless, a small gash bleeding near where his ribs threatened to poke through the thin skin of his chest. He wore blood-spattered blue jeans with brown, buckled leather boots.

Nice boots, Blaine thought as he approached the bed. His own trainers were nearly all worn down and falling apart, not to mention caked with blood.

"Hello Blaine," Darren said as they shook hands.

"Nice to meet you. Are you alright?" Blaine asked, nodding at the wound.

Darren glanced at the cut in his side. "Oh, yeah, I'll be fine. Just cut myself climbing through a broken window." The boy's eyes seemed to sparkle a moment and he searched Blaine's face for something. "I heard you're only a year older than me. That's cool, yeah? It'll be nice not to be the only kid here. Though Beth is only twenty-two so I don't see why *she* calls me that. Have you met her, by the way? Excellent tits, am I right? She can be vicious though, so don't tell her I—"

"Alright, that's quite enough," Helen interjected. Blaine laughed while Darren looked sheepish, and as a blush bloomed over Darren's cheeks, Blaine noticed a small mole just below his left eye. Cute. "Lay still so I can patch you up."

Blaine stood by the foot of the bed while his mother taped a bandage over the wound. Darren actually looked a bit like him—thick, dark eyebrows, light brown eyes, angular nose straight above a mouth that looked like it could stretch right across his whole face when he smiled. The only difference was that Darren's hair didn't have streaks of blond and his head was more round than long. He was also fortunate enough to have a wider gap between his brows.

Blaine's thoughts drifted, and he wondered how Andrew was faring downstairs. Andrew still seemed a bit fragile from earlier, and suddenly Blaine felt guilty for leaving him down there with people he didn't know, people who would be prodding him with questions.

"I'm going to check on my friend, alright, Mum?" Blaine said. "He, er, sort of lost someone on the way here and I'm worried about him."

Helen looked up with concerned eyes and nodded. "Of course, dear. We'll be right down."

Blaine gave his mother a final once-over, still not quite believing he'd actually made it and that she was perfectly well. He brought her into his arms and hugged her again for good measure before turning and heading back downstairs.

He followed the sound of voices to the living room, where he found Andrew sitting among what he assumed was the rest of the survivors his mother had taken in. Elizabeth and Tim were there, along with two other women, one young and one so old Blaine was surprised she was still alive. When he walked in, Andrew looked so grateful to see him that Blaine's heart gave a painful clench.

"She's well," he said, going to sit beside Andrew on the floor.

"That's good," Andrew replied.

"I'm Sarah," the young woman on the sofa next to Tim said with a wave.

She had a strong, firm voice, which seemed to appropriately match her wide face, adorned with a large nose and equally large brown eyes. Long, amber-coloured twists of hair fell nearly to her shoulders, making her pointed chin seem even sharper, and her skin was a lovely shade of peach, smooth with pockets of freckles. Tim's arm was around her and she was smiling happily.

"I worked for Helen down at the pub before... you know. I've heard a lot about you."

Blaine smiled and waved back. "Hello."

"This is Timothy," Sarah said, touching Tim's thigh. "He's from Florida over in America."

"Was vacationing in Europe when the shit hit the fan and I got stuck," Tim explained. "This sofa is where *we* sleep, by the way. Only place left for you two is the kitchen floor."

"Timothy, please," Sarah said gently. Tim sighed, and Blaine and Andrew shared a look.

"We've already met," Elizabeth said from the corner with a dazzling smile. "I'm Elizabeth, the brilliant journalist currently occupying the floor of your room. Sometimes Beth for short, but call me Liza or Lizzy and I'll claw your eyes out."

"Think I'll stick with Elizabeth," Blaine said, blood running cold. He could tell why Darren had been so worried.

"Precisely what I said," Andrew murmured next to him. Blaine chuckled.

"This is Mary," Elizabeth continued, walking over and placing a hand on the shoulder of the frail old woman in the recliner. "She's the one that's taken your old bed, I'm afraid."

"That's alright," Blaine replied. "Pleasure to meet you, Mary."

Mary wore a white nightdress that had turned yellow over time. She had thick grey hair in a single braid that fell over her shoulder, and her skin seemed to be hanging loose from her thin bones. Blaine felt like he'd break her just by looking at her too hard.

Mary lifted a wrinkled hand and smiled. Her voice came out raspy but firm. "Helen has showed me some of your photos. You're an excellent photographer."

Blaine beamed. "Thank you."

Darren walked in carrying a candle, Helen behind him. "It seems we missed the introductions," Helen said. Darren sat on the floor to the left of Blaine and placed the candle in front of them.

"It's fine," Blaine replied. "Why don't you tell me what happened from the beginning, Mum?"

Helen sat perched on the armrest of the sofa occupied by Tim and Sarah and folded her hands in her lap. "Well, that first day I stayed locked inside, of course. I heard lots of screaming and gunfire, but didn't dare look out the window. I kept upstairs. Early the next morning, a man and his wife were knocking on doors. I almost didn't answer it when they got to me, but they looked *so* desperate. I asked them what they needed and they said they just wanted a place for his mother to stay, that they couldn't take her with them."

Helen gave Mary a kind look and Mary smiled back. Helen continued. "I didn't want to leave anyway, in case you were on your way here," she said to Blaine. "So I said yes. Sarah from the pub came about a week later, with Tim. They helped board up the place. Elizabeth and Darren came almost four weeks ago, two days apart. Since then it's been the six of us, getting by on what Tim and Darren manage to scavenge."

Blaine glanced around at the faces of the survivors then back up at Helen. "That's great, Mum," he said, smiling.

"Oh yes, it sure is something," she deadpanned. "Now tell us what you've been up to, I'm sure it's much more exciting. You can share as well if you like," she added, nodding at Andrew. Blaine was grateful she offered, instead of forcing him to.

Blaine sat up straighter. "Remember how I said I was delayed?" He didn't wait for an answer. "Well, after I got out of London, there was this petrol station..."

Chapter 11
First Night

12:39

Blaine told her—and, consequently, the others as well—about how he'd met Merrick and how the old man switched his name on a daily basis. He told them about Paul and Emily and getting to Bristol and how thinking of them made him even more determined to learn what Merrick had to teach him. When Elizabeth asked where an old man learnt to snipe, he backtracked and told her that Merrick had been in the British Army, and had claimed to be the best sniper in the world.

Then he skipped ahead to meeting Andrew, how he'd almost run him over with the Jeep. He skipped the part about Andrew's sister, saying instead that they simply hadn't found her when they'd got to Oxford, but he did say that he'd agreed to let Andrew come along because it was better to travel with someone than without.

"Wow," Darren said with wide eyes at the end of it. "That sounds amazing."

Blaine blushed at the attention and shook his head. "Not when you're there. All the training Merrick made me do was terrible. All the hours of standing with that bloody rifle..."

Blaine licked his chapped lips and swallowed. So much talking had made him thirsty, and he still hadn't really eaten.

"I'll get you a drink," Darren said, scrambling to his feet. "Both of you," he added as an afterthought and went to the kitchen.

"Oh dear, I think the kid has a new idol," Elizabeth said, rolling her eyes.

"Better him than Timothy," Mary remarked. She and Elizabeth

101

laughed, while Tim grunted and glared at them. Sarah laced her fingers through Tim's, and it seemed to help.

"So what about you?" Elizabeth asked Andrew. "You just said you were in the Royal Navy when we met in the kitchen, but not much else."

Blaine gaped at him. "You were in the Royal Navy? You didn't tell me that."

Andrew shrugged. "It didn't seem important. We're all just people now, right?"

"The status may not mean much anymore but the skills do," Tim said. "The two of you... You're valuable."

Darren returned with two glasses of water and handed one each to Blaine and Andrew before reclaiming his seat on the floor beside Blaine. Andrew thanked him with a nod and took a sip before replying to Tim.

"I'm happy to help in any way I can. I can only imagine what it's been like for you to have to retrieve supplies with him," Andrew said, jerking his head in Darren's direction.

Tim laughed. "Oh, the kid's a mess. Sometimes he'll get all brave and try charging ahead, no plan whatsoever, and other times he'll freeze up with fright. Nearly blew my head off the other day when one of those crawlers jumped outta nowhere."

"I did not!" Darren yelled. He was immediately shushed by the lot of them and clapped his hand to his mouth.

Andrew chuckled. "From what I've seen, Blaine's only slightly better. At least with the little training he's had he knows enough to make a plan."

"Oi." Blaine elbowed him hard in the ribs.

"And he's not a bad shot either," Andrew amended.

"Well, thank you for helping get him home safely," Helen said.

"Could've done it on my own," Blaine muttered into his glass of water. He was glad he'd met Andrew, though, and pleased with how easy striking up a friendship was proving. "Even if he was in the Royal bloody Navy."

"You're welcome."

Helen checked her wristwatch. "Right. Sleeping arrangements," she began, getting to her feet. "Tim and Sarah are on the sofa-bed in here, with Darren in the recliner. Elizabeth and Mary are in your old room. There's always the floor of my bedroom, but I doubt you want to share a room with your mum."

"Er, no, thanks," Blaine said. "Tim said we could have the kitchen, and I'm fine with that. Andrew?" he asked, heartbeat quickening.

Andrew nodded. "I've always felt safer sleeping close to where the guns are."

"Great, all settled then," Helen sang. "You're lucky I happen to have two extra blankets. I'll be right back."

Blaine had a feeling his face went red from the thoughts that entered his head, but nobody seemed to notice, as they were all moving around, preparing for bed. He only mourned for a moment—he wouldn't have minded sharing a blanket with Andrew, not at all.

He took his glass of water and followed Andrew to the kitchen. They moved the supplies and chairs out of the way, clearing a space just to the left of the table, so if anybody entered in the middle of the night they wouldn't be tripped over.

Helen returned with two pillows and blankets, handing one to each of them. Blaine set his down and Andrew made his bed right next to it.

"Are you hungry?" Helen asked.

Blaine's stomach rumbled at the mention of food. "Yeah."

"Preferably not crisps," Andrew said.

"We're not sleeping now, are we? It's the middle of the day."

Helen laughed and shook her head. "No, not at all, this is to set you up. Though you could, if you like. Nothing stopping you, and I know you must be tired. There's tinned fruit, if you want some. There's also soup, just don't light the fire at night."

"Where could you light a fire here?" Blaine asked. "There's no fireplace."

"On the roof. You remember when I wanted to start a garden up there and got the entrance built in my bedroom? With the pull-down ladder?"

"You never got around to it," Blaine commented with a nod. "That's rather lucky now, though."

"It is." Helen agreed. "The fruit is in the fridge, but of course the fridge doesn't work, so it'll be a little warm. You're free to help

103

yourselves to a can each, but we usually try to split one between two people."

"Thanks, Mum."

"No problem at all, dear." She pulled Blaine into a hug. "It's so good to see you safe."

Blaine felt more of the weight lift off his shoulders, even if he did feel a little guilty about embracing his mum in front of Andrew, who hadn't been as fortunate. He let himself feel loved a few seconds longer before pulling away.

Blaine got the tin of fruit from the fridge and hoped his mum kept the tin opener in the same drawer as always. After discovering that she did, he opened it and got two spoons for him and Andrew to share, then went back to sit on their makeshift bedrolls.

"So much better than crisps," Andrew said after swallowing his first bite. Blaine hummed in agreement. "Even in the field we got better meals than that."

"I was stuck at a petrol station with a Costa Coffee nearby, not a grocery. I took what I could get." Blaine plunged his spoon back into the tin, knocking Andrew's out of the way. "Were you really in the Navy?"

A line formed between Andrew's brow, but just as quickly it vanished as he smoothed his expression. "Yes."

"Did you like it?"

"Sometimes, I think."

"What was your job? Or position or rank or whatever it's called."

Andrew pushed Blaine's spoon aside and stole a bite. "Commander. Royal Marines."

"Wow. Had to be recent, yeah, since you're so young? And really, a commander? I thought you had to be a lot older to be—"

"Not in times of war. Easier to get promoted then, especially when your superiors keep dying."

"Are we in a time of war, then?"

"The way the government sees it, yes."

Paul would've got a kick out of that, Blaine thought.

"Why'd you leave?" Blaine asked.

"I wanted to find my sister. I don't wanna talk about it anymore."

There was something going on with Andrew. He was handsome, that was obvious. His eyes were such an enchanted deep blue, his lips so full and soft. Without the beard Blaine had, his sculpted jaw was visible, and there was the hint of a dimple in his chin. He had hard features in his nose, cheekbones and jaw, but equally soft, almost feminine, features in his eyes and mouth. Blaine could've spent all day staring at him.

But he was so closed off and sealed shut that Blaine knew there had to be something more. He'd been granted a brief glimpse when Andrew had allowed himself to cry in the car, and it was mostly because of that shared moment of grief that Blaine decided he'd figure it out. He was determined.

"Okay."

16:23

It was strange to Blaine having all these people in the house he'd grown up in. When it had been just him and his mother, the house had seemed large. Now it seemed cramped.

He and Andrew got the gist of everyone's situation from Darren. There'd been the initial introductions, but Darren expanded upon them, telling the two of them what he claimed was everything they needed to know if they wanted to get along.

"Tim's great," Darren said, "but he knows he doesn't fit in. You'd think he'd get over such a thing, being in a foreign country, considering we're all humans just trying to survive, but it seems to unsettle him. The only person he doesn't really keep at a distance is Sarah, his bird. She's got him wrapped around her finger."

They were sitting in the upstairs corridor, Blaine and Andrew with their backs to one wall and Darren to the one opposite. Blaine hoped their voices didn't travel downstairs, where everyone except Elizabeth and Tim were still relaxing.

"Sarah's a good person, though," Darren backtracked, showing his palms. "She kept inventory for your mum when she worked at the pub, I guess? So that's what she does here, and she's fairly serious about it, too. She has a list for everything. If you're thinking about taking even a sip of rum, she'll know. And she notes down everything we bring back from supply runs. Don't let that pleasant smile of hers fool you."

"Is all that necessary?" Blaine asked, shocked.

Darren lowered his voice. "Between you and me, I think she likes it just so she has something to do. It's certainly good to know what things we need more of, what things we have, but does she need to take it so seriously? No way."

"Sometimes people need structure and order to keep their minds off things," Andrew stated firmly. Blaine looked at him in surprise. "If her way of dealing with what's happened is to stay as organised as possible, she shouldn't be scorned for it."

Darren blinked. "Right. Anyway, Mary didn't say much downstairs, but she's a storyteller, really. A lot of the time her stories are just things that happened to her, and they're usually pretty boring. But it's nice, too, you know? Relaxing. She'll just randomly start talking sometimes after dinner and everyone will start listening. And let me tell you, she's lived quite a wild life.

"Helen, well." He glanced once at Blaine, then to Andrew. "Helen sort of just makes the rules, I guess, and we follow them. Usually when I run into her, she's cleaning. I offered to help a few times but she says she likes to do it herself. 'Makes me think of when my boy used to leave things lying around,' she says. 'Easy to pretend things haven't changed.' Now, that sort of makes it sound like she's mental, but I'm not saying that. She's just reminiscing. She knows entirely well what day it is; she's the one who keeps track of the days for us on her calendar."

Blaine nodded, smiling.

"She's also Mary's closest friend here, right before Elizabeth. Which brings me to dear old, Beth," Darren said with a wistful smile. Blaine chuckled. "She's roommates with the old woman, so they're pretty close. Elizabeth reads to her sometimes since her eyesight's so bad she can't read herself. There's also loads of tension between her and Sarah if you haven't noticed, so when the claws come out, you'll want to make yourself scarce. But mostly Elizabeth is wonderful. From what I've seen, she splits her time cooking and writing."

"Because she's a journalist," Andrew supplied. Blaine had forgotten she'd told them what she used to do before all this.

Darren nodded. "That's it. She keeps a journal, writes whatever she feels like, I guess, because she says it's important to record history. Don't give me that look! I've never read it!"

"Liar," a new voice said. Blaine and Andrew both turned their heads to look at the person now at the top of the stairs. It was Sarah. "I know you read at least a page of it before I walked in on you."

"Hi, Sarah," Blaine said. "Darren was just—"

"Telling you what things are like here," she finished. "I understand." Smiling, she walked over and sat down next to Darren, across from Blaine and Andrew. "The rules are pretty simple. We share everything, eating and drinking as little as possible. We relieve ourselves in bottles or buckets up on the roof, though when it gets colder that'll probably change. We don't light the fire at night. We have one lookout posted on the roof at all times. We don't make a lot of noise."

"What if someone gets bitten?" Andrew asked.

"If it happens out on a supply run, they simply aren't allowed to come back. If they try to make trouble, that's when they're dealt with," Sarah explained. "No one wants to shoot another survivor, but we aren't ignorant of the fact that sometimes we'll have to."

"I almost shot him," Blaine said, chuckling as he playfully elbowed Andrew. Andrew didn't seem to find it quite as funny. "An idiot standing in the middle of the road."

"About that," Sarah said, looking directly at Blaine. Her voice had been gentle and calm the whole time, and now took on a more hesitant tone. "We welcomed you here because you're Helen's son. And Andrew because he's your friend."

"But there's no room for anyone else," Andrew said simply.

"Exactly. If you meet any strays or anyone who asks for help... we can't afford to bring them in. It's just the eight of us, unless Helen says otherwise. She has the final say on everything since it's her house."

"Of course, I understand," Blaine said, nodding.

"Good. Just one more thing, and this is more of a personal rule," Sarah said. She looked between Andrew and Blaine, all trace of good humour gone. "Don't gang up on Tim. Everyone here seems to like taking the piss out of him, and I hate it. He's a good man. He just has trouble expressing things."

Beside her, Darren snorted, and earned a slap to the back of his head for it.

"I don't think you'll have to worry about it much from me," Blaine said. "I'm generally a nice person."

Andrew shrugged. "I keep to myself. If people respect me, I respect them, simple as that."

Sarah's face regained its normal, easy-going nature. "Brilliant. In that case, I'm glad to have you both here."

From above, there was the sound of footsteps on the roof, then on the ladder leading down into Helen's room. Elizabeth came into view a moment later, walking into the hallway.

"Oh, hello," she said, shooting Andrew in particular a bright smile. "Dinner's ready."

22:12

"Would you mind terribly if we shared the blanket?" Andrew asked as they prepared for bed later that night.

Blaine's heart skipped a beat. "Why?"

"I think it'd be more comfortable if we slept between the two."

Blaine kept his expression as neutral as possible. "You just don't want to sleep on the bare floor. Not that I blame you. It's seen better days."

"Well, there's also that. So you don't mind? I promise not to roll over and steal it all," he added with a grin.

Blaine stopped breathing. Had Andrew just smiled? Had he almost made a joke? His entire face had changed with the tilt of one side of his mouth.

Blaine gave himself a mental pinch so he could reply. "Nah, I don't mind. But if you do steal it in your sleep, I reserve the right to kick you awake."

Andrew laid out the blankets on top of each other, remaking the bed with near clinical precision. By the time Blaine had toed his shoes off and put them next to Andrew's, Andrew was resting on his side.

Blaine tried curling up on his right, then his left, and finally settled for lying on his back. He wondered how badly he'd ache in the morning. He wondered how badly he'd ache after a week.

There were a few moments of silence, then Andrew said, "It's really great what your mum is doing."

Blaine turned to look at the back of Andrew's head. "Yeah. It's smart of her, too, isn't it? Gathering people?"

"Mmhmm."

Blaine returned his gaze to the ceiling. Why did it feel like that was only an introduction to what Andrew really wanted to say?

"Thank you," Andrew whispered. Blaine wasn't entirely sure he'd heard it until Andrew rolled onto his back, urging Blaine to meet his eyes, and continued. "For earlier today."

The timing was horrible, but just then Blaine dropped his gaze to Andrew's lips and wanted to kiss them. He wondered if they were as soft as they appeared. In the flickering candlelight, they sure *looked* like they were.

"Yeah, it's... it's fine," Blaine whispered back. Andrew made to roll back onto his side and Blaine unthinkingly stopped him with a hand on his arm. "Wait."

Andrew stared at him, waiting. Blaine hadn't exactly made a plan past this, but decided he'd take a chance. Each day could be his last, right? The worst thing Andrew could do was say no, and then they could just pretend it never happened.

Blaine sat up and leaned on his elbow, looking down at Andrew and his eyes that were so blue even in the dim light. "Can I... kiss you?" he asked under his breath. He felt himself blushing and thought about mentioning the fact that he's gay, but remembered what Merrick had said and figured maybe his natural behaviour did make it obvious. If not, then it was obvious now. He just hoped Andrew was into men as well, or at least didn't mind indulging Blaine this one time.

After Andrew's eyes lost their shocked expression, his jaw seemed to clench, and his brow came together the tiniest bit. He didn't look completely opposed to the idea, or even appalled. He looked more like he was in pain than anything.

At first he shook his head, but then he nodded and Blaine's heart soared.

Blaine didn't want the awkwardness of a slow approach, but he also didn't want to do something embarrassing like bump noses, so he raised his hand to cradle Andrew's face and hold it still. Despite that, Andrew tilted his chin up as Blaine lowered his head to press their lips together.

He tried not to immediately think it was perfect. Because that just wouldn't be reasonable, would it? Sure, it sent electricity sparking through his veins and made him almost pulse with pure joy, but that didn't make the kiss perfect. He couldn't pinpoint it at the moment, but he was positive there was *something*. It would just be too... too cliché for this to be the perfect kiss.

His arm, that's what it was. It had to be. Blaine's right arm was still bent so he was propped up on his elbow, and it was really starting to be a pain. He let his left hand drift away from Andrew's face and fall to the other side of Andrew's body so he could push himself up.

Now he was hovering over Andrew and pressing his lips harder down, nudging Andrew's mouth open so he could slide his tongue in and get a proper taste. *Now* it was the perfect kiss.

Andrew's tongue jumped to join Blaine's and his hips gave a little jerk upwards. His hands came up to hold Blaine's face and Blaine could have sworn he heard Andrew moan, maybe just a quiet, bitten-off one, when Blaine let more of his weight drop.

Blaine was just in the process of sliding his leg across Andrew's body in an attempt to straddle him when suddenly Andrew's hands pushed Blaine's face away. Blaine snapped his eyes open and saw Andrew staring up at him with a look he couldn't quite decipher. It was one part puzzled, one part helpless, and one part angry. And maybe—if Blaine searched hard enough—one part mortified. That could have been wishful thinking though, because Blaine was certainly embarrassed enough for the both of them, having taken the kiss much farther than intended.

"Satisfied?" Andrew asked.

Blaine nodded sheepishly. "Very."

"Good." Andrew pushed Blaine off of him. "Go to sleep."

Blaine tried not to look too hurt, but the twisting in his stomach made it difficult. He'd had a decent thing with Andrew, a tentative, budding friendship of sorts, and he hoped he hadn't just ruined it. Or worse, taken advantage of Andrew in a moment of mournful weakness to make him do something he regretted.

Blaine rolled onto his left side, comfort be damned and oscillated between anger, sadness, and self-loathing before he finally fell asleep.

Chapter 12

In Dreams

Andrew's hair looked remarkably golden even in the scattered sunlight that shone through the leaves above. The breeze made his fringe sweep across his forehead, and the movement momentarily distracted Blaine from his task.

"Hurry up, Blaine," Andrew said from where he was leaning back against the tree with his head turned to the left. "I need to scratch my head."

Blaine raised his camera, placing Andrew and the tree in the rightmost third of his shot with the lush green background completing the negative space in the other two thirds. Andrew wasn't the best subject, since he couldn't hold still for very long, and had a habit of moving right at the last minute to purposefully botch up the shot, but he was kind of beautiful and Blaine liked capturing him. He could look like a model even at his worst, with his hair sticking up and his shirt wrinkled from sleep. The way he was now — with a white top half-buttoned and the sleeves rolled up, and dark grey jeans that Blaine had bought him for his birthday — made him look positively delectable. Blaine simply *had* to pause under this tree and take a photo. Or twelve.

Blaine snapped one, waited until Andrew's tongue darted out to unconsciously lick his lips, and snapped another while said lips were still perfectly glistening pink. Andrew's jaw clenched as he no doubt fought the urge to raise his hand and scratch whatever phantom itch had sprung up, and it gave his expression such a wonderfully determined look that Blaine had to snap another.

"Alright, you can move now," Blaine said, lowering the camera.

He scrolled through the shots, studying them while Andrew trod over. The one of Andrew's wet lips turned out brilliantly. The wind had shifted, causing the leaves to sway and the sunlight to dance across Andrew's chest. Blaine already had plans of maybe editing the photo to add a faint blush across the bridge of Andrew's nose and darkening the bark of the tree for better contrast against the white shirt when he felt Andrew's arms wrap around his waist.

"Had your fun?" Andrew asked in his ear.

Blaine abruptly forgot anything he'd planned to do later as Andrew's warm weight aligned itself with Blaine's back and he basked in the touch. With Andrew closeness came the strong scent of old sweat produced from hard work hours before, and Blaine inhaled it deeply as though to get lost in it.

"Yes."

The camera was pulled from Blaine's hands.

"Hey—"

"I want to have a bit of fun, too," Andrew declared with a devious smile. He spun Blaine around and took a few steps back. "Take off your shirt."

Blaine felt himself flush deep red. "Andrew!"

"Come on, Blaine." Andrew waved the camera around. "Isn't it about time you've been objectified a bit yourself?"

"I do not—"

"*Blaine.*"

"Oh, fine." Blaine pulled his shirt over his head and threw it down with a huff. "There."

Only his chest was bare, but he felt completely naked. The wind made his nipples harden and he shivered. On top of that, he hated having his photo taken. He wasn't beautiful like Andrew, had too much hair on his body to be attractive, and he wasn't nearly as photogenic.

Andrew smiled, though. "Great. Now..." He pressed the flat of his warm palm to Blaine's chest and pushed him gently back to the tree. "Lean here, with your shoulders back. Place your feet just here... Arch your back a little."

"Andrew!" Blaine exclaimed when a hand brought Blaine's arse forward, thrusting his hips away from the tree.

"Perfect," Andrew purred. "Just one last thing." He moved Blaine's hands to the waistband of his jeans, hooking Blaine's thumbs inside. "Yes, fuck, that's perfect. Stay just like that."

"*Andrew,*" Blaine groaned as Andrew shuffled backwards. He felt ridiculous posing this way.

"Quit frowning, Blaine, or you'll ruin everything," Andrew ordered as he raised the camera. "Pout if you must, but don't *frown.*"

Blaine glared at him through his eyelashes, but did his best not to frown. He knew it just brought his eyebrows closer together and made him even uglier, made his lips thin like some sort of fish. He supposed he could indulge Andrew just this once, since Andrew had done it so many times for him.

Blaine suddenly heard a rustle of leaves to his left and turned to look. "What was that?"

"Nothing, Blaine. A squirrel probably, or the wind."

Blaine bit his lip, worried. "What if someone sees —"

"So you're a bloke in the park with his shirt off, who cares? It's a nice enough day."

Something didn't feel right, like they were being watched, but Blaine tried to shrug it off. Sometimes he felt even the clouds were watching him. He turned back to Andrew, who still had the camera raised and was snapping away. His big ears were sticking out on either side of the device.

"Undo the zip," Andrew said.

"Wh-What?"

"Please?"

Blaine rolled his eyes. "Oh, well, because you said please that means I *have* to do it."

Andrew lowered the camera just enough that he could peer over the top. "What if I promise to take you sailing again?"

Like a reflex, the image of Andrew bent to work pulling ropes and straining his muscles flashed through Blaine's mind. He saw the spray of water, sparkling with a momentary rainbow, shoot across Andrew's body, speckling his face and hair. He felt the rocking current underneath his feet as Andrew kissed him on the deck of the boat. Oh yes, he definitely wanted Andrew to take him sailing again.

"Alright, fine," Blaine gave in. Andrew's triumphant smile lit up his entire face before he became serious again and raised the camera.

"Keep your eyes up," Andrew instructed.

Blaine took his thumbs out of the waistband, never letting his eyes leave Andrew, and slowly undid the button of his jeans. He took a deep breath and began to pull down the zip, the unlatching of metal teeth piercing the quiet stillness of nature. Every second there was a click of a photo being taken that set Blaine's pulse racing.

Then it was done, finally, the dark grey of Blaine's briefs visible through the parted opening, along with a bulge that was becoming more and more prominent with each passing moment. Blaine had always hated being in photos *because* of the intimidating lens focused on him, and would much rather be behind it than be the subject, but now there was something alluring about its intensity. He wasn't sure if he wanted Andrew to stop.

He saw Andrew's throat swallow hard. "Slide them down," Andrew said hoarsely.

Blaine placed his hands on the side of his jeans and slid them down, until they reached the point where they fell naturally to his ankles. It was much colder now that he was practically nude, but he was sweating a little despite it. His cock was straining against the confines of his briefs, fully hard and aching with the need for touch.

But Blaine kept his hands on his stomach, fingertips dancing along the waistband of his pants as he waited for Andrew's instruction. He could see Andrew's own reaction to the situation clearly outlined in his jeans.

Blaine knew it was a dream when Andrew was suddenly standing in front of him, camera forgotten, with hands roaming over his chest and lips mouthing his neck. Blaine arched his back further away from the tree and sighed at the insistent touch of warm fingers carding through the hair below his navel, while teeth and tongue nipped at his throat.

In the way of dreams, one image melted into another. One moment they were standing against the tree, Andrew's hand finally sliding under Blaine's pants and making him gasp, and the next they were both naked, rolling around on the grass entangled in each other's limbs.

At some point, it had become warmer. There was no longer a biting chill to the air, but instead the sort of comfortable warmth that bathed their skin in the sunshine of a lazy afternoon. Even the grass wasn't as prickly and uncomfortable as it should have been, but a strange kind of velvety softness with an earthen smell underneath.

The earlier worry of someone finding them had gone with the realisation of this being a dream, but Blaine didn't quite have the power to change things or make them happen at will. It was the sort of a dream where he'd awakened to the fact that he was dreaming and now had simply to sit back and see what would happen.

He ended up on top of Andrew, straddling him with a pleased grin. Andrew's hands were large and rough where they'd settled firmly on Blaine's arse, and with a roll of Blaine's hips Andrew was tightening his grip even more, fingers insistently digging into supple flesh.

Andrew's lips pursed with the effort of not giving in right away. He redirected his attention to Blaine's legs, running his hands up and down possessively. As if in revenge, he kept bringing his hands tantalisingly close to Blaine's groin, rubbing the tender inside with his thumbs before quickly retreating back again.

It was becoming less playful and more intense, more deliberate. Where Blaine had thought he'd be able to draw it out and tease Andrew a bit more, he now found that he no longer could. He needed all of the wonderfully golden skin pressed against him, needed the cock that was lying full under his balls to be inside him.

Andrew sat up, sliding his hands over Blaine's legs a final time before they made their way up his back. From there it was easy for him to pull Blaine into a kiss, one that started out with the simple sensuous opening and closing of mouths but quickly became more heated, passionate, dirty. Fingers slid into Blaine's hair as Andrew anchored his hand on the back of Blaine's neck, as Blaine too moved his hands up to Andrew's muscled shoulders to have something to hold while he rocked against him, chasing friction.

Fuck me, come on, get inside me, fuck me.

His mouth was too busy to say anything, but mentally he begged. In his mind he was shameless, wasn't embarrassed to scream for it.

I want it, come on, fucking give it to me.

Andrew seemed content for now with simply kissing and touching every bit of Blaine he could get his hands on. When at last Blaine didn't think he could wait any longer, he pushed himself forward onto his knees, reached behind him for Andrew's cock himself and sat on it with an impatient moan.

The Blaine who was sitting back and watching loved the convenience of dream sex.

Andrew exhaled a sharp huff of air, then let out a drawn out "*oh.*" His brows came together and separated, furrowing and smoothing out as he got used to the sensation.

Again triumphant, Blaine struck up a rhythm. He placed his hands on Andrew's chest and took what he needed.

For the most part it was simply that—to take and take and take, to just have that gaping hole stuffed full, to feel the firm thickness entering and re-entering, pushing so wonderfully deep inside him. A smaller part was to satisfy Andrew, to hear the "Yeah, yeah, fuck yeah, take it," that Andrew panted beneath him.

The part that Blaine clung to, the part that made him clutch Andrew's skin and bite his lip with how much he loved it, was the preciousness of the moment. In the piece of his mind that knew this was a dream, he revelled in the achievement. *Yes, yes, this is what I wanted,* his mind chanted. *This is what I fucking wanted, God it's been so long, fuck yes, fucking finally.* It was the same part that made him go faster, made him force his hips down harder. When that didn't give him the desired results, he leaned back on his hands and changed the angle before plunging down with quick snaps of his hips.

Yeah, that's it, right fucking there, oh God.

Andrew was more or less a blur at this point. He was still there moaning and pushing Blaine on, but there was little else besides the need to finish. Cognizant Blaine was yelling, "Make him touch you, make him touch you" and it seemed that was finally one thing over which he had control, as not long after, Andrew's hand curled firmly around the base of Blaine's cock and began stroking as earnestly as Blaine would have himself.

It was a vicious pace they'd set together, and Blaine could feel the two of them barrelling toward the end as though they'd ceased to be two and had melded into one. Their separate gasps of breath and slaps of skin together made a kind of off-tempo beat. It was the music of fucking, the music of sex, and a crescendo was building, rising steadily closer to the top.

The second Blaine climaxed and spattered, crying out with the bliss of it, he woke up drenched in sweat with his heart racing. It was dark, with not even a single candle to provide a glimmer of light, but Blaine could make out Andrew lying next to him, curled up and snoring softly in his sleep.

He felt a burning shame, like he rarely had before. He felt dirty and didn't know how he could stand to share such a close space with Andrew an instant longer, not when he'd dreamt such shameful and lustful things, and was still hard from the dream even now.

You idiot, he chided himself. *You think you have a chance because he agreed to kiss you once? He just lost his sister. There's no way in hell he's thinking about ugly old you.*

Chapter 13
Settling

Bristol
DAYS 62- 71
08:14

Days went by. They didn't talk about the kiss, and Blaine didn't know whether to be grateful or frustrated. On one hand, he felt he had made a fool of himself. On the other, he thought it couldn't have been his imagination that Andrew had reacted more than just positively, which sent his mind jumping ahead to possible future scenarios between them. He was too embarrassed—and partially ashamed—to bring it up though, and it seemed like Andrew wanted to pretend it never happened.

He didn't know what was going on in that head of Andrew's because the man was so closed off and they hadn't known each other long enough for Blaine to be able to at least make an educated guess.

Though it was Blaine's childhood home, and not a particularly large one at that, Blaine still managed to lose track of him during the day. Half the time, Blaine had his hands full with Darren, who never seemed to give him any space. It wasn't until he heard Tim going on about how lucky they were to have a hardened guy like Andrew around to help that Blaine figured Andrew had been disappearing to the roof all day, taking long hours of guard duty upon himself.

As soon as the sun went down and they retired to their shared blanket, things only became more tense. Andrew was as silent as always, but if Blaine moved too much or tried to say something, Andrew would snap at him.

Some nights they could hear Tim and Sarah having whispered arguments in the living room (though they could never decipher about what), and Darren would join them in the kitchen to sleep away from the fighting couple, forcing Andrew to remain collected. Blaine always worried what Darren would make of their decided sleeping arrangement, two men sharing a blanket when they could each have their own separate space. Most times Darren just gave him a "what can you do?" sort of a grin and plopped down by the fridge, probably too tired to even address what he had to have seen. If he did suspect anything, he was a mate and didn't mention it, even during the day.

Other nights, when it was just the two of them, Blaine heard Andrew crying while he pretended to be asleep. Andrew was not okay.

It was probably around the fourth time Blaine heard Andrew sniffling that he decided to do something about it, taking the risk of making things either better or worse. Tim and Sarah were quiet that night, so there was no chance of Darren showing up. He rolled over and slid closer, pressing his body to Andrew's before wrapping an arm around Andrew's waist and pulling him in. Andrew predictably tensed up and Blaine heard him stop breathing. Blaine closed his eyes and tried to act as though the position didn't affect him as much as it really did. When Andrew finally exhaled, it was shaky enough that his entire body trembled.

"Blaine—"

"I'm just trying to help, Andrew."

Andrew breathed in and out one quick time, before his rhythm settled and his body lost its tension. Blaine fixed his right arm where it was crushed beneath him so it was more comfortable, and Andrew took the opportunity to shift a little closer. Blaine couldn't contain his smile, incongruous as it was, and he let his nose press against the nape of Andrew's neck while his left hand bunched a bit of Andrew's shirt in his fist. Andrew didn't seem to mind.

After that, Blaine started going up to the roof during the day to keep Andrew company. Andrew didn't say anything the first time, didn't even acknowledge Blaine's presence, but the second time Andrew had snapped, "If you insist on being up here, at least cover the other side."

Months ago, the harsh tone might've hurt Blaine a bit more, but

Blaine knew Andrew's type now. He'd grown used to Merrick's biting sarcasm and sometimes vulgar bluntness. Perhaps Andrew could've been nicer about suggesting it, but it did make more sense strategically that Blaine cover the opposite side of the roof if there were to be two of them up there to do it. Blaine had sighed and trudged over to the other end.

He spoke to his mum about it one day, about Andrew's withdrawal and how he should deal with it. She said the best thing he could do was try to be there for him, to try to get him to talk if possible, but not to be too pushy about it. Blaine had never been good with knowing when he was pushing too much, but he decided he'd try.

The fourth day of guard duty with Andrew was when Blaine finally started to get somewhere.

"Hey, Andrew."

Silence. Blaine looked over his shoulder and squinted against the morning sun shining in his eyes to better make out the rigid line of Andrew's back.

"What exactly are we on guard for?" he asked.

"If infected or any other survivors try to attack."

At last, an answer.

"Won't other people know where we are when they see us up here?"

"Tim said there aren't too many others in the city," Andrew explained flatly. "Those that have decided to stay and manage to survive don't go outside too much and don't have access to the kinds of weapons we have. Maybe a pistol at the most, and that's if they're willing to use the ammo. We'll be able to pick them off before they see us."

"And at night?"

"Elizabeth covers it at night."

"It'd be much easier to avoid people if you switched with her."

Andrew said nothing.

Blaine sighed and turned forward again. A walker had appeared below while he'd been talking, and was now reaching its arms up while fruitlessly trying to scale the wall. Blaine swung his calves, kicking the heels of his feet into the wall and dislodging dust. Sprays of it fell to the walker below, dropping onto its upturned rotten face.

Good job it's not a crawler, Blaine mused. Even a hunter wouldn't have been able to get up the side of the house, but a crawler could traverse it easily.

Blaine suddenly scanned the area, both down below and the nearby rooftops. His skin prickled all over with the thought of one of those things coming out of nowhere. He wasn't safe anywhere.

"Why are you avoiding them, by the way?" Blaine asked to take his mind off things.

"I don't like talking."

"That much is obvious." Blaine was hesitant to ask his next question, but he'd been having good luck so far. "You lost someone else, didn't you? Besides your sister?"

His chest was tight with anxiety waiting for the answer. He didn't know why, but he needed to know. Maybe he just needed to hear that he wasn't the only one to have lost his friends, even though he was sure he wasn't. He needed to hear someone else's story.

The fact that he wanted to know Andrew's would just be a bonus.

After nearly a minute passed, Blaine had given up on receiving an answer. He'd gone back to watching the walker beneath his dangling legs and kicking dust at its face. When he heard the strained sound of Andrew's reply, it was easy to reason why.

"Yes."

"A friend or —"

"I loved him."

Blaine winced at the turn that had taken. He recalled Paul's face the moment he'd told him to go and how pained it had been. He felt a pang in his heart in sympathy.

"It's weird," Andrew continued. "We were close friends and I never thought I loved him before, but after he died... It's complicated. I don't wanna talk about it."

"Okay." Blaine tightened and loosened his mouth, considered whether or not he should push his luck. He did want to say one last thing. "Sorry for kissing you, then. I wouldn't've asked if I'd known."

"I could've said no. I almost did."

"Suppose that's true."

It seemed to be the end of the conversation. Blaine wanted to know more about him, of course, but would put it off for another time, maybe another day. He was satisfied with what he knew for now. He was naturally friendly but even for him it was odd to know almost nothing about a man he'd taken into his mother's home.

"D'you have a pistol on you?" he asked a few minutes later. "There's a walker down here I don't wanna waste my rifle ammo on."

DAY 73
21:47

By now their sleeping position was comfortably routine, or at least it seemed that way to Blaine. He'd stopped waiting the few awkward minutes before shifting closer at night. As soon as he slipped between the blankets to join Andrew, he tucked himself neatly against the warm, muscled back, and Andrew laced their fingers together, holding Blaine's hand to his chest gratefully.

On the nights Darren came in to get away from the arguing Tim and Sarah, he still said nothing about their position. Definitely a mate, then. Better than Blaine had given him credit for.

He'd never had this sort of strange, dichotomous relationship before. He'd never even had a friend with casual benefits. He didn't know where he and Andrew stood on the spectrum but as long as he could have peaceful nights, he wasn't sure he much minded.

Andrew seemed to like it that way as well. Where he was curt and aloof during the day, he was softer and more tactile at night. Blaine could tell Andrew wasn't the type of person to let others touch him easily, and was secretly glad to be allowed the privilege. Andrew was polite enough to the others, sometimes more antagonistic than he needed to be, but alone, with Blaine, he seemed to let his guard down at least a bit.

Blaine had given up hope that Andrew would talk about things like a normal grieving person, but apparently that was the night he had finally come to his senses.

"I have no family left," Andrew whispered into the dark.

As before, Blaine thought he had imagined it at first, or perhaps that it had come from the living room and any moment Darren would come shuffling in with his blanket and pillow, causing Andrew to tense up before finally settling down again. Then Andrew's hand squeezed his fingers tighter and he felt Andrew's breathing stutter.

"She used to... she used to joke about how many children she'd have once she found someone. She said she'd breed her own army of little minions exactly like her to torment me. I used to hate the idea of miniature Maddies running around, clawing at my clothes, or tying my shoelaces together, and hiding my things. I never realised I may have actually wanted that."

Andrew inhaled sharply and unsteadily, as if his need for oxygen had sneaked up on him. He raised the hand locked with Blaine's to his face and wiped tears away. Blaine felt like his heart was breaking, and pressed his forehead to Andrew's shoulder.

"There's no hope for nieces or nephews now. And even if there was, I wouldn't want them living in this hell," Andrew said, his voice cracking near the end. "That thing... It wasn't even her. It's like she never existed, like everything before all this was just a dream. Like I was never a good person."

Andrew unlaced their fingers and Blaine worried that Andrew would get up and leave to cry somewhere else, but Andrew surprised him by turning towards him. Andrew's eyes twinkled with tears and his cheeks were wet and Blaine had to push down his own swell of emotions just so he could be the strong one for a few more minutes.

"I've done so much wrong, Blaine," Andrew whispered between them. "I don't even know what I'm doing here, in this house, with these people. I wanted to do something good and be of help to someone while I'm still alive, but I don't want to make more friends if I'm just going to lose them, too."

Blaine didn't know what to say. He was only nineteen, just a *boy* in the whole scheme of things really, as much as he protested otherwise or brought it up when it suited him, like with Merrick. He couldn't give Andrew any sagely advice because he just didn't have any, and he hardly knew Andrew. The sudden outburst of emotion and confession was a little overwhelming.

But Andrew was looking at him like he expected a reply, so Blaine swallowed past the lump in his throat and said the only thing he could think of.

"I wish I could fix everything for you," he told Andrew. "I don't know much about you, because you haven't told me much of anything, but I'm trying to help you, you know I am. All I can think to do is be here for you. Like what my mum is doing, I guess, bringing people together. They've all lost friends and family. Everyone has."

Blaine dared to wipe a fallen tear off Andrew's cheek, and left his hand there. Andrew's face seemed perfect for simply softly holding. "So we make new families to survive. Things may not ever be the way they were before. That's why I cherish those I care about even more now."

Blaine sighed and let his hand drift from Andrew's face to his hip. The blank look in Andrew's eyes let him know he'd failed. "I'm sorry I can only give you such a stupid answer."

Blaine only had time to see Andrew's brow furrow a little before Andrew kissed him. It surprised a gasp out of him, and Andrew took the opportunity to lick his lips before diving back in. Just like the last time, this kiss made Blaine tingle with electricity, right to the tips of his fingers, but now Andrew's hands clutched Blaine's side and brought him close.

Blaine had never thought a kiss could be a cry for help, but that was the way this one felt. Andrew's lips sucked and pushed against Blaine's, very innocently keeping tongue out of the mix, and he clung—yes, clinging was exactly how Blaine would describe it—to Blaine's lithe frame as though desperately trying to keep his head above water. His strong hands gripped Blaine like claws, tight enough to dig into skin and hurt, and Blaine certainly wasn't going to refuse him. He let Andrew kiss him any way he pleased, and it was almost like he could hear *HELP HELP HELP* echoing through his mind.

When Andrew's hands loosened their grip, and his body relaxed, Blaine kissed him to sleep.

DAY 75
08:43

Andrew had never been one for sitting still in a single place. Even though every moment held a little bit of tense fear, he missed the adrenaline of a fight, and *damn it* he missed the sea. After days of inaction, he'd asked Sarah if they needed any supplies, and she'd said they'd acquired enough on the previous run to last them at least two more weeks. It was risky leaving the house, not just because of the infected, but because of the other survivors camped out that saw them as competition.

There went that plan. Andrew had to admit to himself he'd been looking forward to going outside again, as mental as it sounded. Some twisted part of him itched to kill something that put up more of a fight than walkers and the occasional crawler. He wanted something that would require more thinking, something he had to hunt down.

It was strange, being on the civilian side.

But he couldn't just sit around either. It was bad enough that he hadn't been able to keep himself together and had ended up confessing his woes to Blaine, proceeding to kiss him after telling himself he wouldn't do it again.

It had been horrible the first time. Luke hadn't even been dead a day and Andrew had tainted his lips with someone else's, let Blaine kiss him and feel him in ways only Luke ever had. He'd been disgusted with himself for days afterwards, even more disgusted when he'd let Blaine hold him.

I know you hate it, but c'mere, we're having a cuddle.

The first few times he'd pretended it was Luke. He'd closed his eyes and imagined a time before the Outbreak, when he'd always grudgingly given in and let Luke manhandle him into little spoon.

But it was impossible to pretend for long. The floor was too hard to be a bed, the blankets and Blaine smelled completely different, and the hollow ache in Andrew's chest always returned to remind him that no, Luke wasn't alive anymore, Luke would never hold him this way again, and it was foolish to believe otherwise.

He had stopped pretending and started trying to find solace in the fact that *someone* still wanted to hold him this way. Despite everything he'd done, all the people whose lives were lost or ruined due to his actions, this half-Romanian kid with a monobrow found him worthy of being helped.

To make things worse, Blaine kept giving him *looks*, which were fine at night when Andrew deemed it okay to indulge and accept the concern (he was even alright with Darren being there, because the kid seemed able to keep his mouth shut), but during the day it was off-putting. Not just because he suspected Tim might have a problem with something going on between two men, but because Andrew didn't think he was ready to care for someone again just yet. It was disrespectful to Luke's memory, it was too painful to consider, and caring about someone was dangerous even when there *wasn't* the possibility of losing them at any given moment.

He needed to get back on platonic ground with Blaine, because Blaine obviously wanted more, or at least wanted something definitive on which to base their relationship. He couldn't dance over a blurry line of friendship as Luke had, and the longer the whole thing went on, the more Andrew began to dangerously think he wanted something more concrete as well.

He needed to get off his arse and do something productive. The idea came to him when he saw Blaine changing into one of his cleaner shirts.

Blaine had hair all over. He had it across his chest, down his stomach, over his arms and legs and even on the small of his back. It wasn't that he looked childish or even particularly wimpy. Like Luke, he was slender and lean, but unlike Luke, his muscles weren't nearly as well-toned. He moved about like a clumsy, furry collection of twigs.

Andrew's idea to help ease his restlessness would do more than just solidify the friendship — *only* friendship — between him and Blaine. It would simultaneously prove that he wasn't weak, that he didn't need to be comforted nearly as much as Blaine believed he did. Yes, he'd had his few moments of weakness and had broken down on what now totalled two occasions, but he didn't *need* the comfort Blaine offered.

Even if the comfort was pleasant.

There wasn't much room in the house, but the roof was a suitable place for the activities Andrew had in mind. One morning, on the way to start the day's guard, he dragged Darren up there. Elizabeth was making soup, and Tim had followed out of curiosity.

"Blaine," he called out. Blaine was already sitting on the edge of the roof, staring out at the pink horizon, and turned his head at the sound of his name. "We're gonna do something a bit different

127

today."

Blaine grinned and got to his feet. "Yeah? What?"

"Well," Andrew began, "thing is, Blaine, you're kind of weak."

Elizabeth laughed from where she stirred the pot over the fire. Tim poked Darren in the side with a stubby finger.

Blaine's brow furrowed and he blinked, but then tilted his chin defiantly. "Strong enough to survive this long. Merrick made me stand with my rifle raised for hours. *Hours*, Andrew."

"Hey, I didn't say you were useless, I said you're 'kind of weak.' And I'm restless, so indulge me for both our sakes."

Andrew knew it was a bit of a low blow, made even more evident in the way Blaine crossed his arms with a huff, but it got the job done.

"Fine. What do you want?" Blaine grumbled.

Andrew cracked a smile. "Let's see how many press-ups you two can do." He dropped to the ground and held his body up with his arms, waiting for Blaine and Darren to do the same. Tim joined in with a chuckle.

Blaine's face stayed passive and neutral, so Andrew knew he was in for a laugh. He waited until all three of them were in position to say, "Go."

Tim kept pace with Andrew easily. Blaine got to twenty and his arms started shaking on each ascent, but he pressed forward. Darren was reduced to Blaine's quivering state by thirty-three. Andrew was doing them so fast he got to fifty by the time they were all sweating and gasping for breath.

Finally, Blaine collapsed and pushed himself up one last time to sit cross-legged. "You fucking show-off," he panted.

"You shouldn't swear in front of a lady," Elizabeth sang from the fire. Blaine was so out of breath he ignored her.

Andrew stopped, even though he could have gone on a lot longer. Tim's pace had slowed but it was obvious he could do probably twenty more before he too gave out.

"Did you expect any less?" Andrew asked with a smirk just as Darren gave up.

Tim stopped a few seconds later. "Whew," he exhaled. "Haven't done *that* in a minute."

"Alright," Andrew said, getting their attention again. "Let's stretch before we do anything else. I assume you at least know how to stretch, yeah?"

Blaine and Darren groaned and Tim got up, wiping dust from his trousers. "That's my cue, I'm afraid," he said. "I just wanted to beat your sorry asses doin' push-ups. Have fun, kiddos." He ruffled Darren's hair before leaving to check the status of the soup and going back inside.

"Well, what are you waiting for?" Andrew nudged them. "Come on, legs out, lean forward. If you're good, Darren, Blaine will teach you how to use his rifle later."

Darren's eyes lit up, while Blaine glared bloody murder over his shoulder.

Chapter 14

Interaction

DAY 80
10:54

For the most part, it hadn't worked. Every night, Blaine slid close to Andrew and wrapped an arm around him like he was entitled to, and every night, Andrew battled with himself to either shrug Blaine off or sigh and melt back into the pleasing warmth.

Every night, he lost the battle and tucked himself closer, because after a long day of being on alert and forcing himself to appear as though he were perfectly fine, it was nice to feel he could relax. The point of the strength conditioning had been to prove that he *didn't* need the comfort, but it seemed Blaine hadn't got the point. Or maybe he did, but chose to ignore it.

If only Blaine didn't do it so automatically, before Andrew could steel himself against it. It'd be easier to resist that way, but like Luke, Blaine made it so difficult *not* to enjoy.

Mornings were worse. If "perfect" were a feeling, waking up in Blaine's embrace would've been it, at least for the few moments Andrew allowed himself to enjoy it. In the world between dreaming and reality, the secure weight of Blaine around him was heavenly. For the few seconds during which Andrew didn't know who or where he was, what the state of the world was or what could kill him at any instant, lying there curled up and peaceful without a care was a luxury Andrew didn't often have, and had learnt to appreciate quickly.

It was a feeling that he clung to, and because of that, he both loved and hated it.

As if that wasn't bad enough, there were times when he woke to Blaine's erection pressing against his lower back. Other times Blaine would unconsciously rub against him and sigh from the friction, and those times Andrew would always bolt from the bed before Blaine could wake up and realise what he was doing.

But otherwise, when their bodies had moved during the night and were loosely tangled, and there seemed to be no hurry to flee due to arousal, Andrew waited a few seconds, smiling contentedly as he held Blaine's arm against his chest like some sort of child's toy. He enjoyed their synced breathing just long enough for him to start feeling guilty. Then he'd open his eyes and slide from between the blankets, Blaine's fingers curling inward as Andrew left, reluctant to let go even in his sleep. By the time Blaine walked onto the roof twenty minutes later, rubbing his eyes and yawning as he took up his post, everything was normal again.

Some mornings, Andrew wanted more than almost anything to turn over and reciprocate, to roll his hips into Blaine the way he'd used to do to Luke. He wanted that closeness again, not just the holding in comfort, but all of it—the insistent sliding of stomach against stomach, the gasping, the fingernails digging into skin. He wanted the kissing, the thrusting, the moaning. It was always Luke to whom Andrew had gone for cathartic sex, and with Luke gone, *because* Luke was gone, there was no outlet.

Sometimes, sitting up on the roof, Andrew would turn and look over his shoulder at Blaine's hunched back, the rising sun shining through the blond tips of his hair, and have to remind himself why he hadn't just fucked him already.

18:33

They were all listening to Mary tell a story during dinner. Actually, almost everyone had finished their meal, so they sat listening with empty bowls and wandering thoughts. Only Tim wasn't present, as it was his shift to be on guard up on the roof.

Blaine, sitting cross-legged on the sofa with his bowl in his lap, was staring at Mary in the recliner with obvious fascination. If he had a mind to, Andrew could openly stare without the threat of Blaine catching him. He tried to keep his gaze fixed on the floor, anywhere but Blaine, and he ended up catching Darren's eye.

Darren's blush as he lowered his head and looked at his hands was visible even in the candlelight. That was just fine with Andrew. The boy could look and blush all he wanted. It set Andrew a little on edge, knowing his and Blaine's awkward almost-relationship had a silent observer, but Darren had proved trustworthy so far. He admired Darren at least for that.

Letting his gaze drift again, he saw Elizabeth shoot him a glance. He quickly looked away and tried to focus on Mary's story.

"George was always stubborn, though, and wouldn't listen," her raspy voice said clearly. One of her old, wrinkled hands held a fist full of her yellowing nightdress, making the fabric hitch up and show a bony ankle. "I told him Janice had always been good to him. I said, 'That's the kind of woman who'll stick with you through the good times and the bad. That's not the sort of woman you cheat on just because some other tart with big breasts and a small waist sashays by you.' He was an idiot, my son. But I didn't say a word to his wife, either way.

"Wasn't until a few weeks later that Janice asked if there was something going on with him. He'd been acting odd, apparently, snappish for no reason. I still didn't say anything to her. George just didn't know what he was doing, that's all, and I didn't want Janice to leave him while he figured things out for himself. He needed a woman like Janice in his life, and it wasn't his fault he couldn't see how stupid..."

Andrew tuned her out again, not interested in the life and times of her son. He let his thoughts wander again, thought of the sea, the waves, the smell of the ocean, until Mary's voice became background noise.

He could see why the others enjoyed this time so much. It was almost like they could forget the dangers that lurked on the other side of the walls, the soulless monsters shuffling through the quiet city night. For the moment, they were just people sitting around, listening to an old woman drone on.

The next time Andrew looked up, he caught not only Elizabeth's eye, but Helen's. Elizabeth's eyes darted away, but Helen's gaze remained firm. Andrew stared back as long as he was able, and only looked away first because he worried he was beginning to come off as rude.

It was no surprise when Helen came up to him after Mary's story ended. He had to pee, and was heading for the ladder to go up to the roof when Helen pulled him aside.

"Can I talk to you?" she asked.

Andrew nodded. He wasn't about to deny the owner of the house anything. Another part of him — a part he adamantly tried to stomp on — thought that he'd never deny Blaine's mother anything.

She took him up to Blaine's old room. It seemed oddly fitting for what Andrew was sure she wanted to say. Andrew had only glimpsed this room once, and now found his heart racing as he struggled not to look around with too much interest. All of Blaine's childhood things were still here; traces of his past lay around, things like a Rubik's cube sitting on a wall shelf. Everything was Blaine in this room, even though two women currently slept in it.

"Blaine's told me you've been having a hard time," Helen said. "He's been worried about you."

Andrew's stomach sank. As much as he hadn't wanted to talk about the state of his relationship with Blaine, he wanted to talk about his own troubles even less. It seemed worrying about other people's problems was a family trait.

"Everyone's had a hard time," Andrew said carefully.

"Yes, and everyone deals with things differently," she replied, brows furrowing in concern. "I won't lie and say I understand. I have no idea — nobody here has any idea — what you've been through. You've told us next to nothing about yourself, and we've all respected that because you've been a good member of our group. But that's not what I want to talk about. Blaine said he's worked things out with you, got you to open up a bit, and I'm leaving things at that. I only wanted to be sure you were alright; it's not my business to pry."

Andrew knew for certain now what it was she wanted to address, but didn't know what to do — turn himself cold and hard, blocking her off as he would any ordinary stranger, or be charming and warm, open and sympathetic? He knew which he would prefer to do, but he couldn't afford to lose favour with her.

"What did you want to talk about?" he asked. He was still keeping his voice easy and calm, not yet sure which reaction he'd decided on.

"You and my son have become close," she said. Andrew's heart skipped a beat, his pulse stuttering at how simply she put it out there. He suddenly couldn't look in her keen eyes; though they were an entirely different colour than Blaine's, they seemed to have the same perceptive air. "He cares a good deal about you."

Andrew swallowed. "I know."

"I don't want him getting hurt. In any way. I thought I'd lost him once already."

The choice was suddenly easy. He wouldn't be cold and indifferent, nor open and charming; he'd just be himself. "I swear to you I'd never hurt him. I'd never let *anything* hurt him."

He'd known it to be true for a while, that letting any harm come to Blaine was probably the worst thing that could happen, but admitting as much was something else. It made it more tangible somehow.

Helen smiled. "Good."

DAY 82
09:44

Andrew was still restless. He'd never done well being cooped up anywhere, though he was grateful for the space they had up on the roof. It wasn't "fresh" air by any means, but the openness and the wind made it much better than the smoky, oppressive air inside.

Sneaking a look at Sarah's lists in the kitchen one morning, he felt he could make a compelling argument for a supply run. He put his usual morning routine on hold to search her out, and found her sitting by the boarded up window in the living room, reading a book. Helen was there as well, working on something on the other side of the room, something with needles. Knitting?

Andrew went up to Sarah cautiously, wondering how to begin,

and hated himself for his inability to socialise properly. There was a time when he'd been brilliant at this sort of thing; before all this, he'd had as much social grace and elegance as Madison. Now it was as if that part of his brain was broken. He struggled to remember the basics: smile, nod, use the correct tone of voice, maintain eye contact.

"Sarah?" His voice came out too hoarse, too gravelly. He should've cleared his throat first. He did it now.

Sarah looked up and brushed a curly strand of amber hair out of her face. She lowered the book and blinked at him with wide eyes. "Alright, Andrew?"

"I had a look at the inventory. Your lists are quite impressive. Very detailed."

Sarah smiled. "Thank you. Everyone else seems to think they're a bit mundane."

"I noticed we're running low on tinned fruit, bottled water, and, um... other things that I guess you need."

Sarah laughed, no doubt at the way Andrew was blushing. "It's okay, Tim doesn't like saying tampons either."

"We should also probably get loo roll," Andrew said, not so subtly moving on. "I've heard Elizabeth complain that just because it's the end of the world, it doesn't mean we can't be civilised. Also it wouldn't hurt to get more rounds for our pistols. Blaine could use some ammo for his rifle, but 9mm and 5.56mm rounds are more common and easier to find."

"Oh, uh, okay—"

"I also noticed that you've got a list for the places you've looted so far and you've only gone to shops. We might consider going through homes, too, don't you think?"

Sarah blinked, looking lost, and was even gaping a little. Andrew tried to backtrack.

"Sorry if that was overwhelming. I just meant to ask if you think—"

"You still want to go on a supply run?" she finished, bringing her eyes into focus. Andrew nodded. He even attempted a smile for good measure. "Sure. Grab the list from the kitchen and talk to Tim about it. Just remember to leave a gun for me before you leave, since I'll be taking your shift on the roof."

"Oh, and Andrew?" Helen called from the other side of the living room.

Andrew turned to face her. "Yes?"

"Mary's not feeling well. I think she's got a fever. If you wouldn't mind looking for something—vitamins, penicillin. Anything would be appreciated."

"Of course, Helen." Though he doubted they'd find such things at an ordinary shop, not if most places had been ransacked already. He'd have to talk to Tim about it.

Helen beckoned him over with a finger and he stepped around the low-burning candles on the floor to go to her. When she waved a hand, urging him closer, he bent forward and lowered his head.

"I know Blaine will want to go with you. Remember what I said and keep him safe," she whispered.

So many things Andrew wanted to say. *I'd die before I see any harm come to him,* was the first thought that entered his head. He didn't dare say it aloud, even if Helen did suspect his feelings for her son already. Instead he simply nodded.

10:34

Tim set out the map of Bristol on the roof, where Andrew, Blaine, and Darren surrounded it. It was cold and windy out, signs of winter bringing worries back to the forefront of their minds. Tim held the map still with his knees on the bottom corners.

"There's one supermarket we haven't raided yet," Tim said, pointing. "This is where we are on Milsom Street, and here's the market around the corner. No way in Hell is there medicine there, though. I say we go there on foot, grab what we can, then take your Jeep to the hospital."

The hospital. Too much effort for an old woman who didn't have much time left anyway. Andrew didn't think it was worth the risk, but didn't say anything. It might not have been worth the risk, but that didn't mean he didn't want to go. Already his fingers were twitching.

Blaine shook his head, clearly thinking what Andrew did about the distance. He slid his finger to the hospital on the map. "No, no, no. The nearest hospital with what we'll need is here, the Glen. Why don't we just go to the chemist right down the street?" he asked, pointing.

"It's no good. The boy and me been there already," Tim explained. "The place is cleared out, looted, trashed, and looking like a goddamn war zone. I can guarantee every pharmacy in the area'll be the same. Nobody's gone to the hospital, see? Too risky, so nobody wants to. *That's* where we'll find our treasure."

"We could always check the nearby houses, too, see if anyone has paracetamol or something in their medicine cabinets," Andrew suggested. "Hopefully nothing expired. But for the hospital, Blaine and I can go. I'm betting Blaine knows his way around the place more than any of us here, and I'm best equipped to cover him."

"Sounds fine by me," Tim said. "We've been wary of going through any other houses, though, in case we run into anyone. You know, anyone whose flesh is still attached to their bones and they're protective of keeping it that way. Let's just see what you two bring back from the hospital, okay?"

Andrew bit back his reply. *Patience*, he told himself. "Alright," he said.

"My mum'll hate it, but I'm in," Blaine agreed. Darren nodded his affirmation as well.

"Good. Now for the store, I'm thinking sniper boy can cover us from that rooftop there," Tim explained, raising his arm to indicate the spot not far off. "We technically don't even need Blondie; Darren and I have done runs like this before. But the more arms we have to carry stuff back with us, the better."

Andrew gritted his teeth at the nickname, but let it pass.

"We go triangle formation, me at the point with you two at the back," he said, pointing to Andrew and Darren. He looked up, staring straight at Andrew. "Any problems with that?"

Andrew didn't have a problem letting *anyone* lead after what happened at Portsmouth.

"Not at all."

137

Chapter 15

Test

11:22

It'd been a while since Blaine had gone into combat against infected. Not terribly long, and he *had* picked off a handful from the roof, but up close and personal? Eye to eye, with the stench of decaying flesh rushing up his nose? As he retrieved his rifle and ammo from the kitchen, then dashed back up to the roof, he prayed he hadn't lost his edge.

The shop really was just down the street and around the corner, and the houses here were side by side, so as Tim had said, Blaine could follow the three men easily from the rooftops. When he neared the intersection at Stapleton Road, he jumped down to the roof of a lower building, hoisted himself up over the ledge of the shop at the end, then followed their progress perched from there. He had to lie on his side, his elbow half off the edge of the roof, just to keep his sights set on them.

There weren't many infected out roaming today, so Blaine didn't have to do much, since the three of them below could handle it. Tim did most of it, swinging his chair leg with nails riddled through it at the lolling, infected heads. Every so often Andrew or Darren would break from their triangle formation to take care of a walker, but much of their trip down the street was running. Helen had said they'd cleared a lot of the neighbourhood already, and Blaine had to admit that it certainly smelt like it.

He did have to pick off a few walkers that had congregated around the shop entrance when the three below reached it. He was hesitant at first; amidst the flailing arms and distant growls, Andrew was there. To even have Andrew in the view of his scope seemed wrong, let alone pulling the trigger. But the group that had amassed was too much for two blunt weapons and a pistol to handle. Blaine reminded himself to keep a level head and killed a few with well-placed shots to the skull.

As he waited up above for Andrew and the others to loot the store, he kept an eye on the surroundings. Tim's mention of running into other people had him looking over his shoulder every so often, worried about encountering other survivors. So far, there hadn't been any incidents, not in all the days he'd taken up lookout on the roof. Not even the smoke of a fire in the distance. Not at the petrol station with Merrick, not in Oxford, and not even in Bristol, though their presence was certainly palpable here. It was as though they were simply lying in wait.

He knew Andrew didn't have any qualms shooting other people, considering it'd been his job before. Tim and Darren didn't seem to have trouble with it either, but they'd been here mostly from the beginning, and had had to defend themselves from both kinds of enemies for much longer. Blaine had no doubts about whether or not he had the ability to, it was more that he wasn't sure if he was ready to.

He had no problem killing the soulless infected, but humans? People with loved ones, who were just trying to stay alive like him? He didn't know if he could handle taking an actual life. He wished Merrick was there to tell him what to do, how to feel.

Just as Blaine's right arm was starting to fall asleep, he saw a flash of gunfire in the shop from his spot across the street. Andrew being the only one with a gun, Blaine wondered if it was a zombie or human who'd been shot. Or perhaps they'd run into a survivor and one of them had been shot *at*?

Blaine shook his head, chasing the thoughts away. He had to stay focused and keep his eyes sharp. He had to see everything going on at one time, and couldn't have emotions clouding his thinking or giving him tunnel vision.

He shivered in the cold October wind and spared a brief glance at the sky. It would probably rain again soon. Tomorrow, or the day after that, maybe. They wouldn't be able to cook anything on the roof and would have to eat the last of the tinned fruit.

He ran his finger over the radio clipped to his jeans. Part of him wanted to use it to tell them to look for dehydrated or freeze dried food, something they wouldn't have to heat up or eat from a tin. Cereal, maybe, if they could find it. But he was only supposed to use the radio for emergencies because of the noise, and Andrew probably knew what he was doing. He had experience.

Blaine couldn't tell how much time had passed, but his tensed muscles and keen watching made it seem to drag on forever. Then he saw movement, a shadow passing from between houses and darting to the bus stop just below him.

Most of the walkers in the street were dead, but the man below dispatched the ones that came up to him with a long blade, a machete of some sort. He swung it into their skulls, cleaving through bone just enough to take them out quietly.

Blaine's pulse quickened and he tightened his finger over the trigger. He kept the crosshairs trained on the man's head, watching as he leaned against the bus stop and caught his breath. Here at last was evidence that Blaine's group wasn't the only one in the city, someone finally making their presence known. He was simultaneously relieved not to be alone, and fearful of what it meant. It was only when the man twisted his neck around to check the area that Blaine recognised him.

It wasn't anybody Blaine knew personally. They'd only gone to secondary school together ages ago, seen each other in the corridors or in the canteen. Blaine didn't even remember the bloke's name, but there he was, clothed in faded black with grime on his face, fierce determination in his grey eyes. Blaine knew, like a sixth sense, that he was headed for the supermarket.

Blaine wet his lips, took a deep breath, and clenched his jaw. He didn't want to kill the man, but he could tell by the look in his eyes that he was dangerous. It wouldn't be a problem if he got to the supermarket; it would be three against one, and the one didn't even have a gun.

Blaine didn't plan on letting it get that far. He compromised.

When the man took a step out from behind the bus stop, Blaine aimed for just near the man's hand, waited for the wind to die down a bit, and pulled the trigger.

It was a warning shot. The man jumped back, looking around for the source. Blaine shuffled to the side and flattened his body to the roof.

He raised his head to look a few seconds later. The man had started running across the street. Blaine raised his rifle again and shot just past his ear before he ducked behind a car.

Blaine clenched his jaw. If he shot the car, the alarm could go off and it would make too much noise. He had to wait until the man darted out again. He held his rifle steady, prepared to swing left or right depending on which side of the car the man decided to flee.

He was saved by his three comrades finally exiting the building, Tim and Darren carrying one large box each while Andrew, his rucksack stuffed full, scanned the street with his pistol raised. Blaine didn't care what the man did after his friends had made it to safety; he could blow the place up if he wanted. If he moved the slightest bit to harm Andrew, Tim, or Darren... Well, Blaine had no qualms about shooting him anywhere below the waist.

Luckily the man wasn't stupid. He sneaked a look to the left, spying the pavement where the three men were hurrying back, then slid as stealthily as he could around the car, crouching against its side and out of sight. Blaine stayed locked in position and saw the man scour the rooftops before finding him, only noticing Blaine because Blaine let him. The man waved his free hand frantically in a placating gesture with wide eyes, signalling he wouldn't try anything.

Blaine lowered his rifle, pulling his face away from the scope, and held his left hand up, his fingers splayed and showing the palm. He watched as the three from his group neared the corner of the street, and counted down from five for the man below. By the time he pulled in his thumb, Andrew and the others had turned the corner and were already halfway home.

The man nodded once, gratefully, then turned and sprinted for the supermarket. Blaine didn't stay to watch; he shuffled to his feet and navigated the rooftops back to the one with the fire pit and the drop-down ladder. He didn't think he'd share this with anyone. He thought he'd keep this instance, this little act of kindness, to himself. Mostly because the others would've wanted him to kill him.

Descending the ladder, Blaine heard Tim's laughter in the living room. He smiled to himself, already knowing it was a joke at Darren's expense.

"Find anything good?" Blaine asked as he walked in. Everyone but Mary was crowded around the two boxes in the middle of the room, and Darren was holding a container of shaving cream.

"I found this," Darren said, raising it. "Someone had been hiding away back there, and, well, Andrew took care of them." Blaine shot Andrew a glance, but Andrew was busily rummaging through the rucksack he'd set on the floor. "Otherwise I don't think they stocked it," Darren went on. "Couldn't find razors, but Andrew said he learnt how to do it with a knife."

"Not just any knife, mind you," Andrew appended, looking up. "You can't just take any blade to your face. And it has to be extremely sharp. But it's possible. I could teach you."

Blaine was still preoccupied with the fact that Andrew *had* in fact killed someone living, but forced it to the back of his mind. If no one else was going to make a big deal over it, he wouldn't either, especially since he'd nearly done the same thing.

"That's hardly enough for all four of us," he said, eyebrow arched.

"There's more." Darren turned and pulled out six more tubs of it, one for each of them and two left over.

"And thank goodness," Helen piped up. "All that hair on your face makes you look so unclean, Blaine."

Blaine laughed and caught the container Darren tossed him. "Cheers. Anything else? It looks like it'll rain soon—"

Andrew held up a finger and grinned. "Which is exactly what I thought you'd say, so I got extra crisps just for you."

Blaine groaned. "I hate you *so* much right now."

Andrew shrugged. "It was a supermarket, Blaine, they had things like meat and fish and bread, hardly anything meant to survive an apocalypse. We're lucky with what we found."

"It's more canned food," Darren supplied.

"As I suspected."

"Hey, hey, let's not forget the drinks," Tim said, slapping Darren and Andrew's backs. "We got soda, beer, water. Probably gone flat by now, but at least we can get drunk!"

"The last thing you need is to get drunk, Tim," Elizabeth said. "I can only imagine what you'd be like."

Tim shot her a glare, but she held his gaze with icy firmness. Sarah cleared her throat and Tim looked away, mumbling, "Whatever. Bitch."

"We should get to the hospital soon," Blaine said, breaking the tension. His mother looked at him gratefully and Andrew nodded.

"I'll go move our bed aside so there's room for you all to walk in the kitchen," Andrew said, slipping out of the room.

Blaine blushed, but Andrew didn't seem to notice what he'd said. Blaine was lucky enough to be standing out of the ring of candles, so the colour in his cheeks wasn't too visible in the shadow.

Tim, apparently, wasn't as slow as he looked, and tilted his head to the side. "Did he say —"

"Beds," Blaine supplied. "He said beds. Plural."

"Uh huh."

"I heard him say beds too," Darren added.

"Where's the keys for the Jeep?" Blaine asked, grateful for Darren's help, but changing topic nonetheless.

"In the kitchen."

"Right, I'll just get it, then." Blaine adjusted the strap of his rifle slung across his chest and spun on his heel, leaving as quickly as he could.

Andrew had slid the blankets to the side and was rolling up the edges a little when Blaine walked in.

"Have I ever said you're an arse?" he snapped as quietly as he dared.

Andrew froze, his brow furrowing the slightest bit. "What have I done now?"

Blaine sighed and snatched the keys from the worktop before walking to the table where the guns were laid out. He ignored Andrew, wrapping his belt around his waist and seeing if he could use it as a makeshift holster for his pistols.

"Blaine, what is it?"

"Nothing. I'll tell you later. Forget it."

Tim and Darren walked into the kitchen then, carrying the boxes. By that time, Andrew had rolled their blankets up enough that it was impossible to tell whether or not they'd been separated beforehand. Blaine felt a sudden sickening fear that they might have to change the way they slept from now on just to validate Blaine's story should anyone look in during the daytime. And really, it was a wonder only Darren had noticed before, since the kitchen table only partially hid their bed from view.

Blaine stifled the urge to groan. Tim and Sarah's night-time arguments provided enough gossip around the house. Then there was the way Darren alternated between following around both him and Elizabeth like a loyal dog, wanting to impress one and get into the other's knickers. Had there been quiet talk about his and Andrew's relationship, too, knowing looks that Blaine had simply been too ignorant to notice? He remembered Tim's sceptical "uh huh" and fought off groaning again.

He kept fiddling with his belt instead, seeing if he could pull the pistols out quick enough to be efficient. He couldn't. As Tim and Darren unloaded the boxes, and Sarah walked in, her trusty list in hand, Andrew came over and looked Blaine up and down before shaking his head and tutting.

"You need a chest holster," he said quietly. "We'll try to find you one. Lift one off an infected officer or something."

Andrew looked at him like he had such potential, with an undertone of maybe-more-than-friendly affection and pride. Blaine felt like what he imagined one of Andrew's men might have felt when they were shaped into what Andrew needed them to be—strong, able, and willing to prove that they could do anything they were asked, all Andrew had to do was say the word.

But if Andrew kept looking at him like that in front of other people and expecting them not to think something was going on, it was going to be a problem.

Chapter 16
Hospital

12:20

Blaine put the pistols back in the makeshift holster with a huff and brushed past Andrew to the corridor leading to the door. He wanted to leave *now* and just get this stupid hospital raid over with. Then he wanted to beat Andrew with the butt of his rifle until Andrew told him what was going on in that thick head of his, because he was getting tired of dancing around each other, no matter how much Andrew needed time to grieve.

He heard Andrew pick up his gun from the table and was about to open the front door when he was suddenly yanked back and pulled into an embrace. He recognised the form of his mother and blinked a few times before tentatively raising his arms and hugging her back.

Some of the anger toward Andrew melted away as he held her, bending over to rest a cheek on the top of her head. A flicker of a memory pushed its way to the forefront of his mind — the first time he'd hugged her and realised how short she was, or rather how tall he'd grown. He'd been sixteen, maybe seventeen at the time. He'd loved hugging her after that, loved how small and compact she was, how she fit right in his arms. It seemed a lifetime ago, even though it was only three years, but it still made him feel larger, like more of a man, more important.

"Be careful," she insisted, her voice muffled in his chest.

"Of course, Mum."

She let him go and looked past him, to where Andrew was just approaching. She raised her eyebrows meaningfully at him.

"Goes without saying, Helen," Andrew stated, smiling down at her. Helen patted his shoulder and walked to the kitchen, probably to help Sarah update the inventory.

Blaine waited until they were outside to ask, "What goes without saying?"

"That I look after you, idiot."

Blaine rolled his eyes and unlocked the Jeep. The tender moment with his mum having passed, he was back to being annoyed with Andrew's indecisive behaviour. "As if I need looking after," he said as he slammed the door shut.

"We both need looking after, Blaine. I'm expecting you to cover me as well, you know."

"I know that," Blaine snapped. "I just meant that I don't need looking after the way *she* thinks I need looking after." He got into the driver's seat, putting his seatbelt on. Now he was partly annoyed with himself and how childish his last statement sounded.

Andrew gave him a questioning look. "What's with you?"

Blaine halted where he was about to start the engine. "What's with me? What's with *me?!*"

Andrew held up a hand. "Okay, you're clearly about to go on some kind of rant, so let me just stop you by saying we don't have time. If I've done something—"

"Oh, you've done something."

Blaine bit his tongue to keep from continuing. *He's still mourning, don't be a selfish arse, he's still mourning*, he told himself.

"We'll talk about it later, after we've got back from the hospital," Andrew said. "We have to focus on the task at hand right now."

Blaine ground his teeth together and started the engine. He pushed down his irritation and thought of the map. He knew the city well enough. It was just a matter of navigating impassable roads and looking out for other survivor groups. Remembering the man he'd let go not half an hour before, and the fact that he hadn't fought infected up close in a while, sharpened his senses and allowed him to put aside his petty problems for the moment.

The nice thing about not being the only survivors in the city was that the number of dead infected was more than in other places. Blaine liked how simple it was to travel the roads littered with corpses, even if the feeling of being watched and the signs asking for help made him uneasy and the stench of decay made him occasionally want to retch.

There were still walkers on the road of course, and even the occasional crawler latched onto the side of a building. Blaine was keeping his eyes open for a hunter, but didn't really expect to see one.

"Listen, Blaine," Andrew began when they were nearly halfway there. "I know I'm not easy to put up with. Half the time I can't stand myself. I figure you're probably confused, and..."

Blaine glanced over and saw Andrew chewing his lip. He wanted to tell him to quit ruining it; his lips were perfect, and if he kept it up, they'd be gnashed to shreds, and who wanted to kiss lips like those? But he held his tongue again and pushed away the ache in his chest.

"I, um." Andrew rubbed the back of his neck, refusing to meet Blaine's eyes, so Blaine knew a confession was coming. "I know you want there to be more between us and I just wanted to thank you for putting up with me while I figure things out. I think it's safe to say I wouldn't be sitting here right now if it weren't for you, and I know you're trying your best to help me, so, you know... Thanks. I just need more time after... everything that's happened."

Blaine's mouth went dry and he wasn't sure he could respond. He'd thought it'd take some sort of miracle for Andrew to open up like that, and didn't know how to reply.

Then he remembered he was driving, saw the sign declaring the name of street, and hit the brakes hard enough to jolt them both forward.

"Sorry, sorry!" Blaine apologised quickly. "It's nothing, I just missed a turn, that's all."

Andrew snorted and rolled his eyes. "Anyway. Thanks for not telling anyone anything in the meantime."

Blaine wheeled the car around, buying himself time to think of something to say. In the end, he figured Andrew would prefer he keep it simple. The message had been relayed and Blaine had received it loud and clear: *I don't usually show weakness and I want you to know that what you're doing isn't going unappreciated.*

So Blaine just said, "Yeah."

They were close to the hospital now, and saw more infected walking around. Andrew lowered the window so he could shoot the ones trailing them. Luckily, no one had shot their tyres or tried to steal their car or anything. Blaine pulled up as close to the building as he could.

They couldn't linger in the car and make a plan like they had in Oxford. This wasn't a street in front of a flat, it was the front of a hospital. If they didn't get out and immediately start shooting, the car would be overrun with the infected coming in from the car park.

Blaine jumped out the second he turned the engine off. As Andrew ran forward to overtake him, it became clear that they'd fall into the same routine as last time, Blaine picking off what Andrew didn't kill.

"There's a pharmacy in here somewhere," Blaine said as they turned down one of the many corridors that had become brownish-grey over the apocalyptic months. "We could get loads of things, not just what Mary needs. Antibiotics, painkillers, sleeping pills."

Andrew shot an infected nurse between the eyes then leaned against the wall, panting as he reloaded his gun. "Yeah, but it's sure to be locked. We should find the keys first, assuming the staff left them somewhere."

Blaine felt spindly fingers touch his shoulder and yelped. He jerked forward out of its grasp, spun around and shot one of his pistols on instinct, propelling the walker back. He raised his gun and pulled the trigger again, this time shooting through the walker's right eye socket and spattering the nearby wall with blood.

Blaine heard Andrew growl and turned around just in time to see him glowering. Andrew didn't say anything, probably because he knew he didn't have to. Blaine sighed and brushed past, forcing Andrew to follow.

"Bet we could break through the glass and get behind the counter," Blaine said. "It's as good a place to start as any."

"That's assuming they don't have one of those pull-down gates. There's always extra security measures where drugs are involved."

Suddenly, Blaine stopped. He could've sworn he'd heard a quick-paced thumping sound, something like running, or maybe...

Charging.

Hunter.

"Come on, run," he hissed, pulling Andrew.

He didn't pay attention to where he was going, didn't spare a glance for the signs that indicated the direction of the pharmacy. He didn't even take the time to worry much about the walkers wandering around each corridor.

It was much like the time he'd fled Emily's flat, clutching the rucksack to his chest. He simply ran, hoping to outrun anything that came after him. Only this time, he hoped also that Andrew was managing to keep up.

Blaine ducked behind a corner, crouching behind a monitoring system. They were out of sight for the moment, and now Blaine had even less of an idea where they were than before.

"Why are we running?" Andrew asked in a whisper.

AAAAIIIIIIEEEE!

Blaine's blood ran cold at the sound of the hunter's screech. He gripped his pistol, suddenly wishing he had Andrew's SA80.

"H-Hunter," he whispered back. He put a finger to his lips, urging Andrew to stay quiet, and hoped Andrew didn't notice the way he was shaking.

He thought again that it'd been too long since he'd been in a proper fight. He felt out of practice and frightened out of his mind. If the hunter were to come around the corner right that second, Blaine didn't think he'd be able to move at all, let alone quick enough to defend himself. He'd be frozen right to the spot.

Andrew, on the other hand, seemed perfectly fine. He sat beside Blaine, perched on the balls of his feet, with a calmness that was almost unnerving. Shooting a glance at him, Blaine saw his face was completely blank, his eyes seeming to have dulled to a glassy rendition of what they once were.

AAAAIIIIIEEEEE!

Quick, heavy footsteps charged down the corridor perpendicular to them. Blaine held his breath as they neared, fighting the urge to squeeze his eyes shut.

One, two, three, four...

He didn't think he'd ever been more scared in his entire life. It was a million times worse than the first night in the Jeep, because at least then he'd had its metal exterior to provide a layer of protection. What did he have now?

Five, six, seven...

There it went, whizzing past, and Blaine thought for a moment it was sure to have seen them. He thought for certain it could hear the creaking of his bones or the rolling of sweat down his back.

Eight, nine, ten, don't come back this way, for the love of God don't come back this way

The charging had stopped, but a sniffing sound had taken its place. Blaine imagined the dagger-sharp teeth and maroon skin, recalled clearly the low stance in which it prowled, and prayed that it would give up and turn another corner to look elsewhere.

"Nrrnnngh."

Blaine snapped his eyes left. A walker was emerging from the room adjacent, its white doctor's coat stained and ragged. It was one of the more well-preserved infected they'd seen, with its skin still held together and not as deteriorated. Even so, it was a grey, gaunt-looking creature, with a long face and wispy brown hair stubbornly clinging to its scalp.

It skidded its feet over the tiled floor, shuffling forward once it saw what it had discovered. In his new haste, it kicked a discarded pen across the floor.

It was going to give away their position.

AAAAIIIIEEEE!

No, no, no! Blaine couldn't shoot it, for then the sound of the gun, even muffled by the suppressor, would alert the hunter. Beating it with the butt of his gun would crush its skull and still be too loud.

Blaine looked around frantically while it still hobbled across the corridor. There had to be something, maybe a blade like that man in front of the supermarket had.

Andrew was abruptly on his feet, darting to the left. Blaine opened and shut his mouth before he could ask where the hell Andrew was going. It seemed Andrew had deserted him entirely, left him to save himself.

"Aaannngr."

Blaine used the wall behind him to slowly stand. He felt like every nerve in his body was on high alert. One ear was straining to hear the hunter, while the other searched for Andrew. He kept his eyes only on the approaching walker.

He didn't know what Andrew was doing to his left, in his peripheral vision, but it all suddenly made sense when Andrew stepped up behind the infected doctor and slid his knife into the base of its skull. Blaine detected a wet, somehow blunt, noise that made him cringe, but it came and went as soon as Andrew pulled the knife out. He watched silently as Andrew slowly guided the motionless body to the floor, then wiped the blood off the blade onto the white coat.

Andrew's eyes were still glassy and cold when he raised them to meet Blaine's, but in them wasn't the disappointed, derisive look Blaine had expected to receive. Andrew simply jerked his head to the right a bit and cocked a brow, silently asking Blaine to check the corridor for the hunter.

There weren't many other infected in the passage perpendicular to their hiding spot, three, maybe four walkers. At the end, sniffing the air with its head tilted back, was the hunter.

Without taking his eyes off it, Blaine nodded curtly. Andrew took a step forward to move, but Blaine raised his hand, signalling him to stop. The hunter had lowered its head and turned. After a few drawn out seconds, it stalked around the corner, out of sight. Blaine exhaled and dropped his hand.

"Do you want me to take the lead?" Andrew asked in a hushed tone.

"Do you know how to get there?"

"You have no idea where we are, do you? Have you ever even been here before?"

Blaine looked around. He'd had a friend who had a relative get treated here once, but it'd been ages ago. He had no idea where they'd ended up, and Andrew did have about as good a chance as Blaine did at finding the way.

"I've got myself out of more complex environments before, trust me," Andrew added.

Blaine snorted softly. "No need to brag."

Andrew shrugged. "I'm not. Just stating a fact."

Without another word, he poked his head around the corner to make sure it was clear, then waved for Blaine to follow.

Chapter 17

Survivors

13:37

Blaine was tired. Andrew could see it in the drawn resoluteness of his face. Every sound had him on edge, every time he fired it was with reluctant obligation, and it was obvious he wanted nothing more than to be back at home by now.

Andrew was trying to get all his restlessness out in one go. He thrived on this sort of thing — *make your way toward the objective, don't engage unless necessary, look sharp, check your corners, stay alive.* He was looking forward to returning to the others with the medicine, mission successful, victory earned. He was looking forward to later that night when he could lie down to sleep, could close his eyes feeling like he'd done something meaningful.

Blaine would slide an arm around his waist, hitch his leg up a little to get comfortable, and give one last slow exhalation of air (which Andrew could always feel down his neck and even eagerly anticipated) before letting the tension leave his body. Then, right at that moment, that's when Andrew would close his eyes and re-experience only the good feelings of the day before drifting off to sleep.

Very romantic, Big-Ears, but you're forgetting something.

Andrew pulled the trigger of his gun, shooting the walker in front of him just above the left eyebrow. He was running low on bullets and could only carry so many mags with him. He'd seen Blaine reload at least once, but wasn't sure what he had left either.

A sign on the wall directed them to the pharmacy. They were nearly there, Andrew could feel it. It would only be a few more turns.

Blaine must have seen the sign as well, because he heaved a sigh of relief.

Not surprisingly, there was a security shutter over the window of the pharmacy. Blaine groaned in frustration.

"Guess this is when we start looking for the keys to the door," he said, looking up and down the passage. "Shooting it won't help, will it?"

Andrew shook his head. "Not something like this. There's no going through, only around."

Just then, the shutter lifted a bit. Andrew aimed his gun at the new opening. Hesitantly, Blaine mirrored the action.

A pair of wide, dark brown eyes appeared in the narrow gap, eyes nearly the same colour as the russet skin. They were framed with long, thick black eyelashes, and were set far apart in the wide, angled face. Curly brown hair fell on either side of the head, just over the tips of the ears.

The eyes roamed over both Blaine and Andrew, seeming to consider them as much as they considered the eyes. At last, a man's voice said, "I heard the gunfire. You're here for medicine, aren't you?"

"That's right," Andrew answered.

"My name's Elliot. I'm willing to make a deal."

Andrew lowered his gun. "What is it?"

"My sister and I have been holed up in here since the start of the Outbreak. I've been able to leave and get something for us to eat every so often, but we're not doing so well," he explained. "My sister, Jessica... She's pregnant."

"Shit," Blaine hissed.

"You want us to escort you out?" Andrew guessed.

The head bearing the eyes nodded. "Exactly. You can take whatever you need if you help us out."

"Sounds fair to me."

"There's just one thing you have to do before I let you in."

Blaine sighed. "There's always one thing."

"My sister can barely outrun the slow ones in her state," Elliot said. "There's a hunter lurking around here somewhere and I've seen at least two crawlers. She can't leave until those are taken care of."

"And you're not letting us in until they are," Andrew said.

"That's it."

"Do you know how hard those things are to kill?" Blaine asked.

"If you want the drugs badly enough, I'm sure you'll find a way."

The shutter slid shut.

13:50

"I can't believe we're doing this," Blaine muttered later while they hid in a storage room. "This is so incredibly stupid, trying to take out a hunter."

Andrew dug his thumbnail into the tip of his forefinger. "When you think about it, it's the crawlers that are harder to kill."

It was crawlers that darted unpredictably, so quick it was near impossible to track their movements. Witbeck might've been a pansy, but he was a decent shot. He'd've been able to kill something more human. He'd've been alive.

Andrew closed his eyes and dug his thumbnail harder into his finger, hard enough that his hand shook from the pressure. He let out a slow breath.

When he opened his eyes, Blaine was staring sideways at him.

"I just meant hunters are easier to predict," Andrew explained. "Yeah, they're fast, but they charge straight forward. All it takes is a well-placed bullet and they drop like a stone. It's harder to keep a crawler in your sight."

"I left my rifle in the Jeep."

"What's that got to do with anything?"

"I'm not good at CQB."

Andrew nodded. "We'll have to be smart about it."

He'd have to find a position where he could take them out stealthily. That meant no firing, approaching from behind, and killing quietly. It was easier said than done when the whole place was crawling with infected.

A lure would work, he thought suddenly. *Blaine could shoot at it, get its attention... No, not Blaine.*

154

A touch on Andrew's wrist startled him, and it didn't much settle his nerves when he saw Blaine's hand was the culprit. The slim digits were sliding gently over Andrew's skin, down to where he was still applying pressure into the pad of his forefinger.

Wordlessly, Blaine tilted Andrew's palm up and pulled the thumb back before rubbing the indentation away. It was so slow and sensual and not at all appropriate for the moment. Andrew felt a twitch of irritation, less at Blaine for having done it and more at himself for the way he'd liked the gesture. It had interrupted his focus.

"Sorry," Blaine murmured. "I know I shouldn't've, but... if I'm about to die I'd rather regret doing things than not doing things."

"You're not about to die." Not only would Helen kill him if he let that happen, he'd probably be just as lost as before and would end up wanting to die anyway. The idea of going back to such an empty existence was terrifying.

"Wouldn't be too sure about that," Blaine said.

"You've killed these before. You can do it."

"I can try."

"If you don't, then I will. You won't die, okay? I won't let you."

It was a stupid thing to say, a stupid slip of the tongue. It was bad enough they'd been hiding in this storage room for so long, bad enough that he'd confessed his uncertainties about their relationship in the car on the way here. Now even worse was the way Blaine was looking at him, his liquid brown eyes wide and searching, as though he were trying to puzzle something out. His face was so damn expressive, so trusting, and it wasn't helping Andrew to regain his focus a single bit.

Blaine's eyes dropped to Andrew's mouth, and he was close enough that Andrew could see the subtle parting of his lips as he began to move forward.

Oh God no.

"Don't." Andrew put his palm to Blaine's chest, breathing unsteadily as he pushed him back. "There are more important things right now."

The hint of a blush formed on Blaine's face as he swallowed and looked away. "Yeah."

"We need to get to a position where we can see them but they can't see us," Andrew said.

Blaine nodded. "I was thinking we may not even have to kill them. We could just lure them into a room. Elliot wouldn't know."

"That does save ammunition," Andrew agreed. He had to admit he was impressed, though he would've thought of something like that eventually. "The hunter we need to take out for sure, though."

"I doubt the doors would stand against that thing anyway."

"There's that, but it would also help if we need to return here in future."

"So we don't have to deal with it lurking around every time," Blaine said.

"Precisely."

"What happens if we see two of them at the same time? Or the hunter shows up when we're surrounded by a bunch of walkers?"

"Then I'll take care of the hunter while you cover us both. Think you can do that?"

"Yes."

"Good. You ready?" Andrew put his hand on the doorknob.

"Luring the crawlers into a room and taking down the hunter, right? Sounds like a plan to me."

"Any ideas on how we might find them?"

"We could make enough noise to attract a horde," Blaine suggested.

"That's the stupidest thing I've ever heard."

"If you have any other suggestions..."

Andrew didn't. "If we're lucky, we'll run into them without having to resort to that."

For some reason Blaine smiled. "Luck runs in my family."

"That a gypsy thing?"

Blaine shrugged. "Probably."

"Hmm." It was ridiculous to consider, even though Blaine seemed to have a lot of faith in the idea.

"Open the door," Blaine challenged with a smirk. "If we see a crawler within five minutes, I win a kiss."

Half of Andrew wanted to rise to the challenge. It had sparked something in his competitive nature and it seemed too good to turn down. The other half was hesitant. That half still wasn't sure if it was ready to kiss Blaine again.

It's like he wasn't even listening when I confessed all that shit to him in the car, Andrew thought bitterly. It had been a hard enough thing to do and he didn't want to have to remind Blaine of it a second time.

Fuck it, he's right, we could be dead tomorrow.

"Deal."

Andrew opened the door.

By now he had a general idea of how the hospital was set up. He had a tentative map in his mind, constructed from a series of landmarks he'd catalogued on the way to the pharmacy. The area they were in now was all surgical equipment and operating facilities. Judging by the thickness of the doors, it'd be ideal if they could lure the crawlers into the operating rooms.

They sprinted silently to the end of the corridor and stopped. Andrew peered from behind the wall, checking around the corner.

Shit.

He sighed and turned back to where Blaine was staring at him anxiously. "Crawler on the ceiling down there," he whispered.

There was a glint in Blaine's eye, but he wasn't smiling just yet. He stepped forward to look around the corner himself, then stepped back.

"Gimme your rifle, I can take it out from here."

"What happened to luring them into a room? Saving ammunition?"

"There's no walkers or anything down that way. It's not moving so I've got a clear shot. One burst should do it. Come on."

"One burst should give away our position," Andrew countered.

"If you don't give me your gun I'll take it out with my pistols."

"Fucking stubborn," Andrew muttered under his breath. He shoved his SA80 to Blaine's chest. "Here. Do it quickly."

Blaine slid his pistol into his makeshift holster and switched places with Andrew. The crawler had been unmoving when Andrew had looked, its grey hair hanging from its head, and it had been facing the opposite direction. If it stayed in the position it was in now, Blaine would indeed have a clear shot at the head, but with a narrow margin for error.

Perhaps that was why Blaine hadn't fired yet.

Andrew turned his head to look, and saw Blaine with his eye pressed close to the scope. It shouldn't have been taking this long.

"You gonna shoot it or what?" Andrew said.

Blaine fired a quick burst. "Shit." He fired another. Andrew heard a whining screech, followed by a thump. Blaine lowered the rifle and handed it back to Andrew with a sigh.

"Dead?"

"Yeah. You owe me a kiss," Blaine said, finally allowing himself a grin.

"We'll see if your luck holds out a bit longer."

Blaine frowned. "Now you're just abusing my luck."

Andrew shrugged and walked past him, heading down the corridor with the dead crawler. "Come on."

14:34

They were still near the operating rooms when they spotted the hunter. Andrew felt a tap on his arm, and looked to where Blaine's finger was pointing.

There it was, stalking maybe five metres ahead. Andrew raised his rifle and took aim, bringing its head into his crosshairs.

It stopped in its tracks, as though it could hear Andrew's finger curling tighter around the trigger. Slowly, its neck turned and Andrew could see its profile, its dark eyes and hollow cheeks, its mouth open wide enough to display pointed teeth. In the clarity of his scope, he could see the ageing of the flesh, how like worn deep purple paper it was, dried and wrinkled and curling at the torn edges. It seemed to have caught on to something, seemed to be sniffing the air for a familiar scent.

In the blink of an eye its neck twisted almost entirely around and it was staring right at Andrew.

AAAIIIEEEE!

Andrew pulled the trigger. He heard Blaine yelling at him to run even over the sound of the gun, but as the hunter came charging forward, Andrew kept firing. He had to have shot it in the head at least

158

once. He rarely missed.

"Andrew, come on!"

Blaine tugged his arm and a burst hit the wall. The hunter was right in front of him now, taking up his entire sight in the scope, and moving too quickly to have been fatally injured. Andrew swore and let himself be pulled out of the way.

The hunter went charging past, but skidded to a stop once it realised it'd been evaded. They didn't stick around to see it turn; they ran into the nearest operating room and slammed the door shut.

"Will that hold it?" Blaine asked. His voice had a strained quality to it Andrew would've recognised anywhere. It shook almost as much as his hands did.

"It might," Andrew said. He honestly didn't know. He wouldn't be surprised if it didn't.

A screeching behind them made them press their backs to the door. Across the room, perched on the operating table wearing tatted hospital scrubs, was the second crawler.

"Oh Jesus," Blaine gasped. He fumbled for his second pistol.

Andrew aimed and fired just as it leapt from the table and began to skitter toward them. His gun clicked.

"Blaine, I'm empty."

"Shit shit shit." He handed Andrew his Glock as he finally pulled the other from his belt. By the time he'd taken aim, the crawler had shifted its weight to its back legs, about to pounce.

Andrew fired and managed to hit the head, but the bullet lodged itself in the crawler's jaw. Blaine fired, but a jolt from the hunter on the other side of the door behind him made him miss.

"I'm gonna die, I'm never gonna get that kiss, I'm gonna die," Blaine rambled weakly.

Andrew took a step forward. He put himself between Blaine and the crawler and pressed Blaine back against the door. It was the solid wall of heat at Andrew's back, the stuttered breathing on the back of his neck that anchored him and made everything clear.

As the crawler leapt into the air, extending its jaw, Andrew fired one more time, right in the centre of its forehead.

Two down, one to go.

Once more, the hunter charged against the door, but this time it pushed through. In abandoning his position against the second door, Andrew had provided the necessary opening for the hunter to barrel in. It ran straight ahead, zooming past on Andrew's right and leaving broken pieces of wood in its wake.

"Andrew," Blaine whimpered behind him. Andrew felt fingers twist into the back of his shirt, and it only made him more determined to kill the thing he'd failed to kill earlier.

He didn't know how many bullets were left in this pistol, but as the hunter turned on its heels, Andrew figured he didn't have the time to check. He took a deep breath and aimed right at the hunter's head, staring down the sight.

Can't miss this time, Big-Ears.

I won't.

AAAAIIIIIEEEEEE!

It only took one shot. Andrew fired once, stopped the hunter in its tracks, but then fired again as it dropped to its knees. To be sure.

He wanted to finish it off properly. He wanted to walk over there and bash its skull in with the heel of his foot. Instead he turned around and kissed Blaine.

14:55

"Is it done?" Elliot's brown eyes asked.

"It's done," Andrew said.

The shutter slid down and a moment later there was the sound of the door unlocking. Andrew pushed Blaine forward to get him in first.

"Sorry about making you go on a wild goose chase of sorts," Elliot said after he'd locked the door. "But we wouldn't have been able to get out otherwise. I'm sure you understand."

Elliot had a sort of intelligent presence about him, as Andrew figured a chemist would, but he also had a quality of strength Andrew could see right away. He had a defined, square jaw at the end of an angular face, with wide lips and a button nose, and he seemed to be the sort of man who was trying to stay clean and presentable even in the desolated, apocalyptic world. The only thing he was missing were wire-framed glasses and he would've made a right picture.

"One of our group is ill," Andrew said. "We don't know what with, but she's old and we figure some sort of antibiotics ought to help. Penicillin, maybe."

"I could give you all the antibiotics we have but I wouldn't recommend just pumping her full of medicine and seeing what works. I could go back with you and take a look if you like," Elliot suggested.

"That's fine," Blaine said.

Andrew thought they should've asked Helen first, but it was none of his business. He shrugged.

"Do either of you have a bag?" Elliot asked.

Blaine shrugged his rucksack off his shoulders. "I've got one." He handed it to Elliot.

"We were thinking painkillers and such, too," Andrew added.

"Of course. Why don't one of you come with me and the other can go help my sister get ready."

"I'll take the sister," Blaine said. In a lower tone, he added to Elliot. "I'm a better people person. Andrew's a bit stiff."

Andrew glared at him, but it was probably for the best anyway. He did hate talking and meeting new people. He followed Elliot back into the rows of bottles and tried to think about all he knew of medicines.

Chapter 18

Resettling

15:44

When they returned from the hospital, Andrew and Elliot disappeared upstairs, while Helen hugged Blaine again right away. Blaine didn't make a fuss about it. After the experience he'd had, he clung to his mother even tighter.

At first he felt like the same boy who'd been unable to run from Emily's flat months ago, once again frightened and small, wanting nothing but his mother's comfort. There'd been more than one moment at the hospital where he'd nearly frozen up with fear. The memory of whimpering and twisting his fingers into Andrew's shirt as Andrew gunned down the hunter was particularly embarrassing to look back on.

But coming back and hugging his mum, embracing her in arms so much stronger than hers while she smiled gratefully into his chest, made him feel strangely powerful. He was victorious.

"This is Jessica," he said, releasing Helen and gesturing to the woman behind him. It had been no easy task getting her out of the hospital, mostly because they'd run out of ammo right near the end, but they'd managed it. It had certainly helped that Elliot knew his way around better than they did.

What was more, Jessica was beautiful. Like her brother (twin, apparently), her hair was a frizz of thick brown curls, but hers came down past her shoulders, accentuating the heart shape of her face. Even in dim lighting, her dark eyes seemed to shine bright. She looked gentle and wild at the same time, with a childishly rounded nose contrasting the sharp arch of her eyebrows. She had the sort of innate beauty and grace that Blaine would've loved to photograph were it any other time but the end of the world, and perhaps it was because of that that they got on so well right from the beginning.

"Hello," Jessica said, smiling. It brightened her face even more. "Fine boy you've raised here."

"Thank you, I like to think so myself," Helen replied, beaming.

"Jessica's brother Elliot is a doctor," Blaine explained. "He went upstairs with Andrew to help Mary."

"Of course. Did you two need a place to stay?" Helen asked. "I'm sure we have enough room for two more."

"I wouldn't want to make anybody uncomfortable."

"Trust me, dear, if you were going to make anyone uncomfortable, I wouldn't've offered. You and your brother are both welcome to stay if you wish."

"Thank you, that's very kind. We'll do our best to pull our own weight, I promise."

Blaine made for the stairs. "I'm going to see how things are going," he announced. He darted up the steps without waiting for a response.

Andrew was leaning against the wall in the corridor, as Blaine had hoped he'd be. He glanced up at Blaine's arrival, but dropped his eyes the second they met each other's gaze.

"Hey," Blaine said.

He didn't know where things stood between them anymore. Andrew had said he wasn't ready for things to escalate yet, but he seemed content to jump back and forth over the line they'd drawn in broad daylight now. He'd even agreed to a kiss, and had done it more gently than Blaine thought possible for him.

Now he was back to being quiet and aloof.

"Elliot figure out what's wrong yet?" Blaine asked.

"Don't know. I didn't go in."

"Why not?"

Andrew shrugged. "I don't like going in your room. It has your things in it... I dunno, it didn't feel right."

"You can go in if you want."

"I'd rather not."

Blaine sighed and leaned against the opposite wall. "Where are we, Andrew, 'cause I can't tell."

"We're where I said we were," Andrew snapped, still not looking him in the eyes. "You did things at the hospital because you thought you were going to die, and now that it's over, everything's as it should be. End of story."

"Could you stop being so damn closed off and just talk to me? You can come to me about your sister but you can't come to me about whoever this guy was that you loved before? Do you think I don't want to hear about it or something, just because you can't help still having feelings for him?"

Blaine supposed he should've predicted Andrew would try storming away, but he reached out to grab Andrew's arm before he could make it to the stairs anyway.

"Andrew—"

"Take your hand off me before I break it."

Would Andrew do that? Blaine didn't think he would, but he didn't want to wait to find out. He reluctantly released his grip on Andrew's arm and let him hurry down the stairs.

"Excuse me."

Blaine turned. It was Elliot. "Yeah? Is it bad?"

Judging by Elliot's solemn expression, it seemed to be. Elliot came closer and lowered his voice, furrowing his brow as he spoke.

"Looks like a common cold, and it's entirely possible she could recover," he said. "But she's old and susceptible to all sorts of things. The medicine will only keep her alive for so much longer, and with the state we're in—"

"It'd be better to save them for someone else," Blaine finished. Of course. It was only a matter of time before Mary passed, and why waste valuable resources on her when someone who had a chance of recovering more permanently could use them? Not to mention Elizabeth had already been exposed and could probably pass on the virus to the rest of the house. Though of course they all had better immune systems than an old lady.

"I'm afraid so," Elliot said. "As far as I'm concerned, it's up to you and Andrew. You two are the ones who went to all the hard work of getting them, and Mary... Mary doesn't have to know. She could take a placebo and go quietly, peacefully."

"You're some kind of doctor."

"We've all had a rough time. I wouldn't have suggested anything like this before, of course. Now I'm just a realist."

Blaine nodded. "Okay. Give her a placebo."

"You're sure? Do you want to talk to Andrew?"

Blaine snorted. "Andrew doesn't care."

16:52

Blaine swirled his spoon around in his soup. Most nights he was so hungry that he ended up tilting the bowl to get as much into his mouth as possible, but tonight it seemed not enough. The broth was too thin, too watery and tasteless. He would've preferred something more substantial, something he had to chew, but Elizabeth said they were saving the canned food for heavy winter. Blaine thought it was stupid, but apparently Elizabeth was the food authority.

He knew he was being morose. It wasn't usually his style; he was like his mum in that he was peppy more often than not, while others dragged themselves down in pessimism. He hoped he didn't get cynical after all that had happened. He'd been fine with Merrick's training conditioning him into the survivor he needed to be, but he hoped living in a wasteland wouldn't make him cold and unforgiving like Andrew.

So why had he told Elliot not to give Mary the medicine?

A sigh across the living room echoed his own feelings. Looking up, he saw it was Tim, frowning down at his bowl much the same way Blaine was.

Tim seemed to know people were looking at him, and glanced around before smiling apologetically. "Sorry. Just thinking that it's so damn quiet. I miss my guitar."

"You played guitar?" Darren asked, eyes wide. Blaine was surprised, too. Even Andrew had an eyebrow raised.

Tim grinned. "Lots you don't know about me, zombie-bait." Sarah smirked into her soup. "But yeah," Tim sighed again. "Miss plucking those old strings. I had an acoustic. Black with a white trim. Got it on my fifteenth birthday."

"Sounds nice," Helen said.

"It was."

There was silence again, dragging seconds into what felt like minutes. Then Jessica said, "I miss libraries."

All eyes turned to her in the recliner. Blaine had noticed that she'd clung to a paperback the whole way through their escape from the hospital—a relatively thin book called *The Stranger*. During the short time they'd gotten acquainted with each other in the small pharmacy, packing her and Elliot's things, he'd discovered her love for books and reading. He could tell right away she was intelligent. Both she and her brother had a strong, wise grace about them.

"The experience more than their existence," she clarified, bringing a spoonful of soup to her mouth. "If that makes sense."

"I miss football," Sarah said. "Not your kind of football, Tim. Sorry."

"What team?" Darren asked.

Elizabeth shook her head, snorting. "Here we go."

Sarah grinned. "Premier League? Chelsea."

"Ouch," Darren said, wincing. "Stoke here."

Sarah's face contorted in a grimace. "I'll have to ask you to leave."

"None of that," Helen warned. She was clearly fighting a grin herself, though. Blaine couldn't help laughing, and when everyone joined in, he felt his earlier mood lift a bit.

"I miss tea," Elizabeth said when everyone quieted down. It only served to start them up again; there were nods and murmurs of hearty agreement, even from Andrew.

Blaine figured he might as well say something. "I miss my camera. I'd give anything to be able to walk down the street taking photos without worrying about having the skin torn from my limbs." He earned a stern look from Helen for that, but he didn't care.

"I had a closer look at the photos in your room after Mary complimented you on them," Elizabeth remarked. "You really were quite talented. *Are* quite talented, I should say."

"Thank you."

Jessica nudged Elliot. "What about you?"

Elliot smiled wistfully, not looking up. "Music. I agree with Tim.

The world seems so quiet without it."

"And we can't even bang on drums or anything 'cause that'd just alert the infected," Darren added mournfully. "But me... I miss computers. God, I could use an internet fix."

"A porn fix, you mean," Elizabeth muttered.

Darren blushed. "You know me too well."

She actually guffawed, putting a hand over her mouth to muffle the noise. Blaine couldn't blame her. He and everyone else was doing the same.

"Alright, it's only fair then, since I embarrassed you," she said. "That's another thing I miss — vibrators."

Darren turned an even deeper shade of red, and Blaine thought for sure he saw the boy's gaze drift downward.

Helen, always the one to settle things down, piped up, "I miss running the pub. Talking to my regulars."

Sarah nodded. "Those were good times."

Helen's eyes shifted to Andrew, who Blaine noticed seemed to have sunk in on himself with the way his shoulders were hunched. "Anything you miss, Andrew?" she asked. Blaine was grateful, since he didn't think he could've asked himself.

Andrew was quiet for a while. Almost to the point where it was awkward. Then, in a voice that was louder and more firm than Blaine thought he'd reply in, he said, "Showers. I miss showers."

Blaine struggled not to imagine Andrew showering. In the end, he failed.

"Amen to that," Elizabeth said. "Showers, hot water... Hell, *running* water. Hell, *clean* water."

"Yeah," Andrew said. "Hygiene in general, really."

"Thanks so much for taking us in, by the way," Elliot said, putting his empty bowl aside. "I don't think we could've lasted much longer in the hospital, let alone on the outside."

Blaine knew it had been bold of him to assume his mother would welcome them, especially with Sarah's warning of not bringing back strangers hanging over his head, but he couldn't have just left them, not with Jessica being pregnant. They were also the first survivors besides his group that he'd met, and they seemed genuinely nice people. Despite the initial cold silence the group had displayed upon their entry, they seemed welcoming enough now. Blaine thought he could see the wheels turning in Sarah's head as she went over her mental inventory, but even she was being outwardly polite toward the newcomers.

"Hey, it's all good, man," Tim said, shrugging. "I think I speak for everyone when I say as long as you contribute, it's not a problem. We're a little tight on space, but we've got enough for you. Barely, but enough."

"I know, and we do want to contribute," Elliot said. "I'm no good at fighting, I'm afraid, but if anyone feels ill — "

"We know who to ask," Tim finished with a nod. "And don't worry, we'll have you beheading walkers like a pro in no time. Our boy Andrew's got Navy training. Even has the kids run drills up on the roof."

Andrew snorted, but remained silent. It wasn't the reaction Blaine would've gone with. He felt a flare of anger, strangely more irritated by the dig at Andrew than by the one at himself.

"Don't worry, Jessica, we'll find something for you to do," Helen assured her. "I've been thinking we should start washing some of our clothes. The Avon's a bit of a journey, but perhaps Elizabeth could go every so often with an escort while you take up her cooking duties."

Elizabeth didn't seem to like the sound of that, but kept her mouth shut. Jessica gave Helen a soft smile and said, "I was a terrible cook before all this, but I'd certainly be willing to try."

"Oh, so was I," Elizabeth said. "But survival cooking is different. There's no complicated spices, no measurements. As long as it's hot and looks edible."

Tim froze with a spoonful of soup before his mouth.

"Fuck off, Tim," Elizabeth said without heat.

"Elliot," Helen began hesitantly. "About Mary." Blaine's stomach lurched. The atmosphere in the room turned decidedly less cheerful. "What did you think of... How do you think she'll..."

Elliot seemed to understand her loss for words. While everyone looked deep into their bowls, Blaine tried to watch the exchange discreetly. Surely Elliot wouldn't give away what they'd done?

"She's very old, Helen," Elliot said solemnly. "I gave her an antibiotic, but she's weak already. I won't lie to you — it doesn't look good. I'm sorry."

Glancing up, Blaine thought he saw tears forming in his mother's eyes. None fell, but they were certainly there. She thinned her lips and nodded, then suddenly got to her feet, her brown curls bouncing.

"Right then. Sleeping arrangements."

21:11

Jessica ended up getting the recliner, while Darren and Elliot got the living room floor. A look passed between Darren and Blaine as they parted ways to settle down for the night. There was no way Tim and Sarah would argue now, not with two new people in the room. Blaine didn't even know what they argued about, but mostly it seemed to be Sarah yelling at Tim for letting people think he was cruel and tough when he actually had a soft, reasonable side, and why couldn't he drop the alpha male act for one bloody second? Either way, the look from Darren spoke clear enough: *Things'll probably be quiet in here from now on, so have fun with your newfound privacy.*

It would've been perfect if Andrew wasn't still being a pillock and if Blaine wasn't still sore at him. It was the first night in many that he turned his back on Andrew, not sleeping curled around him.

It didn't take long for Andrew to notice the change. Their backs still pressed together for at least that little warmth, Blaine could feel the tenseness in Andrew's body. The same tenseness that usually left with a contented sigh now kept him locked and rigid.

Though still upset, still hurt, Blaine didn't have it in him to hold grudges. He never had. It hadn't been five minutes and he already missed tucking his arms around Andrew and holding him close. But he told himself this was for the best. Throughout the awkward, dragging silence of each of them trying to get to sleep, he ignored the urge to roll over and whisper apologies in Andrew's ear. When Andrew shifted uncomfortably, one of his legs sometimes catching Blaine's and causing him to jerk away, Blaine clenched his fists and willed away the ache in his chest.

Andrew wanted Blaine to back off while he got his baggage sorted? Blaine would back off. Andrew had asked for this.

169

Chapter 19

Preparation

DAY 83
10:13

The morning after Elliot and Jessica's arrival, Andrew woke up late. He hadn't been able to get to sleep well the night before, and didn't want to think about why. By the time he'd checked his guns and went up to the roof, Blaine was already at his usual post, feet dangling over the edge with his rifle across his lap.

"Morning," Blaine said. Andrew noted the tone wasn't unfriendly in the slightest. Not warm and bubbly, but not antagonistic. There was at least that.

Andrew stood with his feet planted to the spot, halfway between his own position and where Blaine sat staring out onto the city. For a moment he just longingly looked at the back of Blaine—his hair, his slouched posture, his neck. He stood long enough for Blaine to look over his shoulder and give him a questioning look, wondering why his footsteps hadn't crossed the remainder of the roof.

"Why didn't you wake me?" Andrew asked.

Blaine shrugged. "It's not as though you needed to be anywhere. We had a tiring day yesterday. I thought I'd let you sleep in, get some rest."

Andrew crossed to the other edge and plopped down in his usual spot without a word. He hated this view. The front of the house looked out on the neighbourhood, on the streets littered with stinking corpses. He had to stare at all these other houses, imagine the lives that the people there used to have, day in and day out. Blaine had the much better view, but Andrew wouldn't ever ask him to trade.

Blaine sighed. "Not to mention sleep is a nice escape from all this."

"Only if you have good dreams," Andrew said.

"You don't have good dreams?"

Without looking, Andrew could tell Blaine had turned around to look at him, to stare at the back of his head while he waited for an answer. It made Andrew itchy, made his skin prickle a bit.

"Not really," Andrew said. "If it's not a nightmare, it's something I know I'll never have again."

He generally tried not to dwell on the few dreams he could remember. Even before the Outbreak, he'd paid his dreams little attention. It came from months, maybe years, of training. After what he'd seen in the Royal Navy, he'd learnt to shake such things off. Or to at least try.

"I had more nightmares during my stay with Merrick than I do here," Blaine chattered on. "I usually have nice dreams here, I guess because this is my home. Last night I had a nightmare, but that was probably because of the hospital run."

Andrew didn't say anything. He sort of wished Blaine would stop talking, but he also sort of felt guilty for Blaine's nightmare.

"What about you?" Blaine asked. "Did you sleep okay? Any dreams?"

Andrew fought off the quickening of his heart and the building sweat in his armpits. No, he hadn't slept okay. It'd been awful, and he knew Blaine knew that.

"Can't remember. I just know I was cold."

"Yeah," Blaine said wistfully. "It is getting colder."

Andrew frowned. How the hell had Blaine made it seem like the changing weather was his fault? It was as if he'd said, *It is getting colder... You should do something about that.*

16:45

It was just about time for dinner, the time when Andrew had Blaine and Darren going through their conditioning again. Tim sometimes

171

came up as well, joining in when he felt like it, but for the most part he didn't push himself the way the others did. Andrew could understand that. Life in the apocalypse was beyond boring, and Tim probably had little better to do.

Today, however, something seemed to be wrong with Darren. He was giving up too easily, huffing in exasperation over seemingly nothing. It wasn't irritation with Andrew's orders so much as it was a reluctance to do them. As though his body was just going through the motions while his mind was otherwise occupied.

"Darren." Andrew knelt beside him and put a hand on Darren's ankles, lowering his straightened legs. He looked Darren in the eyes and immediately saw there was something else on his mind. "Get up, I wanna talk to you."

Darren's brow furrowed in confusion, but he did as Andrew asked. Andrew ignored the curious looks of the others and led Darren over to the nearby roof, away from Tim, Blaine, and Elizabeth at the fire.

He could hardly believe he was going to do something like this, when he was the last person who should be looking to give advice. But if he couldn't solve his own problems, it seemed something to at least help someone solve theirs.

"You alright?"

Darren frowned at his feet. Whatever was troubling him had to be serious. The boy looked up to Blaine so much, and was so earnestly interested in being his friend that there wasn't much he hadn't told him. Blaine rambled on about him during the day when they were on guard. If Blaine didn't know, nobody knew.

"It's about Elizabeth," he muttered at last.

That did make sense to Andrew. It was hardly a secret that Darren was into her, though Andrew didn't think Elizabeth herself knew. Or perhaps she did but she was too busy batting her eyelashes and trying to get Andrew's attention to care. Andrew would really have to remedy that soon. He'd just been so caught up in his own worries.

"What about her?" Andrew asked. He stopped himself from glancing over at her, but in the corner of his eye, he could see her shivering under a too-thin jacket, cold in the October air.

Darren wet his lips before continuing, still not meeting Andrew's gaze. "I expected she'd be a little sick, since she's sharing a room with Mary, you know? I mean, I expected that. But it seems worse than just a cold. She's always been pale and, and a little on the bony side. I'm just worried."

"So tell her you're worried? Ask her if she's alright?"

Darren shook his head, his frown deepening. "I can't. She's so... You know how she is. Intimidating. And she thinks I'm a *kid*. I just. I like her, and I don't want to mess things up. But it's killing me not knowing how she feels. She looks so unhealthy, and — "

"Okay, calm down," Andrew said, putting a hand on his shoulder. It might've been his sense of duty rising to the surface, but he was suddenly determined to see this resolved. He also was all too familiar with liking someone and not wanting to mess things up. "I'll talk to her for you."

Darren looked up, eyes filled with hope. "Would you?"

"Of course I will. Don't worry about it."

Darren smiled. "You know, you're a lot nicer than the others give you credit for."

Andrew didn't know what to say. Inwardly, he thought, *You should've seen me a few weeks ago.* Aloud, he just grunted and said, "Thanks."

18:29

Andrew waited until after dinner, when he knew he could find Elizabeth alone and writing in her journal. He still didn't like going in Blaine's room, so he knocked lightly on the open door to get her attention.

Mary was resting in the bed, with Elizabeth leaning against the side and writing intently. She looked initially annoyed at being interrupted, but her features softened when she saw who it was.

"Hi, Andrew," she said, tucking a strand of hair behind her ear. She put her pen in her notebook to save her place then put it aside.

A fleeting moment passed where Andrew regretted agreeing to do this. She certainly was intimidating, all blue eyes and perky breasts.

She stared at Andrew and demanded his full attention. He shifted uncomfortably, wanting to turn and walk away.

"Hi. I was wondering if I could talk to you for a minute."

Getting the hint, she got to her feet and padded softly into the corridor, closing the door behind her to let Mary rest. Andrew thought about how he should begin, wondering if he should mention right away that it was Darren who was concerned, less so him.

"How are you feeling?" he asked.

Elizabeth gave him a crooked smile. "Worried I'll catch what Mary's got? Don't worry, I know the whole house is thinking about it."

"We also know that you're stronger. Mary has a cold that she's too weak to fight. If it does pass to you, and therefore to us, we'll be able to take it," Andrew explained. "But I wasn't talking about a simple virus. You seem... frail, if you don't mind my saying." At Elizabeth's sudden shift in expression to anger, he quickly clarified. "Almost like you're malnourished. I was just wondering if there was maybe another health issue. Something you had before the Outbreak that you aren't being treated for now, maybe?"

Elizabeth pursed her lips thoughtfully. "Is it because I'm pale? I've always been pale, you know."

"If you don't want me to tell anyone, I won't. I can keep secrets."

Elizabeth chuckled. "Oh, I know you can. Alright, I'll tell you."

She looked around, checking to see that they were still alone. Straining his ears, Andrew heard the others downstairs, but no footsteps threatened to interrupt them.

"I've been feeling really weak," she said. "For quite a while, actually, even before Mary got sick. The kind of weak that makes you feel light-headed and dizzy. And sometimes my heart beats fast—really fast, for no reason. I can't seem to get warm, and I get these terrible headaches."

Andrew didn't know much about health, but it did sort of sound like malnutrition. Low blood sugar, maybe?

"Elliot's a doctor," Andrew said. "You could talk to him."

Elizabeth nodded. "I know. I considered doing as much as soon as I heard. I just wanted to let him settle a bit first. How rude would it be to ask for help and he hasn't even been here a day?"

"He wants to help. Trust me, he won't mind. He and Jessica are good people."

She nodded again, this time smiling. "Listen, Andrew." A slim hand touched his wrist and lingered, caressing. "You're a good person, too. I could tell right away. Quiet, a little aloof, a bit sarcastic at times, but a good person. The only one who noticed something was wrong with me, anyway."

Andrew withdrew from her touch as politely as he could manage. Jerking away as though burnt would've just added animosity between them and he didn't need to feel even more estranged in this house.

"It wasn't me, Elizabeth," he said. "It was Darren. Earlier today, you saw me take him aside during training while you cooked dinner. He was worried about you and asked that I say something. It wasn't me who noticed. I'm sorry."

"Then why didn't *he* say something?" Her face was twisted in confusion, the desire to understand written across her features.

"He was too frightened." Andrew knew it wasn't his place, but he also knew if he didn't say something, no one else would. "You intimidate him. He fancies you."

"Oh." Elizabeth blinked. "I knew he found me attractive, but I wasn't aware it was so... That he also fancied me."

Andrew shifted again. With his mission complete, he once more wanted to walk away.

"I think I..." She hesitated, seemingly searching for words. "I wouldn't say I like him quite that way, but then I've never considered it. I was sort of hoping more that there might be something between you and I?"

Thankfully, she didn't touch him again, having got the message the first time that he wasn't into touching. However, she apparently completely missed the underlying message that he wasn't interested at all.

"That's flattering, Elizabeth, really, and you're certainly stunning, but I don't find you attractive the way Darren does. I'm sorry, but I'm gay."

"Oh!" Elizabeth blushed and looked away. "Would you believe I forgot that sort of thing existed?" she said, chuckling nervously. "It being the end of the world, so much else to worry about and in the midst of it all you just assume. Sorry."

"It's fine."

"I'll, um. I'll talk to Elliot."

"I'll tell Darren. It should put his mind at ease."

"No, no. I'll tell him myself. Thank you."

Quietly, she went back into the room she shared with Mary, closing the door shut behind her. Andrew hoped she wouldn't write about him in that journal of hers, but if she really had been a journalist before all this and wanted to record as much of history as possible, there was no doubt she would. With a sigh, he trudged downstairs, trying not to think about the night ahead and whether or not Blaine would hold him again.

DAY 86
12:37

"Andrew."

He was on the roof, ignoring the demands of his growling stomach, when he heard Tim call his name. He looked over his shoulder and saw Tim's head poking up out of the entrance.

"I wanna talk to you. Come down inside so we can at least be warm."

Blaine gave Andrew a questioning look that Andrew didn't address. Truthfully, he was just as curious to know what Tim wanted to talk to him about. He couldn't think of a single thing he'd done wrong or deserving of "a talk."

"I've been thinking about what you said," Tim began when Andrew had descended into Helen's room. "About doing home supply runs. I still think running into other survivors is a concern, but after talking to Helen, we think this street is pretty much cleared out. If other people were living in these houses, we'd know by now."

Andrew nodded, pleased his suggestion was finally going to be put to use.

"And you took care of that guy in the market the other day," Tim continued. "You didn't hesitate and I need someone like that if we're going to do this."

"Did you want to go today?"

Tim smirked. "How did I know you'd already want to go back out there? You're a crazy son of a bitch, you know that?"

Andrew shook it off. "I do what I have to to survive."

"Uh huh. Well, the sooner we get it done, the better. It's not getting any warmer out and Sarah wants to stock up a bit more for winter."

"So today, then."

Tim nodded. "I'm thinking we don't need the other two on this run. What d'you say?"

Andrew thought about Blaine back up on the roof and Darren downstairs. Darren he didn't want to bring, for the sole reason that he'd looked more than a little shocked when Andrew had so quickly shot the man in the shop. Darren thought he was good man now, and Andrew wasn't so ready to give up that image, not when Blaine, on the other hand, thought him selfish and cold-hearted.

But he didn't want to take Blaine either. He didn't plan on bringing a gun with him this time. This time, he was taking the axe that would one day be Elliot's but was for now sitting unused. He'd been able to get much of his nerves settled in the hospital, but not all. He needed to get the urge to beat something to a pulp out of his system, and he didn't want Blaine there to see him.

"Blaine should probably stay to keep watch on the roof," Tim suggested. "Not to mention that with Mary on the way out, Helen doesn't need anything else to worry about."

"I agree."

"We could just ask Darren, see if he wants to or not and leave it up to him."

"Alright."

Tim patted Andrew's arm in a friendly gesture. "See you downstairs in a few minutes, then."

Andrew took a deep breath and readied himself before climbing the ladder back up to the roof. He wasn't surprised to find Blaine looking over at him as he ascended.

"Tim and I are gonna go on a run."

Blaine frowned and looked like he wanted to protest, like he was trying to understand. "You want it that way?" he asked. "You want to go with just Tim?"

"Helen needs you here," Andrew explained, going with Tim's reasoning. "She's already upset about Mary. She doesn't need to be worried about you."

Blaine didn't seem convinced, but Andrew knew Helen was a weak spot with him. Even though Blaine might not have looked affected, Andrew knew he was inwardly thinking it was a valid point, and that he would want to be here for his mother.

"What about Darren? Why isn't he going?"

"We're not going through shops. We're gonna try a few houses on this street. Tim thinks it's probably clear, but if there are other survivors staying holed up somewhere, he doesn't want Darren to have to see us take care of them. He seemed a little shaken up the last time."

"Andrew—" Blaine started and stopped, cutting himself off as he seemed to search for words. Andrew could hardly look at him, his face scrunched up as though in pain. "Just please be careful."

Andrew swallowed. He didn't trust himself to speak so he just nodded and turned to meet Tim downstairs.

Voices came up to meet him on the staircase. He recognised Elizabeth's and instantly his stomach sank. He didn't want to walk into an argument involving her, but there was no other way past.

"You just think I'm weak!" Elizabeth hissed. She wasn't yelling, but the way she injected venom into her voice to get her point across was almost worse. "You said it yourself, Darren—more arms means you can carry more bags. Even if I don't fight, my arms are perfectly capable of carrying things." She even stuck out her twig-thin arms as proof.

Darren shook his head. "I don't think you're weak at all. You survived weeks on your own before coming here, and anyone who can do that isn't weak. I just don't want you to get hurt. I'll feel better knowing you're here."

Elizabeth flushed red, but Andrew didn't doubt that at least some of it was still from anger. She had her mouth poised to throw a reply back when Elliot interjected, entering the hallway from the living room.

"Elizabeth," he said, voice clear and authoritative. "I have to disagree with you. You know you're in no state for this. Though your mind isn't weak, it's a simple fact that your body is. It's no fault of your own."

"But—"

"Beth," Darren said, putting a gentle hand on her shoulder. Andrew only realised then that they were nearly the same height. "There'll be other opportunities to prove yourself. Helen said you'll be taking clothes to the river to wash them, yeah? And that you'll go with an escort? That'll be dangerous enough. We'll have to keep looking over our shoulders just to make sure nothing tries to take a bite out of us."

He finished with a smile, and Andrew was amazed at how he'd made it sound like an adventure, something to look forward to. It calmed Elizabeth enough that she kept quiet and bit her lip, but she still seemed reluctant to stay behind. Andrew caught Tim's eye on the other side of the group and Tim shrugged.

"I'll stay here, then," Darren said finally. "Just the two of you can go, like you planned. I'm sure it'll be uneventful anyway."

Andrew exhaled and slid past them to the kitchen to put away his guns. He was glad that was settled.

Chapter 20

Home Invasion

13:08

Andrew hated this part. One would think that with his career being what it was, he could ignore the stench from the streets. The truth was that even the visual aspect of it, the gangrene and milky eyes, he was only mildly used to. He'd never been able to get used to the smell, and it seemed a thousand times worse coming off of these walking corpses.

He could put up a good front, though. As he waited for Tim to break down a door, axe in hand should he need to bash in a skull, he kept his face as smooth as possible, not letting the smell get to him. He did wish that they would make a plan to clean the area up somehow, if not finding a place to burn them, then at least dragging them all into one house to keep the stench contained.

The door busted open, bringing Andrew back to the situation at hand. Tim turned around with a smile and gestured for Andrew to head in with his chair leg of nails.

"Why don't you lead this time?"

Andrew stepped in and scanned his surroundings. A staircase was on his right, with a living room on his left, much like Helen's house. He gripped his axe tighter and peered into the living room.

A large flat-screen television sat on an entertainment unit, video game cases scattered about the floor in front of the sofa. Half eaten bowls of cereal were on the table, the milk having thickened into a curdled bluish green and the cereal itself turned to floating mush. Andrew wrinkled his nose in distaste at the smell and stepped back before taking in any more details about the room. It was empty of infected and that was good enough for him.

"You take downstairs," he said quietly to Tim. "I'll get upstairs, check medicine cabinets." Tim nodded and walked further down the corridor toward the kitchen.

The second step on the staircase creaked under Andrew's foot, and he took the rest slowly, carefully. He strained his ears to hear any sounds coming from above but heard none. If they were lucky, the entire family had evacuated.

The staircase turned left at the top, leading to a narrow hallway. All but one door was open, light from the windows in each of the bedrooms spilling onto the carpet and allowing Andrew to see. He quickly poked his head into the first bedroom on his right—master bedroom with a large bed, an impressive vanity, and an equally impressive wardrobe—then carried on.

The next bedroom, again on his right, was across from the closed door which he now figured to be the bathroom. It was a girl's room. Stuffed animals sat in a neat line across the bed, nail varnish was lined just as neatly along the mirror on the chest of drawers, and a lava lamp was next to the bed on a nightstand. For a moment Andrew was envious; he'd wanted a lava lamp when he was younger but had never gotten one.

Saving the bathroom for last, Andrew went to check the final open door, the room at the end of the hall. A boy's room, perhaps a bit older than the girl. More video games in here, as well as a collection of snow globes perched on wall shelves around the room. Nothing useful.

Back in the corridor, Andrew stepped close to the bathroom and put his ear to the door, listening. He could only hear the light shuffling of Tim raiding the kitchen downstairs. Slowly, he raised his hand and tapped a knuckle on the wood.

Nothing.

Andrew stepped back, axe ready, and quickly twisted the knob to push the door open.

It was as empty as the rest of the house. The glass shower door showed no one in the bath tub either. Andrew hurried in, took off his rucksack, and popped open the medicine cabinet.

He grabbed everything that looked the least bit useful and shoved it into his bag—paracetamol, antiseptic creams, aspirin tablets, even nasal spray. He also picked up toothpaste and—thank God—a pack of six shaving razors. He hadn't yet taught the others how to shave with a knife, and if they found enough razors it'd be a while before he had to.

The medicine cabinet cleared out, he went through the drawers. Under the sink was mostly shampoos, lotions, and acne creams. Seeing the box of tampons in the back and remembering Sarah, Andrew grabbed that as well. On second thought, he added a couple bottles of lotion to his bag. Winter meant cold, cracked skin, and though he personally thought lotion a bit of a luxury, he knew at least Elizabeth would appreciate it.

He was less careful as he took the stairs down. He found Tim still in the kitchen, just about done by the looks of things. His rucksack was only half full, but cans were heavy.

"One more house and we should be good for today," Tim said, zipping up his bag and hefting it up. "I'm thinking next door. Anything good upstairs?"

"Some good stuff in the bathroom. Razors, even."

Tim nodded and hurried past Andrew back out into Milsom Street. Andrew followed him, quickly looking around to check for infected. It was still quiet.

The door to the second house was unlocked, probably left so in the haste to get out. It was noticeably different inside, mainly because of all the baby toys strewn about. At first Andrew thought they'd been a large family, but all the photos showed a smiling young couple with only one child, a baby boy. A spoilt baby boy, it seemed, with all the toys he could ever want. Andrew nearly tripped more times than he could count.

Andrew took downstairs this time. The layout of this house required him to traverse the living room to get to the kitchen, so he carefully stepped around the wooden blocks, stuffed animals, and colouring books. An image from his nightmares flashed through his mind, and he wondered what he'd do if he came across the child, infected and crawling through the toys to tear off his flesh.

There were much fewer toys in the kitchen, and those there were seemed to be restricted to a single corner. Andrew set his axe on the worktop and started opening cupboards, searching for things they could still eat.

Peas, corn, carrots. They even had canned mushrooms. Andrew's stomach growled and his mouth watered, but he knew they'd still be having thin, mostly tasteless soup tonight. That, however, had been when Elizabeth was in charge of cooking. Jessica was much more easily swayed, or at least she seemed more reasonable. Surely he'd be able to convince her to give them a treat just this once.

There were only a few more cupboards left to check. Andrew slid his heavy rucksack across the worktop and opened the next. His jaw dropped when he saw a red package on the bottom shelf, and before he could hold them back, tears started to form in the corners of his eyes.

Maryland Gooeys Chocolate Cookies. Maddie used to love those.

Andrew blinked back the tears, angry that they were there at all, and reached up to take the package.

"Unnnnhh."

The guttural groan made Andrew's heart stop. He spun away from the sound and picked up his axe. It seemed he was just in time. The husband from all the photos — infected now, with sunken, cloudy eyes and gristle dripping from his teeth — was making his way around the centre island.

Adrenaline shot through Andrew, making his heart pump faster and his instincts kick in. He held the axe with both hands, pivoted quickly around the advancing walker, and brought the blade down on top of his skull, splitting it open with a sharp cracking sound. The body dropped instantly, hitting the floor with a thump.

Andrew raised the axe and swung it down again, blinking against the light spray of dark blood. The crunching noise made him cringe, but he did it again anyway, this time striking between the shoulder blades and sinking the axe into decaying meat.

Once more, and he nearly severed the head from the neck. Again, and his strike went so deep into its back that he had to step on the body to yank the axe-head free. One more time, just once more, because his arms quivered with the need for some sort of physical release and this was too good to stop. He couldn't do something like this often, and who knew when he'd next get the chance? He swung again, then again, until he was sweating and wheezing, but he was keeping everyone safe, this was one walker who was never going to get up—

A hand gripped Andrew's wrist, halting him mid-swing. Another walker, surely. Maybe the wife. But when Andrew turned, scowling and ready to give her the same treatment, he only saw Tim's face, full of caution and warning.

Andrew lowered the axe and wiped his face with his sleeve. "Sorry," he said, bending down to clean the blade of the axe with the dead walker's shirt. There was a corner that wasn't drenched with blood that worked well enough.

"You okay?" Tim asked.

Andrew thought about ignoring him. It was what he'd been doing for ages every time someone tried to get him to talk about himself, only Helen and Blaine ever really succeeding in slipping past his boundaries. He figured he did owe Tim some explanation, though.

"Better now." He shoved the Maryland cookies into his bag and zipped it closed. "Find anything upstairs?"

"Oh yeah," Tim said, chuckling through his reply. "Found some condoms in the master bedroom."

"Brilliant."

"Yeah. So all this." Tim gestured to the dead walker on the floor. "This about Blaine?"

Andrew definitely wasn't responding to that. He didn't even want to think about how Tim knew. He went back to the living room, not taking care to avoid the toys and instead kicking them out of the way, and looked over the titles on the bookshelf.

Something Jessica would like. Something to sweeten her up, he thought to himself.

Tim, of course, had followed. "Kinda hard to miss the way you two look at each other," he said. "If it's about lack of sex or something that's got you strung out, I can relate. I mean, I've got these condoms now but when the fuck am I gonna be able to use them? Me and Sarah have tried three times and all three times I couldn't get it up just because I kept thinking people were gonna hear."

"For God's sake, shut up!" Andrew snapped, whipping his head around to glare at him. He must've looked frightening, because Tim recoiled. "Blaine and I aren't like that."

184

He turned back to the bookshelf. *Something literature-y. Why's there only stupid romance novels on this bloody thing?*

"At the risk of getting my head cut off, it's pretty obvious that you want things to be like that. Is it that Blaine's just being difficult?"

Andrew snorted, despite himself. "Far from it," he muttered.

"So you're the one being difficult. Well, that doesn't exactly surprise—"

"I'm *not* talking about it."

"Why the fuck not? You just going to keep taking it out on infected and leaving the poor boy looking miserable? What kind of idiot sees a problem that can be resolved with a few honest words but decides to draw it out instead?"

Andrew grit his teeth, clenching his hands. He kept scanning the titles on the shelves, but none of it registered, not really.

Finally he bit out, "I just need to wait a little longer."

He should've expected Tim to question that. "What're you waiting for?"

Andrew didn't want to think about it, much less say it. But he'd already said so much... "I don't know. A respectful amount of time, I guess."

Tim laughed, a real belly laugh, which made Andrew more than livid. What the fuck did Tim know? What did any of them know? He smothered the voice in his head that said they would know if only he told them and gave Tim his darkest look.

Tim sobered quickly. "Sorry. I just don't think Blaine is exactly a blushing virgin. Not like he needs to be courted or anything."

"It's not out of respect for him, you dim wit! It's out of respect for the dead."

"Oh."

Andrew felt like a hole had ripped through his chest. He took in lungfuls of air and massaged the ache sorely, his palm right up against the hole in his shirt where a bullet had entered into Luke's body and never left.

"I dunno," Tim said slowly. Andrew closed his eyes, wishing he would shut up already. "I think it being the end of the world, we can afford to be a little hedonistic."

Andrew opened his eyes to glare at him again.

"What? You think 'cause I'm a stupid American, I don't know what hedonistic means?"

Andrew didn't laugh.

Tim sighed and walked up to the bookcase. He looked it up and down, then stood of the tips of his toes to reach up to the highest shelf. He pulled out three books, each by the same author.

"Can't go wrong with *Lord of the Rings*," he said, handing them to Andrew.

Andrew was still angry, but he had to admit Jessica would probably like them.

Chapter 21

The Root

DAY 87
16:37

Blaine didn't know what had happened on the supply run the day before, only that Tim had apparently warmed up nicely to Andrew. Actually, Sarah seemed to like him a lot more, too. Even Elizabeth, who Blaine had caught snogging Darren in the kitchen last night after dinner, looked at Andrew with less apprehension.

What the hell was Andrew playing at? Making friends with everyone *but* him?

"He's just figuring things out, Blaine," Helen had said when he went to her with the problem. "Don't push him, not yet."

Blaine didn't like it, but there was at least something he could do. With Darren all newly preoccupied with Elizabeth, Blaine figured he could get closer to some of the others as well.

He chose Jessica, mostly because of how well they'd already started hitting it off. This was the first night that she would cook for them, and Elizabeth would help her the first few times. Jessica had spent the whole day reading one of the books Andrew had brought back for her (a gesture that made Blaine roll his eyes and want to gag), but she managed to climb backwards up the ladder to the roof around half four.

"We have to use a small fire because otherwise it's hard to put out quickly, not to mention all the smoke," Elizabeth explained. "Here's the lighter, just light it here."

Blaine's shift usually ended when the sun went down and right before dinner. For the last hour or so before sunset, Elizabeth joined him and Andrew above the house and they sat in mostly silence. Tonight, with Jessica there, Blaine left his post and went to stand by the two women.

"You want to learn as well, Blaine?" Elizabeth asked. She grinned up at him. She'd been noticeably happier since yesterday, even though she still looked a bit ill.

"No thanks, just thought I'd stand by the fire for a bit of warmth," he said. "Think I've got the windier side. He gets all the sun." He nodded in Andrew's direction. Andrew didn't move.

"Okay, now since this is rain water, I usually let it boil a couple minutes to make sure it's safe," Elizabeth said. Jessica nodded. "Here's the thermometer to check the temperature if you want."

"You like the book Andrew got, then?" Blaine asked Jessica. A gust of wind made him shiver and suddenly he was inching closer to the fire, crouching down and wrapping his arms around his calves.

"I love it," Jessica said with a wide smile. "Adventure books are perfect for a time like this. If you're not trying to survive, you're sitting around bored out of your mind."

Blaine chuckled and nodded in agreement. With most of his days spent staring out into space, nose scrunched up from the smell while he scanned the area for movement, he understood completely.

"I see you've used your gift too," Jessica said, pointing at his face. "Shaved."

Blaine rubbed his jaw. It hadn't been the best shave, but it'd been refreshing. "Yeah."

"I meant to tell you—and I hope you don't take this the wrong way; I really mean it as a compliment—but you pull off the monobrow really well. A lot of people can't, but it looks good on you."

Before Blaine could think of anything to say, he heard quiet laughter coming from the other side of the roof, and when he looked up, Andrew's shoulders were shaking. Blaine didn't realise he was smiling himself until he heard Elizabeth snort and snapped his head back to look at her. Seeing her smirking down into the pot, Blaine schooled his dopey grin back into a simple smile.

"Thanks, Jessica. I actually don't really like it myself." He rubbed the space between his eyes, over the bridge of his nose and up to his forehead. "I usually shaved it, before all this. Now that I have this razor, I'm thinking of doing it again."

"Now that'd be weird," Jessica remarked teasingly. "I can't imagine you without it."

"Was just thinking that myself," Elizabeth murmured. "Okay, now just a tiny sprinkle of basil," She handed Jessica a small shaker. Jessica tapped a bit into the pot. "Maybe a larger sprinkle than that. That's good." Elizabeth stirred the broth slowly.

"I look loads better." Blaine stretched his arms out, though he knew they couldn't see his skin because of his sleeves. "You think I like being this hairy?"

The two of them laughed, and Blaine caught Andrew peeking over his shoulder in his peripheral vision, but paid him no attention.

"Helen did mention something about Romanian ancestors," Elizabeth said. She handed Jessica the spoon to take a break from stirring. "That probably doesn't help."

Blaine cracked a crooked smile. "Both she and my father were half Romanian, half British. I can't remember exactly how they met, but it was at some gathering when they were both teenagers. Both of them wanted to be more English than Romanian, fit in with their friends, I suppose, but their parents kept insisting they embrace their heritage. Must've brought them closer together, being rebels and such."

Elizabeth nodded. "The story sounds familiar. Your father was named Greg, right? Helen talked about it one night, after Mary told us about how she'd met her husband."

"Yeah. Grigore, but he went by Greg. He was great, a big teddy bear of a guy who absolutely dwarfed my mum." Blaine smiled at the memories of being picked up and carried around in his father's large arms. "Didn't tell me I'd inherit all this hair from him, though. But then, he died before I started puberty, so I can't really blame him."

"And did he have a monobrow?" Jessica asked.

Blaine frowned. He tried to cast his mind back, to see his father's face, but it was all blurry. His mum was sure to have photos somewhere, he'd have to look at them.

"I can't remember."

Jessica's expression shifted. "I'm sorry."

"It's alright. What about you? What did you do before the Outbreak?"

"Teacher. I taught primary."

Elizabeth smiled. "I can see that."

"And you two?"

"Photography student."

"Journalist."

Jessica lowered her voice and pointed to Andrew. "And him?"

Blaine followed her finger, looked at Andrew, then turned back. "Royal Marines," he replied quietly.

Jessica nodded. "Explains a lot."

DAY 91
19:53

Jessica was easy to get close to, and soon enough she and Blaine spent almost all their free time together. Mostly they talked about books and art, their favourite things before the Outbreak, but there were many times where they simply sat looking at old magazines, ogling all the fit men.

Blaine also caught on quickly that though Jessica was nice to everyone, she didn't like everyone. More than once, Sarah asked her about her baby, even cooed over her and talked about names. Jessica indulged her, but as soon as she left, Jessica turned to Blaine and said she really didn't like Sarah. Blaine, who didn't have positive or negative feelings for Sarah one way or the other, simply nodded.

"So you and Andrew share a bed?" she asked warily one evening. "But you're not together?"

Blaine shrugged and thumbed the pages of the magazine in his lap. Truthfully, he'd been hoping to be able to talk to someone other than his mother about this, but didn't want to dump all his troubles on his new friend.

"It's a bit complicated. I wish it wasn't."

"How?"

"He's being a thick-skulled Marine, is all. We both know we want to move things along but he says he's still grieving or something. I've tried to help him, you know, get him to open up and talk about it but he refuses." Blaine sighed and turned the page. "So we're in limbo until he decides otherwise, I guess."

"That is a bit odd."

"Yeah."

What made it worse was the fact that sometimes Andrew had a way of looking at him, all full of exasperation, as though it were Blaine's fault. He had a way of saying without saying that Blaine was being selfish and impatient, not giving Andrew the time he needed, which only served to make Blaine feel guilty. He tried to tell himself that that wasn't it at all, that he wasn't being selfish and impatient and that he really did want to help Andrew get over the loss of his friend. But then he had to ask himself *why* he wanted that so badly.

If he was being honest with himself, only a small part of him wanted to help Andrew for purely selfless reasons. Most of him simply longed to make his lustful dreams a reality and have Andrew all to himself once and for all.

"Do you want me to try talking to him?" Jessica offered.

"I doubt he'd say anything. He doesn't really know you like I do."

"You never know. Sometimes it's easier to open up to a stranger. I'm sure that's why he's hesitant to speak to you about it."

"If you think it'll work, I won't try to stop you. I think at this point I'm willing to try anything."

Jessica smiled. "I have an idea."

DAY 92
06:55

Anyone could've seen Andrew had a routine. The exact time he awoke every morning wasn't always the same, but his daily actions were.

Wake up, shave if his face seemed to require it, check his guns, head up to the roof for the day.

Today was a day Andrew went to the bathroom to shave. Jessica seemed to have known it would be, and told Blaine to wait outside the door while she talked to him. If Andrew ended up walking out in the middle of their conversation, exiting in a fit of frustration as Blaine had said he liked to do, Blaine could simply say he'd been waiting for Andrew to finish, not eavesdropping at all.

"Morning, Andrew," she sang as she waltzed into the bathroom. From his place outside the door, Blaine could hear her sit on the edge of the tub.

"Uh, morning. Did you need something?" Andrew asked gruffly.

"Just wanted to talk. We hardly know each other, yet here we are staying under the same roof. You risked your life to save me and I don't think I've ever properly thanked you."

A few seconds of silence passed during which Blaine held his breath and clutched his razor tightly. At last, Andrew said, "I'll tell you the same thing I told Elizabeth. I'm gay."

"Oh," Jessica laughed. "I didn't quite mean a thank you like that, but that's good to know I suppose."

"How far along are you, anyway?" Andrew asked.

"Hmm? Oh, I've lost track of days, but I reckon about five months or so."

"Just in time for winter."

Blaine frowned. Why would Andrew say such a thing? He knew Andrew could be cold, but he wasn't cruel, not for no reason.

"I'm aware there's not much of a chance for her survival," Jessica said. Blaine was surprised to hear a note of bitterness in the tone.

"Her?"

"I don't know for certain, but something tells me it's a girl." A moment of silence between them, no sound but the quiet drag of a razor across skin, then Jessica continued. "Some days I think about killing myself, if only to avoid the pain sure to come later."

Blaine gaped, but made sure to remain silent. He couldn't imagine how Jessica could consider such a thing. Even when he'd found her on the floor of the pharmacy she'd seemed strong.

"What stops you?" Andrew asked.

"I couldn't do it to Elliot. We're twins, did you know? If I lost him, then I might consider it more seriously. We're family and we're all we've got left. I have to keep going even if it hurts. That's what I told myself after my husband died and I know that's what he would've wanted me to do."

Blaine's chest tightened with the weight of her words. If he ever lost his mum, the only family he had left, he wasn't sure what he'd do. After Paul and Emily, he'd been distraught, but the thought of his mother had carried him on.

He had Andrew now, or he did in a way, but would that be enough?

Blaine didn't want to think about it. He already felt tears stinging his eyes and tried to will them back, swallowing past the lump in his throat.

"Sorry," Jessica said, "I didn't mean to burden you. You look young. You shouldn't be troubled with such things."

"Not that young," Andrew replied hoarsely. "I've talked to Elliot, so I know he's thirty-three. If the two of you are twins, you're only eight years older than me."

"Either way, still young."

"*Either way*, I've been burdened with worse things."

"Like what?"

Oh God, here we go. Blaine swallowed again. He shifted his weight from one foot to the other. He waited.

There was the soft sound of a razor running down the side Andrew's face again, then a sigh. "I'd rather not get into it."

"That's fine. You don't have to say anything if you don't want to."

"Talking about it means I have to think about it, which is something I try to avoid doing."

"I get it," Jessica said easily. "I don't like thinking about how my baby could be dead inside me already and I'm just carrying around a corpse. Unfortunately I've got this huge stomach to constantly remind me."

Blaine winced. It was a low blow, and no doubt Andrew knew it, but it did the trick. After about a minute, Blaine heard the clink of Andrew putting his razor down on the sink.

"If I tell you, you can't tell anyone else," Andrew said.

"I promise I won't."

"Alright." Andrew took a deep breath. "I've killed a lot of people."

"Of course. Royal Marines and all, yeah?"

"Yes, but... Afterward. During the Outbreak. There were ships that people paid to get on. You remember?"

Blaine did.

"Yeah."

"I was in Portsmouth. My superiors told me to secure and guard all possible entrances. Anything that tried to get through was to be killed on sight."

"Anything?" Jessica echoed.

"Anything. Anyone. Children, infected, old, young; it didn't matter. If it tried to get into the naval base, it was killed. They gave me my orders, they put me in charge, and then they left."

Blaine was speechless. He didn't want to be able to imagine Andrew in such a heartless position, but he remembered easily the way he'd looked when he'd taken out the walker at the hospital with a scalpel. He remembered the hollow gaze and unwavering determination. There'd always been an element to Andrew that was a bit frightening. Blaine hadn't wanted to believe it, because he'd seen Andrew cry and seen his humanity, but this confirmed his suspicions.

"I had a, a friend. Luke," Andrew went on. "He told me before the Outbreak to leave and get to my sister. He knew what would happen. But I wanted to stay and help the civilians; I couldn't abandon them when they didn't even know what was coming. Then they promoted me that morning and gave me all these responsibilities..."

"You lost him, then?" Jessica asked. "Luke. You said you *had* a friend."

Blaine could hear the unsteadiness in Andrew's exhalation from outside the door.

"Yeah. He was... he was shot."

Andrew's voice was thick now, and Blaine didn't need to imagine very hard how he must've looked. He'd seen Andrew try not to cry before. His face got red, his lips thinned, his brow furrowed in agony. Blaine wondered how Jessica was holding herself together.

"They hated me," Andrew said. "The people in Portsmouth. They hated me because I wouldn't let them into the base. And this woman... She said people were dead because of me, worse than dead. It was me she was trying to shoot, but she — Luke got in front of me."

Oh my God. Blaine couldn't think anything else. *Oh my fucking God.*

"Is that when you left?" Jessica asked.

Andrew sniffled, and his voice was even more full of emotion, more than Blaine had ever heard it. It broke his heart to hear it.

"I have to go. Someone should be up on the roof by now."

Blaine's pulse jumped when he thought Andrew might be about to leave, and he took a step left.

"No," Jessica stopped him. "Come on, tell me everything. You can't just start a story and then end with someone dying. You've got to give someone a bit of hope."

"Hope?" Andrew repeated angrily. "There is no 'hope.' A few hours later I found out my sister was infected and I was the one to kill her. There's no hope in this story."

Oh, fuck. It was no wonder Blaine found Andrew trying to off himself. He'd lost his friend, he'd been wearing the man's bloody shirt, then Blaine had come along trying to make small talk in the car.

Blaine wanted to beat his head against the wall. If he'd known the loss had been so recent, he wouldn't have made such an arse of himself.

"What about how you got here?" Jessica asked. "How'd you end up with Helen and Blaine?"

Andrew sighed. "On my way from Portsmouth there was a car pile-up across the motorway. I couldn't get through or around, so I climbed the hill to see what the other side was like and that's when I saw Blaine's car. He gave me a lift the rest of the way to Oxford to find my sister. When we found her the way she was... Anyway, afterwards I came back here with him. The end."

"That's why you two share a bed? Because you arrived together?"

"Yeah, guess so. Look, I have to —"

"I don't understand. If you're gay and Blaine's gay and you both sleep —"

"I *can't!*"

The volume made Blaine flinch. He hoped no one else had heard the outburst and woken up, but he was eager to hear if Andrew had anything else to say. This was why he'd enlisted Jessica's help in the first place — he had to hear the explanation.

195

"I kissed him," Andrew said, lowering his voice again. Blaine's heart raced. "I *loved* Luke. I kissed him while he died in my arms, and then I kissed Blaine that same fucking night. You think I deserve any sort of happiness, or any sort of hope? I don't even deserve to be alive!"

Blaine shuffled away when he heard the door slam open, but luckily Andrew was so insistent to get to the roof that he didn't notice Blaine at all. He stormed from the bathroom and didn't see Blaine standing off to the left as he turned and went right.

"Christ," Jessica said, poking her head out of the bathroom to look in the direction Andrew had gone. She turned her head and looked at Blaine sympathetically. "Think we got to the root of the problem."

The door to Blaine's old room opened and Elizabeth stepped into the corridor looking stunned.

"Mary's dead."

Chapter 22

Confessions

09:45

Blaine thought he would've felt worse when Mary died. He thought he would've been blaming himself somehow, as it was technically his fault. Mostly, as they lowered her body into the Avon, his thoughts were, *Would've happened sooner or later,* and *Does this mean I get my bed back?*

But his thoughts were also on Andrew. Andrew had opted to stay behind with Jessica while the rest of them held as respectful a ceremony they could at the river. The reason he'd given had been that someone needed be there to protect the house. Jessica, of course, simply wasn't able to make the walk.

There'd been a moment of more intense guilt as they'd put Mary in the water, when Elliot had caught Blaine's eye. No one, not even Andrew, knew of Blaine's decision, and definitely not Helen. To everyone else, it was just that the antibiotics had simply not been enough. Only they two knew the truth.

But like the clouds above, blocking out the sun of the grey morning, the guilt hovered over Blaine's head and quickly passed.

"She was a kind woman," his mum said. "She was remarkably strong, and even in these terrible times she sought out the best in a bad situation. She's free of all this pain now. She's free of the danger we face every day. May she rest in peace."

The tears she'd been holding back burst free, and Blaine moved to put an arm around her. She turned her face into his chest to muffle the sound of her sobs, careful even now of drawing the attention of infected. The embrace reminded Blaine of the time he'd done the same for Andrew, when Andrew had broken down in the Jeep and let his emotions come cascading out. Blaine took the open folds of his coat and wrapped them around her, keeping her warm. Her tears soaked through his shirt, leaving a damp spot on his chest.

It was almost funny. Among Paul and Emily, Blaine had been the emotional one, the weakest of the three. They'd comforted him countless times, and here he was, the last of them, now staying strong to comfort others. He supposed he had Merrick to thank for that.

"She was a good storyteller," Darren muttered. "Not always the most interesting story, but she told it well enough."

"And a good listener," Elizabeth added. She especially was shivering, and was doing her best to disappear into one of Blaine's old coats. "Not just the books I read her, but all the... all the shit I told her when I was sad or angry. She was good at reminding me what was important in life and what you just have to deal with."

Blaine swallowed, trying to keep himself numb. The weight of his actions seemed to increase, then slide off his shoulders.

"Yeah, she wasn't too bad," Tim said. Sarah elbowed him and shot him a glare, but he was still smiling. "I didn't think too many folks her age would survive something like this. Caught me by surprise the first time I saw her, how thin her bones were. But she had a strong spirit, like Helen said, that kept her going. Definitely the kind of old person I wanna be if I ever make it to that age."

"I didn't know her long," Elliot said, "but I agree there was a strength in her, even in her weakened state, and I admired that."

Blaine hadn't realised, but at some point his mother had stopped sobbing, her cries reduced to sniffles. She was resting the side of her face against his chest now, and when she looked up at him through her eyelashes, eyes still wet and puffy, he felt obligated to say something as well.

"I didn't talk to her much," he admitted. "Too caught up in other things, I guess. I'm not sure if..." He trailed off, unsure if he should continue. The words in his head suddenly seemed inappropriate.

"Go on, Blaine," Helen nudged.

Blaine frowned. "It sounds terrible. I wish I'd spoken to her more and got to know her better, but at the same time, it hurts less losing someone I wasn't as close with. I'm sorry, I know it's—"

"It's fine," Elizabeth assured him. "I understand. I think it's safe to say all of us do."

Blaine nodded stiffly. Elliot was staring intently down at the ground and Blaine thought for certain he could feel the man's judgement emanating off him. However, when Elliot looked up to meet his eyes, there was only pity.

Walking back, Blaine covered one side of the group while Darren covered the other, and Tim took the rear. Their strategy most of the time was for Blaine to snipe any infected ahead and clear as much of a path as possible before dealing with any stragglers with their knives. Blaine was surprised to see even Sarah take out a walker on their way back. He knew she was capable, but had never seen her in action. Seeing Elizabeth was envious, Darren shot a few walkers down and let her finish them off with his knife.

When they turned a corner close to home, Darren managed to slip briefly to Blaine's side and ask, "You don't think Andrew'll make us do conditioning today, do you? I mean, I wouldn't put it past him."

Blaine wanted to snap at him. *What the hell do you know about Andrew?* he thought bitterly.

Instead he kept his voice firm and replied, "No."

When they got back to the house, Blaine was anxious to go up to the roof right away. For a month he'd been almost constantly near Andrew—sleeping, fighting, surviving. It was only when he was any significant distance away that he realised how much he missed Andrew's presence. It unsettled him not having Andrew close by, even if he was still wary of him after what he heard earlier that morning.

Blaine made sure his mother was okay first. She was still teary-eyed and quiet, but she said she was going to clean up a bit, go on with her duties. There were empty tins to be collected and thrown out, dishes to be wiped clean. She wanted to take her mind off things. Blaine left her downstairs with everyone else.

Andrew was visibly tense when Blaine ascended. Blaine took a deep breath. He'd already decided on the walk back what he was going to say. He wouldn't keep dancing around the subject and drawing things out, not when their time could be up at any moment. He went to where Andrew sat on the edge of the roof and plopped down next to him, the same way he had the first day he'd decided to help keep watch.

Andrew gave him a funny look, wordlessly asking what he was doing.

"Hey," Blaine said. "I need to talk to you."

Andrew sighed and returned his eyes to the empty street below. It smelled worse on this side, Blaine noticed. Andrew squinted into the sun rising over the buildings but didn't much try to avoid the harsh light. "Thought I told you I don't like talking."

"Just listen, then."

"What is it?"

"On the day of the Outbreak," Blaine began, "when I lost my friends, I just... I wept and wept. I curled up in the back of the car and was a complete mess. I was certain my life was over."

"I'm sure a lot of people felt the same."

"That's no excuse not to feel it. I still get all depressed when I think about it, even though it's been a few months and I know I'm incredibly lucky to even still be alive. But that's not the point."

"What *is* the point?" Andrew asked impatiently.

"The point is, I wasn't who I am now. I was weak before I ran into Merrick. I wasn't... I wasn't equipped to live in this world. Now that I am, I have to sometimes make decisions that I wouldn't have before."

Andrew sighed. "Blaine..."

"There was a man," Blaine said. "On the run to the supermarket, before we went to the hospital. There was a man about to run into the shop, and I could've killed him, but I didn't. I let him go, because you and the others had left already and I thought it made no difference to me."

Andrew turned to look at him, frowning. "Why didn't you say anything?"

"I thought the three of you would've told me I should've shot him."

"No. Would've been a waste of a bullet."

Of course, Blaine thought wryly.

"But later that day, after we got back with Elliot and Jessica, I made another decision," Blaine continued. "Elliot told me the antibiotics would help Mary, but that sooner or later she'd die. We could give her the antibiotics and give her more time, or give her a placebo and save the antibiotics for those who needed it most."

"What'd you say?"

"I told him to give her the placebo. Now Mary's dead. The only people who know it's my doing are me, Elliot, and now you."

"You did the right thing."

"I did what I had to. But back to my point. I've changed and I know I've changed, maybe not for the better, but it's what's kept me alive. I wasn't strong enough to kill the man in front of the supermarket, but I was cruel enough to kill an old lady. We all do what we have to do. It doesn't make us bad people."

"Why the hell are you telling me this?"

Now Andrew was getting defensive. He looked angry, suspicious, and much like he was about to try and push Blaine off the roof.

It was time for the leap of faith.

"When I went to the bathroom to shave this morning, I—"

Andrew swung his feet back onto the roof and stood up before Blaine could finish. He was fleeing, he was running away like a coward, and that just wouldn't do.

Blaine shuffled to his feet and darted after him. "Andrew!"

"Leave me the fuck alone, Blaine," he snapped over his shoulder.

"I know about Portsmouth. And Luke."

"Don't fucking say his name!"

Blaine grabbed Andrew's wrist and yanked Andrew around to face him. "You could've told me. You told me about your sister, didn't you?"

"That was a mistake." Andrew snatched his wrist back. "It was all a fucking mistake."

Andrew moved so quickly after that that Blaine only managed to catch up with him when he'd neared Blaine's old room. He'd suspected Andrew would try to lock himself up somewhere, and with Elizabeth being downstairs and Mary no longer inhabiting the bed, Blaine's room would certainly be available for moping purposes. He put his foot in the door before Andrew could slam it shut.

"Blaine," Andrew growled.

Blaine clenched his jaw. "Andrew."

"You don't know when to quit, do you? What the hell do you

want from me?"

He wanted Andrew to stop making things hard on himself when things didn't have to be hard. He wanted Andrew to at least *try* to be happy and move on like the rest of them were doing. He wanted to show Andrew that they could be happy *together*.

What ended up coming out of his mouth was: "Have sex with me."

Andrew gaped. "What?"

He couldn't take it back now, and every second that passed was another second that Andrew had to think too hard about it.

Blaine looked down the corridor to make sure no one (his mum in particular) was coming up the stairs before leaning in closer and speaking through the narrow space in the doorway.

"Have sex with me. Right now while everyone's downstairs."

"You're mental. Go away."

Andrew tried to close the door again, putting more force into the swing, but Blaine only bit his lip against the pain on the side of his foot and kept it there. He slid his hand through to place it on Andrew's chest — *Jesus that's a lot of muscle* — before Andrew could retreat.

"You'll feel better afterwards," Blaine insisted. He let his hand trail down Andrew's torso and was pleased to see Andrew's lips part just a little with a hitched breath. "Trust me. Come on."

He could see the wheels turning in Andrew's head. Cracks were forming in the walls of Andrew's resolve, and it would only take a little more pushing. As Blaine lowered his hand more, nearing the crotch of Andrew's jeans, he began to believe his words himself.

Andrew *would* feel better afterwards. They both would.

"You're forgetting this is my room," Blaine said, his voice low. His hand was right where it needed to be by this point, and Andrew was hiding his face behind the door as Blaine applied the tiniest bit of pressure. "I know where everything is. For example, I know I keep lube in a box under the bed, and I'm pretty sure the condoms haven't expir — "

"Fine."

Andrew grabbed a handful of Blaine's shirt and pulled him in so quickly that Blaine tripped.

Chapter 23

Love in the Time of Zombies

10:48

Andrew still thought it was a bad idea, but he was trying not to think about it too much. He so rarely indulged himself or let himself have a lapse in good judgement, surely just this once he could act without thinking too much about the consequences?

As soon as Blaine had his shirt off—which was almost immediately after he fell into the room—it was easier for Andrew to distance himself from all the voices in his head that insisted it wasn't right. He blocked out everything but the feeling of Blaine's skin on his and the heat of his mouth.

Sex felt good, and for once, Andrew wanted to feel good. Nothing else mattered.

Everyone only had so many clothes, and Blaine was no exception. Andrew had seen him change maybe three or four times, and every time he had to ball his hands into fists, holding back the desire to touch. He didn't hold back now. Though they were both less than the cleanest they'd ever been, Andrew set to learning every contour of Blaine's body as soon as Blaine had all his clothes off.

He started with the chest, mouthing a pebbled nipple, then pushed his nose deep into skin and made his way down. There were times when the hair on Blaine's torso was a bit prickly, but for the most part it was surprisingly soft. It didn't curl up in tufts, but lay flat and smooth. As Andrew's hands clutched Blaine's thighs, pulling them tighter around him, he left kiss after wet kiss across Blaine's stomach.

It was almost a sort of game. Blaine arched his spine, offering himself up, but with each flick of Andrew's tongue to his skin, the muscles in his stomach fluttered, as though in surprise. Andrew did it again and again, just to see how many times he could tease until Blaine became used to it.

You haven't looked at him, Andrew thought. *Not once since this began.*

Andrew knew it. He hadn't met Blaine's eyes a single time, not when they'd been kissing and taking each other's jeans off, not when they'd fallen onto the bed to do things thoroughly and properly. He'd been focusing on Blaine's body, because it wasn't Blaine's body that would jolt him out of his comfort zone and snap him back to his senses.

With a growl, he shut out the voices again. He concentrated on the want, and Andrew wanted. He hoisted Blaine's legs up and went at the smooth skin high on his right thigh.

Blaine tensed. "Ah!"

Christ, Blaine was all limbs. He was all spindly, flailing limbs. Andrew suddenly wanted them around him, clinging to him while he buried himself inside.

Now, now, fuck him now.

"Get it," Andrew ordered hoarsely. He moved back to give Blaine enough room, but still kept his eyes down while Blaine poked around under the bed. He traced the wrinkles on the sheet and listened to the shuffling noises as he waited.

"Can't believe these are still here," Blaine's muffled voice came from under the bed. He emerged and tossed everything to Andrew before standing and swinging a leg up to lie on his stomach.

Luke.

The name shot like a lance through Andrew's heart all of a sudden. The last time Andrew had been about to rip open a packet of lube was two years ago, before he'd gone to Africa, before the Outbreak, before Luke had—

Don't think about it, don't fucking think about it.

Andrew snatched up the packet and rubbed his cock against the back of Blaine's thigh to bring the pleasure back into focus. Yes, there it was, that's what he wanted. He did it again as he tore the foil, kept doing it as his fingers slid over the exposed hole. He was back to eyeing the form of Blaine's body and wanting to devour every little piece of it. He bent forward and put his lips right at swell of Blaine's arse, sucked a bruising kiss into it and nipped the supple flesh greedily between his teeth as he pushed his finger just the slightest bit deeper.

He could feel the tenseness in Blaine's muscles as he struggled to stay relaxed. Every sigh and moan made Andrew want to go faster, and at last he caved and searched the folds of the sheets for the condom. As he opened it and slid it on, Blaine turned over onto his back again.

That's when Andrew made the mistake of letting his eyes slip, and instead of the expected aching pain in his chest or the lurch of his stomach, there was only warmth and desire. His gaze drifted up to Blaine's face, and it was only by luck that Blaine wasn't staring back at him, but at Andrew's hands. His cheeks were flushed red and his lips were parted as he breathed through his mouth, and as he propped himself up on his elbows and lifted his hips, his eyes seemed to darken with lust. His tongue darted out to wet his lips as he lowered a hand to his cock and started stroking himself back to full hardness. He was so gorgeous, everything that Andrew wanted in that moment, and he hated himself for denying it so long. He wanted to stare at Blaine forever, drink in the sight of him, then hold him and kiss him senseless.

Pushing in was bliss. Blaine's head fell back as a low moan was pulled from his throat. Andrew wasn't particularly large, certainly not bigger than average, but big enough that he worried if Blaine could take him right away, or if he should've stretched him with another finger. It felt too good for Andrew to want to pull out now. Maybe if he just stayed in one position a bit longer...

"Keep going," Blaine panted. His fingers were twisted in the sheet and one hand was clutching the pillow beside him, but he was determinedly easing himself forward, taking in more before Andrew moved forward to give it.

Oh fuck yes, oh fuck yes!

The heat just swallowed Andrew up, and he gave one experimental pull out before thrusting back in. He gasped along with Blaine at how incredible it felt, then did it again, pushing deeper this time.

After a few more repetitions, Blaine let his arms go limp and fell flat to the bed. He was still breathing deeply, but seemed finally relaxed. Andrew thrust in a bit harder the next time around and forced a whine out of him.

His hands came up and he dug the heels of his palms into his eyes as he moaned again. He was biting his lip and now a rhythm was starting, he was hitching his legs up to open himself wider.

"Slow," Blaine exhaled. "Want it to be good."

Andrew stifled a snort. *Oh it'll be good.*

Pushing Blaine's knees up and hooking his arms around Blaine's thighs, Andrew shuffled forward, then began rolling his hips in earnest. His own head tilted back with how sweet it was, how wonderfully smooth and tight, and he let out a contented sigh. When Blaine's legs curled in on him, clutching him closer and clinging like his bony limbs were made to, everything clicked into place and became perfect.

Andrew wanted to do it all day. As he fought to hold back his orgasm, he once more felt stupid for not giving in earlier. He forgot where he was, and anything that wasn't in the room didn't seem to exist. As Blaine's breathing grew heavier, his moans louder, rising right along with his, he forgot why they should keep the noise down. He knew there were other people in the house, he even knew it was still the end of the world, but for the life of him he couldn't seem to care.

"You can... go faster now," Blaine gasped out.

Andrew sped up instantly. He snapped his hips forward in quick, sudden jerks, trying to shove in as deep and hard as he could, as fast as he could. Beneath him, Blaine was stroking his cock furiously, his mouth a perfectly rounded O, and he looked just as close to finishing as Andrew was.

Just a bit longer and — *Oh God, oh God, oh God* — Andrew could feel it rising — *here it comes* — and after a dozen or so more quick thrusts, he was over the edge, spurting out his release and again feeling like a complete idiot for not having put his cock in Blaine earlier.

With one last "Hnnngh," Blaine squeezed his eyes shut and burst over his stomach. He was still weakly spilling as Andrew pulled out.

As Andrew sat back on his heels and pulled off the condom, he realised he did feel better. He felt lighter, less stressed out. He had a feeling that Blaine would be a bit annoying about it later, but at the moment, it didn't bother him.

"Oh my *God*," Blaine moaned. He stretched his arms and legs out, looking like some sort of contented, fuzzy octopus. When he relaxed and looked back at Andrew, he was grinning suggestively. "Feel better? I do."

Andrew looked away. "You've got come on your stomach."

Blaine's smile disappeared. "Come on, don't be like that."

"Yes, I feel a bit better, but this doesn't change anything." It couldn't change anything. Being with Blaine felt too good, and that made him feel too guilty. He tied the condom and dropped it next to Blaine's knee. "Here, deal with that since you're the one who wanted to do this in the first place."

Blaine sighed as Andrew moved to get off the bed, and suddenly Blaine's legs were wrapped around his waist again, trapping Andrew and pulling him in. "Andrew."

I know you hate it, but come here –

Oh God no no no

"What?" Andrew asked, his mouth gone dry.

Blaine's brow furrowed as he looked up at Andrew in confusion. "There's no need to look so scared, I'm not gonna hurt you."

"I'm not scared. Let go of me."

"No."

"I'm stronger than you."

"What are you so worried will happen if you just lay down with me for a bit?" Blaine asked.

"I'm not worried about anything, I just don't want to." Andrew made to move away again, but Blaine's legs were stronger than they looked. They clung on mercilessly, not letting Andrew escape.

"Why don't you want to?"

"Because it's too similar! Let go of me!" Andrew wrenched at Blaine's ankles behind his back, but all of a sudden the legs fell away.

"Too similar to Luke."

Andrew's stomach twisted. That was the second time Blaine had said the name, and it was wrong coming from his mouth. It was more than just anger that flared in Andrew hearing it again; it was anguish and guilt and that horribly heavy sadness. But anger was the most acceptable, and it was anger that Andrew lashed out with.

"I told you not to—"

"That's all you had to say, you know," Blaine interjected. "I get it."

"No, you don't! You don't get anything!"

"So then tell me."

It wasn't a conversation Andrew wanted to have naked. It wasn't a conversation he wanted to have with Blaine at all, but particularly not now, after he'd started feeling so much better.

Knowing Blaine, that had been his plan all along. Seduce him, get him to drop his guard, then try to make him spill all his woes.

It wasn't going to happen. Andrew finally managed to get both feet on the floor, and picked up his clothes to dress. He heard Blaine sigh, but thankfully that was all. He seemed to have deemed Andrew a lost cause for now, which Andrew thought was just fine.

He retrieved his gun from the floor and opened the door. As he closed it behind him, he started to feel better again, like by leaving the room he was leaving behind the thoughts Blaine had tried to bring to the surface. Part of him knew he was only putting it off, but mostly he was relieved to have been able to finally engage in the act and not feel as plagued by guilt as he'd worried he'd be. He could return to the roof to take up his watch feeling a bit mentally refreshed.

He just hoped Blaine wouldn't follow him up there.

Chapter 24

Bed Situation

17:53

Blaine was half miserable, and it seemed to be obvious since everyone kept shooting him glances. He knew he was moping, cleaning his rifle in the darkest corner of the living room with far too much attention, but he didn't care. He wanted to talk to Andrew, who'd fled to the roof as usual, but knew Andrew would probably be even more closed off now. No, Blaine wouldn't get a word out of him.

He was somewhat glad when Darren finally moved to come sit next to him. Darren most of all had been glancing over at him, and had most of all failed at being covert about it. Blaine figured they all knew *something* had happened between him and Andrew, because otherwise he would've been up on the roof as well. He'd been expecting questions, and was relieved Darren at last decided to offer himself up to ask first.

"Hey," Darren said, sitting across from Blaine with a smile. The mole below his left eye quirked up as his stretched mouth lifted his cheeks. In the dim candlelight of the living room, his brown hair seemed black. "I've been meaning to speak to you."

Blaine blew down the barrel of his gun. "Yeah?"

"It's about the whole bed situation."

"Uh huh?"

"Well, Mary slept in your bed. You know that. And now sleeping arrangements have shifted a bit."

"I don't mind if someone else takes my bed," Blaine offered. "I'm sure Jessica would prefer it to the recliner."

Darren dropped his eyes and rubbed the back of his neck. "Yeah... We talked about it earlier. The rest of us."

"Oh?" They talked about Blaine's room without Blaine present?

"Jessica said the recliner's sometimes better for her back. I dunno, there was some medical explanation Elliot gave but she decided against the bed."

"Okay."

"And anyway we figured that you sort of, er..." Darren coughed. "Reclaimed it."

Blaine froze. "Sorry?"

"Earlier today," Darren said, still looking down. "First Mary died in it, then you and Andrew... you know. So it's pretty much yours again. Elizabeth said she's fine with the kitchen, so you and—"

"Wait, are you saying..." Blaine darted a look at Sarah and Tim and the others, but nobody was looking his way. He lowered his voice to a whisper. "Are you saying everyone *heard* us?"

Even in the low light, Blaine could see Darren blush. "Yeah. Yeah, that's what I'm saying."

"Even my mum?"

Darren nodded.

Shit. Blaine hadn't thought they'd been too loud, but he'd forgotten how far sounds carried in the house. He'd also hoped people would just be too preoccupied to be paying much attention to muffled noises coming from upstairs.

"Shit."

"Sorry, mate. But, um. Congratulations, too, yeah?"

One long moment passed, but then they both ended up laughing.

20:34

Andrew walked into the kitchen after dinner that night feeling a bit lost. His and Blaine's bed was there, and he hadn't been looking forward to the awkward conversation sure to occur, but Blaine was strangely absent.

Elizabeth was there in his place, curled up on her right side, arms stretched out in front of her. She'd already blown out the candles, and was barely visible in the shadowy interior of the room, but Andrew would know that blond hair anywhere. It too often reminded him of Madison.

Andrew furrowed his brow in confusion as he approached the laid out blankets on the other side of the table. "Elizabeth?"

Elizabeth's eyes snapped open and quickly searched the dark for him. "Andrew? Is that you?"

"Yeah. Did I miss something?"

She sat up, propping herself on her right elbow and looked blearily up at him. "Did Blaine not tell you?"

Andrew stomach sank. "Not tell me what?"

"We gave Blaine his bed back."

She looked at him like it was obvious, and Andrew supposed after what had happened today, it should have been.

We gave Blaine... and you... his bed back.

But a bed was different. Sharing an insignificant spot on the kitchen floor was nothing like sharing a bed, especially a bed they'd fucked in. Andrew hadn't done it earlier today and he wasn't about to do it now.

So he played dumb. "So now it's you and me sharing the kitchen?" he asked.

Now Elizabeth looked confused. "I thought... You don't want to go sleep with Blaine?"

"Is that what you want?"

Truthfully, Andrew was surprised Darren wasn't in here next to her, but maybe they weren't at that stage yet. Elizabeth looked down at the blanket, seeming to consider the situation. Even if Darren wasn't here, to be sharing a bed with another man (gay or not), had to look a bit odd.

"I'm not against you sleeping here," she finally said. "I guess I just assumed—"

"Great."

Andrew pulled off his shoes and moved to slip under the blanket. Elizabeth shuffled to the left to make room, looking more than a little shocked by the abruptness of it. Andrew tried to pretend he didn't care either way who slept on the other side of him, as though this wasn't as weird and awkward for him as it surely was for her.

After maybe five minutes that seemed to never end, during which Andrew had been able to hear every tense breath they both took, it began to be unbearable. Sleeping here, like this, next to Elizabeth, wasn't right. Andrew tried to fill the darkness behind his eyelids with pleasant dreams, images of his happy place, on a boat at sea, drifting easily on the water in the sun, but too often his mind flooded with Blaine's face, wondering how he was managing upstairs in his reclaimed bed.

Did Blaine feel as empty without him as Andrew did? It'd been what seemed liked ages since Blaine had wrapped his arms around Andrew at night and held him close, all because Andrew had told him on the way to the hospital that he'd needed time, but Blaine's presence had been worth something at least. Andrew had still known he was there, at his back, even if they hadn't been touching.

After another maybe ten minutes, Andrew gave up with a sigh.

"Yeah, you're right," he said into the dark, knowing Elizabeth was still awake. "This isn't what I want."

20:46

Blaine hadn't told Andrew about the arrangement change, mostly because he hadn't thought Andrew wanted to sleep in his company anymore. He'd left Elizabeth's old blanket and pillow just outside the door, and there were other floors in the house to sleep on if Andrew so chose. He could sleep in the corridor if that's what he wanted. Blaine just had a feeling that wherever Andrew ended up sleeping, it wouldn't be with him.

He hadn't counted on feeling so bereft. He'd laid down to sleep happily at first, in heaven at being in his own bed again at last. It didn't smell the way it used to—in fact it smelled much like old lady and a bit of sickly sweat—but it was damn comfortable. He didn't know how he'd been managing to sleep on the hard floor for so long, especially someone as bony as him.

But then as the minutes ticked by, a hollow feeling had set in. *This isn't right,* he'd thought. *This doesn't feel right at all.*

He needed Andrew. Even if they couldn't touch, because of Andrew's foolish rules, it was enough to know that he was close by. Sleeping without Andrew was like trying to sleep and knowing a window was left open downstairs or the water running in the sink. It was an itch in the back of his mind that wouldn't let him fall asleep.

When the door suddenly clicked with the motion of the knob turning, Blaine hoped. He hoped and hoped that it was Andrew coming to him, even though he knew it was a stupid thing to hope for. When the door creaked open, and Andrew's face peered through the crack, Blaine's heart soared.

Yet he couldn't speak. He remained silent and stunned as Andrew hesitantly approached the bed. In the soft light of the moon, only barely let in through the boarded window, Andrew looked diminished. He was still large in the muscular sense, and still guarded in his face, but the way he walked forward, with tiny, uncertain steps, and his hands in loose fists, made him almost seem like a child coming into his parents' room after a bad dream. He was the same Andrew Blaine knew, and yet completely changed.

By the time Andrew had reached the bed, Blaine had come to his senses enough to move over. He raised the duvet and let Andrew in. He didn't say a word, knowing Andrew preferred he didn't speak.

He was surprised yet again when Andrew turned on his side, grabbed hold of Blaine's arm, and pulled it around him. It was the same position they'd used to sleep in before Andrew had forced distance between them, and its sudden return was more than Blaine had dared to hope for when Andrew had walked into the room. But here Andrew was, sliding back into the curve of Blaine's form and lacing their fingers together over his chest again.

Blaine was too excited to sleep. His heart was beating too fast for him to even consider it. He knew Andrew probably felt the frantic thudding against his back, but thankfully Andrew didn't seem to mind. There were times when Blaine felt like such a kid around him, even though he was pretty sure Andrew wasn't more than five or six years older than him, and now was definitely one of those times. He was so clearly more excited than Andrew to be doing this again.

"Luke used to hold me like this."

The confession made Blaine's racing heart stutter. He felt a nervous flutter in his stomach at the same time he felt a wretched guilt in his chest.

The picture was all coming together, becoming clearer, and it only made Blaine want to help even more.

"Do you want me to stop?" Blaine asked, not wanting to stop at all. "Or we could switch?"

Andrew hunched his shoulders and pressed more firmly back. Beneath the duvet, his leg found Blaine's and hooked around his calf, as though staking a claim.

"No."

DAY 93
06:39

Andrew awoke slowly. He woke to the feeling of warmth and comfort, and realised abruptly that he was in a bed. For the first time in a while, he awoke feeling safe.

The feeling didn't last for long, but when he finally opened his eyes, there was still the element of warmth and comfort. Blaine was beside him, pouting the slightest bit in his sleep, and suddenly everything seemed to click into place.

He knew now why he'd been so resistant to take things further. He'd told himself before that it was because he needed more time to get over Luke, but that was only part of it. He wasn't sure what his feelings were for Blaine—he hardly knew the boy, and couldn't even ascertain whether or not he particularly liked him—but he knew he was attracted to him, and at the very least that he cared about him. That fact, the caring about him, was a crucial part in why he hadn't let things escalate sooner.

There was still the painful memory of Luke. There was still the guilt of all the things he'd done in Portsmouth. He didn't want to bring all that into a relationship with Blaine. It would taint everything and make it imperfect. He couldn't have that happen, not when he cared so much.

But after last night... It'd been nice to be in Blaine's arms again. A bit therapeutic, Andrew supposed. If Blaine already knew the things of which Andrew was so ashamed, perhaps it wouldn't spoil the relationship after all. Andrew had to remind himself again that he didn't know much about Blaine besides what was immediately visible on the surface. It was possible that Blaine wouldn't react negatively at all, or mind so much about having to deal with Andrew's past. He hadn't so far.

Either way, Andrew was tired. It was exhausting having to resist and resist. Maybe it had even been a bit of pride that kept him from going to Blaine for comfort, but now even that seemed ridiculous. Andrew *wanted* the comfort. It was stupid to not let himself have it, especially in a world where it was so precious and rare.

You're a fool, Peterson.

Andrew sighed. *Yeah. I know.*

06:46

Blaine woke to the sight of Andrew staring at him. Andrew's right arm was extended upward, draped across the pillow, while his head lolled in the opposite direction, his eyelids blinking lazily as he gazed at Blaine's face.

He seemed simultaneously bored and mesmerised. It was the sort of expression Blaine imagined a younger version of Andrew might've made in school, sitting in the back of a classroom enduring a lesson. His eyes seemed to be staring intently at a subject, but Blaine couldn't tell if he was looking at him or at a fixed point in space.

He knew exactly what Andrew was staring at when their eyes met and Blaine's stomach flipped.

Andrew's arm raised from its relaxed position and fell in slow motion to reach across his body. For a moment Blaine thought he must have been dreaming. Andrew was never gentle and caring in his waking hours. In fact he'd only seen Andrew smile a handful of times.

But now Andrew *was* being gentle. He was cradling Blaine's face in his right hand, stroking Blaine's cheek with his thumb. Blaine didn't

215

dare say a word for fear of ruining everything. The slightest noise or movement might cause Andrew to realise what he was doing.

With an abrupt shift of weight, Andrew was suddenly pressed against him, nearly lying right on top of him. A small noise escaped Blaine's throat that he instantly wanted to pull back inside, but it was out now, unable to return. He couldn't worry too much about it however, not when the solid mass of Andrew's entire body was warm and rubbing him in all the right places, certainly not when the next instant Andrew was pressing their lips together.

Yes yes yes! Blaine finished trying to hold back. He slid his free arm around Andrew and tugged at his shirt, trying to pull him further on top at the same time he opened his mouth just wide enough to let a tongue slip in.

In a moment Andrew was sitting astride him, grinding their groins together as they kissed, and Blaine didn't care what Andrew would think of him, he simply dug his heels into the bed and raised his hips, then slid his hands up Andrew's thighs, over the swell of his arse, up his back and into his hair.

Besides the very prominent evidence rubbing against him, Blaine knew Andrew had to be liking it when he moaned and twisted his fingers in Blaine's shirt. In the midst of tongue sliding and hip rolling, Andrew was gasping for breath, and even — if Blaine detached himself from the moment long enough to pay close attention — shaking a bit.

Blaine didn't know what had changed Andrew's mind. He didn't know if this was going to be another one of Andrew's occasional indulgences or if this was Andrew finally giving in, and even though it had the feeling of being the latter, Blaine didn't take his chances. He cherished every moment as though it would never happen again, because for all he knew, it wouldn't.

When Andrew started placing kisses along Blaine's jaw and down his neck while pressing a firm hand to Blaine's chest, Blaine figured perhaps this time it was for good, after all. He arched upward and tilted his head back, and at last he heard Andrew's breathless voice.

"Want this." A hand slipped under Blaine's shirt and up his chest. "All of this. But there's gonna be a few rules."

Blaine wasn't sure he trusted his voice to be particularly steady at the moment, but spoke anyway. "Alright."

Andrew seemed even larger when he was straddling Blaine. In all Blaine's dreams, it had always been Blaine on top for some reason, making it odd but not unpleasant for the positions to be the opposite now. When Andrew raised himself to sit upright, his face flushed and looking as though he were coming up for air, Blaine let his hands fall to Andrew's thighs, and felt the flood of happiness as he looked up at the giant form above him.

"The first rule is simple," Andrew said, staring in Blaine's eyes. "If there's something you want to know about me, you can ask, but if I don't want to tell you, you're not allowed to push. I'll tell you when I feel comfortable telling you and there's no negotiating."

It didn't sound like a terrible rule, but Blaine knew already there'd be numerous occasions on which it would pop up. Reluctantly, he grunted and nodded in acceptance.

"The second rule is don't do anything stupid for me. If we're in a life or death situation, or I dunno, something risky needs doing in order to save me, don't bother. I'm not worth the effort."

"These rules are getting more and more ridiculous," Blaine muttered. "But alright."

"There's only one more," Andrew said. "The last rule is..." He dropped his eyes and furrowed his brow, as though it pained him to get the words out. His hands clutched Blaine's shirt tighter, tight enough that Blaine thought Andrew's hands were shaking. "The last rule is, until I say otherwise or tell you to, you can't ever *ever* leave. Do you understand?"

Blaine swallowed. His gaze flicked to the bracelet around Andrew's wrist and back up again, and he suddenly had to fight back tears. Andrew raised his eyes to Blaine's, and the intensity was almost too much.

"I asked if you understood!" Andrew exclaimed, leaning over Blaine. "You don't ever fucking leave me. You got that?"

Blaine nodded vigorously. "Yeah. Never. I got it."

Andrew exhaled and dropped forward, burrowing his face in Blaine's neck again. "Good."

Chapter 25

We Grope Together and Avoid Speech

DAY 99
13:44

For about a week, everything had been incongruously amazing. The days still consisted of guard duty on the roof, but they were no longer boring stretches of silence. Blaine still did most of the talking, but Andrew answered loads of things Blaine didn't expect answers to.

"How old was your sister?"

"Twenty."

"Was your family wealthy? Since she could afford the flats in Oxford?"

"My mother did come from old money, and had some saved just for me and my sister, never touched it the whole marriage. My father had inherited my uncle's houses, which he sold, and that helped us a lot. It's not as though Maddie and I grew up in a posh neighbourhood. They were just, economical, resourceful, and smart with their money. We got the best of everything without being too spoilt, and had plenty of money to look forward to when we wanted to make a future for ourselves."

"Did you get along with your parents? Did they know you were gay?"

"We got on alright, more so me and my mum. I knew I was different and into blokes at a pretty young age, so even though my mum died when I was only eleven, I'd been confident enough about it to

218

tell her. My dad died before he could find out, back when I was a midshipman and still hadn't gotten around to telling him. He was too busy being proud that I was in the Navy in the first place and I didn't want to ruin it for him. He could be really traditional sometimes."

The distance between one side of the roof and the other seemed to have shortened. Sometimes Blaine looked over his shoulder and was surprised at how many yards were between them. It had started to feel like they were sitting right beside each other.

It was only when the occasional walker wandered down the street that Blaine remembered where he was and what had happened. There was the city, of course, and how it was so quiet and seemingly empty, and how the sun rose and set on crumbling buildings, how the rain fell on rotting corpses in the street. But it was all able to fade into the background of Blaine's mind with Andrew.

Then it was time for another supply run.

Tim's hulking body lumbered onto the roof. When he finally reached the top, he said, "We're low on dry food. And Sarah says they need more women things."

Blaine twisted his neck to look up at him. His black hair had grown longer, looked even more unkempt than usual, and Blaine wished he would cut it.

"You want us to go?" Blaine asked.

"We're all going," Tim said. "Need the hands. Sarah'll take over up here."

"Any idea where we're going this time?" Andrew asked.

"Helen gave me directions to a place she thinks will have what we need. It's not too far."

Andrew got to his feet, so Blaine did as well. "Guess we better get going, then," Andrew said.

14:07

They stuck to deserted side streets and alleys as much as they could, staying clear of the main road. When they saw signs for help and bullet holes that looked new, Blaine scanned the area with his rifle, making sure nobody was around before they sprinted past. He always had a nagging fear that one of the boarded up doors would suddenly open or someone would jump out from behind a car and shove a blade through his chest. Or worse, through Andrew's chest. But they knew how to fight together better now, staying in line formation with Tim at the front and Blaine at the back. They four were a team.

It wasn't too cold out, not like it would be when winter really set in, but Blaine was still shivering. He was sure his ears were red, and his nose felt like it was about to fall off. He could hardly hold his gun properly in the frigid air. By the time Tim said they'd reached the place, an out of the way shop with a lock on the gate, Blaine was looking forward to returning home and not having to go back out for while.

"Hey!"

Blaine froze where he was. He couldn't see who'd spoken from his position behind Andrew, but he knew for a fact that that voice didn't belong to anyone from his group.

Blaine took a step to the right to look over Andrew's shoulder. He could tell from the way Andrew had suddenly tensed that he was now on high alert, ready for anything. He could see the reason why just up ahead.

There were three men, each looking as dirty as all of them, and none too friendly. Two of them had small handguns while the third had a crowbar, and all three were large, barrel-chested men, not unlike Tim. The first thing Blaine noticed was the hardness of their faces, and how their eyes seemed to shine maliciously, standing out from their grey, dust-speckled cheeks. Though they all had different appearances — one shorter, one with multiple chins, one with more grey in his beard — they seemed to be all the same person, three replicated shadows looming closer.

The second thing Blaine noticed was the clothes. One of them, the one with the grey beard, wore a black hat with ear flaps and Blaine immediately thought of Andrew. His own ears were cold in the chilling air, but Andrew's ears looked positively glowing with how red they were, sticking out from his head like flushed saucers. Andrew could certainly use the hat. Another had a blue coat that looked like it'd be huge on Blaine, but comfortable nonetheless. The sort of coat that would swallow Blaine whole and trap in the warmth. It may not have been the most ideal for movement or speed, but it was better than nothing.

Darren took a few steps back to fall into place next to Blaine. It was he who had the shears in his rucksack that would allow them to break the lock on the gate to the shop, which the three men would be needing if they intended to get in themselves. He shot Blaine a look that said he was just as scared as Blaine was, but remained silent as Tim brought himself to his full height and addressed the man who'd called out to them.

"Yeah?"

"We were here first."

It was the one with the crowbar who spoke. He approached as he talked, and Blaine could see the strategy as clearly as if Merrick was there yelling it in his ear, pointing it out to him with neon lights.

He's closing in, he's sizing up, predict his movements.

Blaine saw it play out in his mind in less than a second. The man with the crowbar would try to strike first, save ammo if possible. If that didn't work, one of the others would raise their gun, threatening to shoot. It was only if any of them continued to resist that they'd open fire.

They had to be at least decent shots, but there were fewer of them. Sarah had Blaine's Glock while she kept watch at the house, and Tim had come out with Blaine's shotgun. Blaine had his rifle, as well as a pistol in his belt, Andrew had his SA80, and Darren was using the axe. If the three men thought they stood a chance even then, there had to be another factor somewhere.

"You saying you want first pick or something?" Tim said.

The man with the crowbar was close now, and Blaine found himself thinking, *Someone shoot him before he attacks, someone shoot him so I can take his coat.*

"That's exactly what I'm saying."

Blaine didn't see Andrew move—he only heard the burst of fire then saw one of the men with the pistols suddenly falling to the ground. Like Blaine, the man with the crowbar darted his eyes to look at his fallen comrade, and by then Andrew had his gun aimed at the grey-bearded man in the hat, the one with the other pistol.

It didn't seem to be really happening, and Blaine couldn't believe it *was* happening. His heart was racing and his fingers twitched restlessly where they were numbed from the cold, holding onto his rifle, and he felt as though he should offer to shoot as well, but wasn't quite sure he'd be able to.

He just shot him. He hadn't even said a word and he just shot him.

It hadn't been a leg shot or chest shot either. It'd been right in his face, one of the bullets even catching his throat.

Grey Beard didn't seem to know what was happening. He looked like he wanted to raise his pistol to defend himself but didn't know if he'd live long enough to get his arm halfway up. Meanwhile, Crowbar Man had wheeled on Tim in anger, looking ready to strike him across the face.

Blaine could tell Tim was as stunned by the sudden turn of events as the rest of them, but he did well not to let it affect him too much. "We're going in first," he said.

Crowbar Man looked behind him at Grey Beard, and it was then that Blaine realised who was the one in charge. With a subtle shake of his head, Grey Beard made the decision, and Crowbar Man turned around to respond to Tim.

"Yeah, alright."

Blaine heard a piece of debris fall from above, though he seemed to be the only one who did. While Darren reached into his bag for shears and headed for the gate, Blaine slowly combed his gaze across the rooftops and nearby buildings. He was reluctant to take his eyes off the men ahead of him, but Tim and Andrew seemed to have a pretty good handle on the situation, and if any infected were headed their way, it was Blaine's job to detect it.

Blaine raised his rifle and stepped a few yards away. It sounded like it'd come from across the street, maybe down a little ways. He looked through the scope, his ears perked for the slightest sound over the wind, and tried to separate the sounds of Darren's shears from everything else.

There was the loud snap of metal as Darren broke through the rusted lock, and Blaine looked a few more seconds, moving his sight over each building. A raspy voice made him flinch.

"You see something, boy?"

Blaine knew without looking that it was Grey Beard who'd spoken. He took his eye away from the scope and frowned. Andrew still had his gun trained on him, so Blaine wasn't sure how replying would go over, but he did anyway.

"Thought I heard something," he said. "Maybe a crawler on a roof. It sounded like those skittering noises they make. You know?"

Grey Beard nodded and flicked his eyes up. Blaine thought he heard the shifting of building matter once more and swung his rifle toward the sound.

"Blaine," Darren called, "c'mon, let's go in so we can get out."

Blaine reluctantly lowered his gun. He edged toward the open door, backing inside along with Darren and Tim. Andrew was the last to enter, closing the door behind them to shut the two men outside.

"Yes, more shaving cream!" Darren exclaimed excitedly. "And more razors! What store are we even in?"

Tim shrugged. "Not a clue. I'm gonna check the women's aisle in the back. Blaine, look for loo roll, and paper or wood or anything flammable. Darren, get as much of that as they have and be on the lookout for anything else you think'll be useful."

Blaine shouldered his rifle and started searching the aisles for loo roll, ears on alert for the dragging footsteps of walkers and one eye on Andrew, who was gathering bottles of water. He found what he needed not too far from where Tim was stuffing feminine products in a bag, and gave a short whistle to get the man's attention. He pointed his finger down and Tim made a sign telling him to wait a minute.

Blaine started taking the rolls from the shelves and putting them on top when he heard the crash of glass breaking. He winced at the volume, but quick as a flash he had his rifle up, searching for the source. He wouldn't have been surprised if those two men had decided to take their chances after all, still upset by Andrew's attack beforehand.

It wasn't a man who had burst through the shop's door. It all happened so fast. Darren and Andrew were in the front, but Darren was closest to the entrance, and that's who the crawler jumped first. Blaine looked through his scope, but the image was too close, magnified too much. All he saw was the blur of Darren's coat and the crawler's crooked limbs, its elbows poking out of its blue hoodie at odd angles.

Blaine didn't know how it had got in. They should've heard it go for the two waiting outside first, should've heard some sort of an encounter. The fact that there'd been none was what made Blaine suspect they had seen the crawler and decided to hide, letting it do the work of taking out Blaine and his friends for them.

"Shoot it, shoot it, shoot it!" Darren cried.

"Quit moving so much, just hold it off or I might shoot you, too!" Andrew yelled. The SA80 was accurate, but a burst still had the potential to catch Darren somewhere. The spray of bullets at such a close range would surely leave Darren with a fatal wound.

Blaine took his eye away from the scope and darted a glance at Tim, who'd gone pale. It wouldn't do any good if they all froze up. Blaine whistled again, and Tim's head whipped around to look his way.

"Barricade the door, make sure no more get in," Blaine ordered. Tim didn't even blink. "Now, damn it!" Tim sprang into action.

Blaine returned his gaze back to Andrew, and the flailing Darren on the shop floor. Andrew's eyes were wide, but his face was bunched up in a frown of concentration, and his chest was heaving with each breath. He didn't look like he could move at all, or if he was sure he wanted to.

Waste of a bullet, Blaine's mind supplied. *That's what Merrick would say, too.*

Darren screamed, a sound so full of agony and hopelessness that Blaine was sure he'd have nightmares. But it was the sound that gave Blaine the nudge he needed, and he swung his rifle over his shoulder, drew his pistol, and aimed for the blur he hoped was the crawler's head.

It only took one shot for it to stop moving, but Blaine shot once more, just to be sure. The entire shop was silent for a few tense seconds, and Blaine had a brief moment of panic. He couldn't believe the past minute had actually happened—it felt a little surreal, like a bad dream—but everyone's heavy breathing proved it was real.

Finally, Darren pushed the sprawled body off with a groan, and Blaine came back to his senses. He ran over as Andrew lowered his gun, and Tim turned around from barricading the door to face the scene.

"It's okay, it's okay," Darren said breathlessly, getting to his feet. "I think I'm okay." But his eyes were shifty, looking between the three of them nervously.

Blaine knew Darren well enough to know better. His coat was shredded, especially in the sleeves where Darren had his arms raised to hold the crawler at bay.

"Take it off," Blaine said quietly.

Darren's brow furrowed in pain. Blaine saw him struggle to swallow. "It's just—"

"Take off the fucking coat, Darren!" Blaine raised his pistol, aiming right at Darren's forehead.

Darren's lip trembled, but he didn't move. Blaine felt Tim and Andrew's gaze on him, and he half didn't know what he was doing himself, but he kept seeing Emily's lightless eyes in his mind, how he'd watched her turn in the course of a few hours without his and Paul even knowing it, putting them both in danger. He wasn't going to have that happen to him again, not when he had someone like Andrew to think about now.

"I'm sorry, Blaine."

Blaine didn't know what Darren meant, and was still trying to figure it out when Darren reached out and twisted his wrist, wrenching the pistol from his grasp. Darren shuffled back with his prize quickly, until his back hit a shelf.

Blaine's blood ran cold, and he held his breath, waiting for what Darren would do, who he would shoot first. He didn't think Darren had it in him to shoot any of them, though, not really. It was probably just to keep them off while he legged it out the—

Darren put the gun to his head with wide, frightened eyes and pulled the trigger. Blaine couldn't squeeze his eyes shut fast enough and the moment replayed over and over behind his eyelids, the gunshot seeming to echo inside his skull.

"No," Blaine heard Tim exhale. "Kid..."

Blaine felt like he was going to be sick. He felt it boiling up inside his stomach, preparing to force its way out. He gagged, put his hand over his mouth and curled his arm around his stomach, but couldn't fight it no matter how hard he tried. He ran as far away from the scene as he could before he heaved onto the floor.

He stayed bent over, taking deep breaths with a hand on the nearby shelf to steady himself. He opened his eyes when he heard footsteps walking up behind him, and was relieved to find Andrew there.

"Here," Andrew said, holding out a bottle of mouthwash. "Use this." Blaine took it gratefully and swirled a mouthful around before spitting it out beside his sick. He took another swig and gurgled this time. His mouth burned.

"Thanks."

"Are you—"

"No. I'm not. But it doesn't matter. We have to get going, don't we?"

Andrew sighed and rubbed Blaine's back. "Yeah. And we should strip Darren of his things, before someone else does."

Blaine's stomach lurched again, but not enough that he felt he was going to be ill. He swallowed past the lump in his throat and nodded, letting Andrew lead him to the body.

Walking back down the aisle, the only thing Blaine could see of Darren were his boots. Blaine glanced down at his own trainers, seeing once again how torn up they were and how they barely kept his feet warm in the harsh cold.

Darren wouldn't be needing his boots anymore.

Tim was already piling up all the goods they'd be carrying by the door, working mechanically and emotionlessly. Andrew squatted down beside Darren and retrieved the gun, sliding it across the floor to where Blaine was kneeling at Darren's feet. Blaine holstered it and set about the task of removing Darren's boots.

Fear and worry crept in slowly. Were the two men outside still waiting for them? What would happen now that they were one person short? How would Blaine tell the others, tell Elizabeth what had happened? How would he explain that it had been him who'd pushed Darren to do what he did?

Because it had been him, hadn't it? He'd only been thinking about what would happen if they took Darren home with them, how he would become infected and risk hurting everyone, hurting Andrew and his mother. Darren had done nothing but look up to him, and Blaine had never once said a kind word of praise, only tolerated being

226

the boy's idol. A few minutes ago their greatest worry had been not being shot by other survivors, but it was an infected who'd caused the most damage in the end. Now Darren was dead, his last words an apology because he felt he'd failed Blaine.

Blaine fought back tears, and as he threw his old shoes to the side and slipped into Darren's boots — *his* boots, now — Blaine realised they probably ought to put Darren in the Avon like they had Mary. It was what the others at home would expect them to do.

But glancing at Andrew and Tim, Blaine saw they were just as reluctant to do that as he was. He didn't *want* to take the time. He wanted to go home, out of the cold, and try to put this behind him. As shameful as it was, he wanted to leave Darren here, get as far away from the danger waiting outside as possible and try to forget him.

Andrew shouldered Darren's bag, having relieved him of his weapons. The shredded coat was ruined, so he left it, and the gloves were fingerless, but better than nothing. Blaine finished buckling his boots, and when he stood up, Tim had done gathering all their supplies.

They stood around Darren's body in strained silence a few seconds, no sound but the wind against the side of the building. Then Andrew cleared his throat, preparing to speak.

"You two will have to carry the supplies. I'll shoot."

Blaine frowned. Darren's death had ruined the formation. It was more dangerous with just one person defending.

The radio at Blaine's hip crackled with static, and his hand flew to it. He detached it and cupped his hand over the speaker to muffle the sound.

"Blaine? Blaine?" Elliot's voice came through.

Blaine pushed down the button to transmit and hoped his voice came out steady. "I'm here, Elliot."

"You guys are gonna wanna get back here right away. Sarah and Helen — Well, I'll explain when you get here."

Blaine looked at Andrew and Tim. "We'll be right there."

227

Chapter 26

Last Broadcast

15:15

"You remember that radio I had in the pub?" Helen asked Blaine after they'd set the supplies down. "That I kept in case of emergencies?"

"Yeah."

"Tim brought it back on one of their first supply runs. It's always been a little spotty, and there was nothing but static when we tried it back then. But Sarah figured it's been a while so we gave it another shot."

"You heard something? A broadcast or something?" Blaine ventured hopefully.

Helen nodded and turned up the volume. Andrew and Tim leaned forward eagerly.

"*— for anyone in the Bristol area. It's time to stop targeting each other and start going after the real monsters. Humans have killed other humans for far too long, and it only makes us as feral as the infected. It's time we start working together, be a civilisation again. Anyone interested is welcome to come to Haven —*"

"Where's Haven?" Blaine asked.

"It's what they're calling the sanctuary," Jessica explained. "It's by a river and everything, so we don't have to go so far to wash clothes. And the houses —"

"Where is it?" Andrew interrupted. "How many people are going there?"

"We don't know how many others have heard the broadcast," Helen said. "It seems to be recent, and it's doubtful they'd still be

228

playing it if there were too many people. But it's not far. It's actually in a good neighbourhood with nice houses."

"Could Jessica get there?" Blaine asked.

"We have your Jeep," Jessica said. "Not all of us could fit in it, obviously, but we'd be able to bring more of our belongings than if everyone took just what they could carry."

Blaine nodded. However, he was still worried about Andrew, who was frowning thoughtfully to himself.

Elizabeth suddenly pushed herself off the wall in the corner of the room, emerging out of the shadows. "Where's Darren?" she asked.

Tim went pale. Blaine's heart clenched.

When no one answered immediately, she repeated it more frantically. "Where is he? He came back with you, didn't he?"

Nobody said anything. Blaine kept his eyes down, and had a feeling the others were doing the same.

Before Blaine could process what was happening, Elizabeth had rushed over and started hitting Andrew, swinging her fists down in an arc. Andrew held his arms up to block the blows, but she kept at it anyway, not caring where her hands landed. Andrew didn't say anything, just silently held out as long as she did it.

"You should have been watching him, you should have—you should have—"

Blaine tried to reach out and grab her arms but she swung and pushed him away. He would have fallen to the floor if his mother hadn't caught him, and he was surprised Elizabeth was that strong.

"You keep out of this!" Elizabeth shouted at Blaine. "This is your fault just as much as his. If he hadn't been so focused making sure *you* stayed alive, Darren would be here."

The words hit Blaine like a whip, and Andrew spoke for the first time.

"That's not true!" he yelled. "Sometimes these things just happen, no matter how hard we try to prevent it. I know that better than anyone here, much better than you."

He got to his feet and held Elizabeth's thin arms in his hands, looking her in the eyes and willing her to understand.

"It was nobody's fault he was bitten. He's the one who shot himself. It couldn't be helped."

Elizabeth's eyes were wild with anger. "You just *left* him there, didn't you? Didn't even give him the burial Mary had."

Blaine wanted to scream that she wouldn't understand. She hadn't been there, couldn't possibly know what it had been like. Instead, there was silence again, and Elizabeth was still staring furiously into Andrew's pained eyes.

"Look, just calm the fuck down, Beth," Tim burst out. "It wasn't nobody's fault. If you wanna blame someone, blame the guys we ran into on the way into the place. It was them that probably attracted the damn crawler anyway."

Helen sighed and walked up to Andrew, who still had his hands clenched around Elizabeth's arms.

"Andrew, dear, let her go and take the supplies to the kitchen," she said gently. She looked at Tim. "You help, Timothy."

Andrew let Elizabeth go and she stepped back, rubbing where he'd held her. He and Tim disappeared with the supplies into the corridor.

"We could get a van or something," Elliot suggested. "There's one right down the street..."

Blaine didn't stay for the rest of the conversation. He'd had enough, and didn't think he could stay in the house a second longer. He took his rifle and went up to the roof.

15:28

She was wearing a black dress, the slimming kind to wear on a date, the kind that suggested she'd been single for a while and was just getting back into the swing of things. She wanted to look impressive, interested but not too desperate. One of the straps was hanging off her shoulder, exposing part of her equally black bra.

The skin on the bottom half of her face was missing, like when someone tried to peel the price sticker off something and only managed a half job of it. Blaine could see every single one of her teeth, and part of the bone under the meat of her chin.

It was a shame, really. The top half of her face was beautiful, her blond hair matted and stringy with blood, but long and otherwise attractive.

Blaine shot her left calf.

The force of the bullet had the calf bone sticking out the back of her leg, but she kept walking, not feeling the pain, dragging herself along.

Blaine shot the other one.

She fell, looking around in confusion. Not that her eyebrows had the capability to draw together anymore, but she whipped her head from side to side, searching for the source of her fall. Eventually she just started dragging herself forward again, using her arms to crawl along the pavement.

Blaine followed her through his scope, keeping her in his crosshairs. Sometimes other walkers would trip over her, sometimes she stopped and just stared ahead blankly.

When she was neared the point where Blaine wouldn't be able to see her, he shot her in the head.

He picked another one at random, this one an old man in a business suit. Blaine wondered what business he'd worked for, if he'd had children. He was old; his children probably weren't children anymore, but people with their own families and careers. As Blaine shot the back of the man's knee, he tried to imagine the man's life before the infection. What had he looked like without rotten skin barely clinging to his old bones?

But life could change so quickly. The old man down there probably knew that. He'd had a lifetime of experience, and had probably been thinking it in his final moments.

Blaine knew it. It was only a few months ago he'd woken up on a perfectly sunny day in July, carefree and oblivious until he'd walked into the living room and looked out the window.

And after Darren had been bitten, he'd known it as well.

Blaine tried to clear his mind and shoot.

The sun was disappearing behind the buildings by the time he heard footsteps. He hadn't gone too far, only to the end of the street, walking over the rooftops to get some distance between himself and everyone else. He'd known Andrew would come to bring him back sooner or later.

He heard Andrew lie on his stomach beside him. Andrew was quiet a few minutes, watching as Blaine reduced walker after walker to a crawl, saying nothing.

"Waste of bullets, you know," Andrew said eventually.

Blaine saw a hunter then. The long hair suggested it was a girl, and the body build suggested it was a child. The maroon skin made it hard to tell. As she sniffed the air, hunched over in a predatory stance, Blaine pulled the trigger, going straight for the headshot.

"It gets easier," Blaine said, exhaling steadily. "Doesn't it, Commander?"

Andrew didn't immediately reply, but Blaine hadn't expected him to. He put down his rifle and turned to look at Andrew, who was biting his lip hard, the way he always did when he was frustrated or deep in thought or upset. Blaine shot his hand forward and pulled the bottom lip out from under Andrew's teeth.

"Quit that," he said firmly.

Andrew gaped at him, blinking uncomprehendingly a few times. He frowned and shook his head. "The experience—when you first see the body, just lying there—that gets easier. You get accustomed to the smell, the sight, the blood seeping from gaping wounds. At first it's hard to see something that was once full of life and memories reduced to nothing but a pile of rotting meat you just walk around to avoid stepping on. Then you get used it, as much as anyone can get used to something like that. But the aftermath—the thoughts and memories and emotions and the fact that it's their death on your hands... That only gets harder. It grows inside you like a cancer, changes you."

Blaine folded his arms and rested his head over them, sighing. "Great."

"You know," Andrew began hesitantly. "Your mother still has a calendar."

Blaine hummed disinterestedly. "Does she?"

"She showed it to me."

"Let me guess. Today's special. Or something."

Andrew put a hand on Blaine's back, his spread palm on Blaine's shoulder blades. It was rare for Andrew to touch him so openly, so Blaine knew it had to be important. "Blaine, it's... It's the twenty-fifth of October. It's your birthday."

Blaine expelled a huff of air through his nose. "Of course it is. Of course it's my bloody birthday."

Not that it mattered. Twenty years old, that was all—another year, another 365 days lived. What was one day in the scheme of things?

The day was half over anyway. The sun had reached its pinnacle in the sky and was making its way across the other side of the horizon, getting ready for its descent over the city skyline.

"Is it really my fault Darren died?"

Andrew flipped Blaine over so quickly the air left his lungs. Just as quickly, Andrew's face hovered above his, icy blue eyes staring at him with desperate intensity.

"If it's anybody's fault, it's mine."

"Andrew—"

"The same thing happened in Portsmouth to one of the men under my command," he said harshly. "A crawler jumped on him and I did nothing. I let it maul him to shreds because I knew he'd already been bitten. I didn't shoot two bullets when I knew I could just shoot one."

"Jesus."

"This time I hesitated. I thought about shooting it, because Darren was just a kid who didn't know anything. I could've done something to get its attention maybe, before it was too late, but I took too long deciding. If it's anyone's fault, it's mine. Don't even think about putting the blame on yourself, because I won't let you."

He's right, Blaine thought. Andrew could've fired a single burst, maybe closer to the crawler's middle and away from the limbs, where it would've had less of a chance of nicking Darren. He could've done something to try and get the crawler's attention to draw it away. It'd been Andrew who'd been closest to begin with; the fact that Blaine had seemingly pushed Darren over the edge afterwards was meaningless if it was Andrew who'd let it happen in the first place.

Blaine lowered his eyes and moved his hand to Andrew's arm, sliding it up over the shoulder, up the back of Andrew's neck and into his hair. He was still a little in awe of the fact that he could touch Andrew this way now, that Andrew wouldn't jerk away, but looked back at him with eyes full of affection.

"There's something I want to give you," Andrew said suddenly.

233

"Let's call it a birthday present."

He shuffled back and sat on his heels, rolling up one of his sleeves. When Blaine saw the silver and gold bracelet, his breath hitched in his throat.

"Andrew, you can't—I can't accept—"

"You can," Andrew insisted.

He took Blaine's hand, rolling up the sleeve of Blaine's jacket, and slid the bracelet onto Blaine's wrist, the same bracelet he'd pried from his sister's corpse. The bracelet was a bit too narrow at the widest part of Blaine's hand, but with a little push it cleared the resistance and rested perfectly in place.

Blaine thought it should have been a bit morbid, but it was strangely the nicest thing anyone had ever done for him. It was a reassuring weight on his person that he knew he would cherish forever, would wear proudly.

"I shot her, you know," Andrew reminded him quietly. "I killed her like she was just another one of those mindless ghouls, nothing but a threat."

Blaine curled his fingers into a fist, his heart clenching at the hollow tone of Andrew's voice. He'd told Andrew afterwards that Andrew had freed her, but it never really hit him, never really stuck in his brain. Andrew had *shot* his sister. He'd emptied a whole fucking mag into her without even knowing.

"Darren took that responsibility away from you, Blaine. He killed himself because he knew what he would become and what we'd have to do. It was incredibly brave of him."

Blaine shivered from a sudden gust of wind, and Andrew lowered Blaine's sleeve over the bracelet before returning to lie over him, protecting him as much as he could from the cold. Blaine felt Andrew's heat like when he used to walk into a warm cafe out of a storm. It was welcoming and comforting and Blaine did feel a lot better when Andrew put things into perspective like that.

"I watch you," Blaine admitted, sliding his hands between their bodies to keep them warm. "When we're out there. I've always watched you more than the others. If Elizabeth had accused me of what she did you, I'd be guilty."

A corner of Andrew's mouth twitched. "I know. If it wasn't for years of training, I would be too. Sometimes I still am." Andrew cupped his face. "Don't linger on it. It won't help, trust me, I know. It's okay to be happy, Blaine. Such moments are rare nowadays. I think... I know Luke would want me to be happy. Don't you think Darren would want you to be happy?"

Of course Darren would. He always tried to lighten Blaine's burden and make things better if Blaine seemed sombre. Because they were close in age, the two youngest, and had to stick together.

Blaine was twenty now. Darren hadn't even made it to nineteen. He wondered when Darren's birthday was.

He'd been doing a good job not crying, even when Andrew had given him the bracelet, but a single tear escaped then. That's when Andrew kissed him.

Chapter 27

Happy Birthday

15:36

Everything else in Blaine's mind sort of flew out as Andrew's lips touched his, because no matter how often they'd done this, it was still so wonderfully new. Andrew flicked his tongue to the inside of Blaine's upper lip, making Blaine's body pulse with excitement, and he gave in with a mix of reluctance and eagerness.

His hands seemed to move themselves from between their bodies, past Andrew's hip, under his coat where he felt the warmth of Andrew's skin on his palm. He curled his fingers inward a little, feeling the muscles of Andrew's back as he pulled him close.

Andrew's feet made a scraping sound against the roof as he slid closer, slotting his leg between Blaine's and pushing their groins together. Blaine felt another jolt of lust shoot through him, and he jerked his hips upward before he could stop himself. Andrew grunted and gave a forceful shove back.

"Is it okay if we do this here?" Andrew asked breathlessly. "I know it's cold and a bit in the open."

"Yeah, yeah, it's fine." It wasn't like there were many people left alive in the world who could come spy on them. Blaine thought suddenly of his dream, where they fucked in a sun-speckled park, and laughed deliriously as Andrew kissed him again.

This time it was messy, heated, and a little bit desperate. His tongue dove inside and claimed Blaine's mouth, their lips sliding over each other and making Blaine's head spin. Blaine arched his back without thinking, wanting more of Andrew's touch on him. When Andrew pulled away, his lips were glistening with saliva, and Blaine felt the cold wind passing over his equally wet chin.

"There's something I wanna do for you. As another birthday present."

Blaine nodded, curious to see what Andrew had in mind.

Andrew's mouth twitched in a smile before he leaned forward to kiss him again. He sucked at Blaine's bottom lip, drawing it out, and he gave a slow roll of his hips, grinding against Blaine in a way that dragged his warm thigh over the growing bulge in Blaine's jeans. Blaine trembled at the touch, and Andrew kept it up, kept rocking into him languidly, before he gave up kissing Blaine's lips for sucking his earlobe. Blaine wrapped both arms around him and clutched him closer, embracing the heat between them.

Andrew's hand went between their bodies, fiddling with the button of Blaine's jeans. Blaine's heart raced when he thought he knew exactly what Andrew wanted to do for him.

He gasped at the shock of cold to his cock once Andrew pulled it out, then tilted his head so he could look down and see. It was usually pale, only a shade pinker than the rest of him with a subtle brown tinge at the base, but in the frigid air it had started to turn a bit red. The blue veins twisting around the shaft began to look purple.

Andrew slid down, until his face hovered between Blaine's legs. As Andrew brushed his pursed lips over the reddened shaft, as he licked from base to tip and suckled the head teasingly, as he pressed kiss after kiss into the curved underside, Blaine thought he was going to burst right then, all over Andrew's face. He took deep breaths, trying not to focus too hard on the movements of Andrew's lips and tongue. When Andrew finally took him in, pushing himself up a little for a better angle to sink down, Blaine let out a long exhalation and struggled for control.

The feeling crept up on him slowly. At first it was numbing desire and bliss as Andrew sucked his cock with beautifully hollowed cheeks. Blaine buried his fingers in Andrew's hair, which was soft despite not being washed in so long, and Andrew kept his hands on Blaine's hips, holding him down. It was as though Blaine was riding a wave of pleasure, working his way steadily up to the crest.

As Andrew sped up, wrapped a hand around the base and moaned enough to send the sound buzzing through Blaine's skin, the feeling made itself known entirely. A soothing serenity, a peaceful calm, right at the top of the wave. Blaine's chest heaved with each breath. Warmth radiated from his groin, shooting outward to the rest of his body, and nothing else mattered. There *was* nothing else, just the pleasure, the calming ecstasy that Blaine could feel in his bones.

If he could ride the wave there, at the top, forever, he would have. He tried to, but a swirl of hot tongue around the tip undid him. He put his fist in his mouth and bit his knuckles to muffle his scream. He came long and hard, squeezing his eyes shut so tightly that colours danced behind his eyelids as he shot his orgasm into Andrew's mouth.

He didn't come down right away. Even as he felt Andrew tuck him back in, and heard the slapping flesh of Andrew getting off quickly beside him, he felt deeply sated. It was like sliding down a mountain in slow motion, and he was still very much near the top. Not in regards to pleasure, but in serene, numb satisfaction.

"We can go back whenever you're ready," Andrew said a few minutes later. "The others are still discussing whether or not we should leave for Haven."

Blaine straightened his clothes and picked up his rifle. He could feel the edge of the silver bracelet against his wrist, and knew it'd be a while before he'd get used to the feeling, but he liked it, liked having a token of Andrew on his person.

"Yeah. Let's go."

15:50

Everyone else was still in the living room when they returned. Helen crossed the room as soon as she caught sight of Blaine and brought him into a hug.

"Everything okay?" she asked.

Blaine wanted to push her away, embarrassed by the display of comfort, but endured the embrace so as not to hurt her feelings. "Yeah, everything's fine."

He tried to step away as politely as possible, taking a seat on the floor against the wall beside Andrew. He was confused when Andrew started pulling his arm, dragging him closer, then surprised when he ended up between Andrew's legs, sitting back to front.

A pleasant surprise though. Andrew rarely showed affection even in private, so it was nice that he was finally choosing to acknowledge their relationship around the others.

"We've decided on taking a vote," Tim said. He sat with arm securely around Sarah, while Elizabeth was chewing her nails in the dimly lit corner behind them. "There's only eight of us now, so if it ends up even, I suppose we'll split off into two groups."

Blaine could tell by the look on everyone's faces that nobody liked the thought of that.

"Are we all ready to vote now or should we take a day to think about it?" Tim asked.

"I'm ready to vote now," Elizabeth said.

"So are we," Elliot said for him and Jessica.

Everyone else nodded. Blaine hesitated. He would miss his home and his familiar bed, but they were just objects now. It wasn't the time for being sentimental. If Merrick had taught him anything, it had been to do what was necessary to survive. He nodded as well.

"Alright. All for going to Haven, raise your hand," Tim said.

It was unanimous. Elizabeth was the last to raise her hand, but then all eight were in agreement.

"How about that. It's decided then," Tim declared. "We'll take tomorrow to get our things together, figure out the travelling arrangements, then, day after that, we'll head out."

"Sounds good to me," Helen said.

All were in agreement again. They were going to Haven.

DAY 100
11:34

For the first time in what felt like a while, Andrew was looking forward to the future. He didn't have much to pack himself, so he devoted most of his time to helping where he was needed. Mostly it consisted of watching Blaine pick up and put down various things in his room.

"The duvet has to go for sure, because even though there'll be beds, that duvet has kept me warm for years, and I refuse to—"

"It's the same one Mary died under, you know."

"Oh, shut up, that's beside the point."

Andrew chuckled. Blaine rambled on, pointing at things, turning them over in his hand and furrowing his brow in contemplation.

"Don't you have anything?" Blaine turned to him and asked. "All you have is that one rucksack full of clothes that don't even fit you."

Andrew shrugged and looked at the bag between his feet. The clothes had stopped smelling like Luke long ago, but Andrew still felt a tug on his heart every time he thought too hard about where it had come from and how.

"They're Luke's things," he muttered. "I didn't take the time to go by my hotel room before I left. I just..."

"You don't have to say."

Andrew exhaled. He hadn't wanted to say.

"Did you not have a permanent home? Why were you in a hotel room?"

"I had a flat further away from the base, closer to the edge of the city, but I liked staying nearby after just getting back. I didn't really have much of value in it, though. Nothing I miss. I try not to develop attachments to things."

Blaine turned over the small box in his hand. "Oh."

"What's that thing?"

Blaine looked up. "This? It's a pinhole camera. I made it when I was younger."

"Hmm."

"I had a great digital one back at Paul's place. Couldn't take it in all the hurry, though. It was so sudden how everything happened. Well, Paul thought it made sense because of the quarantines and weird news reports. You should've seen him when they said people were gonna be able to pay to get out of here on those ships, he was absolutely furious. I thought about trying to sneak onto one before I remembered—"

"What else do you think you should take?" Andrew asked, springing off the bed.

Blaine blinked, then looked around one final time. At last, he sighed. "I don't know. I might just not take anything, you know? It might be better to start over."

Andrew nodded. That was the reason why he was looking forward to moving on, after all. Starting over with his new family, building a new life in a new home, putting Luke out of his mind to make more room for Blaine.

"Yeah," he said. "Get new things and all. Start from the bottom up."

Blaine took a few steps forward to rub his knuckles over Andrew's chest and grin. "You should get new things too. Maybe some clothes that actually fit you."

"I planned on it."

"I was thinking a hat as well, to keep those big ears of yours warm."

Andrew was sure to keep his face as blank as he could. Despite the fact that the statement was meant to be playful, he worked to keep the pain from showing on his face.

"I was worried about them when we were out in the cold yesterday," Blaine continued, seemingly determined to get some sort of reaction. "I thought to myself, 'poor Dumbo's ears are gonna fall right off if they get any redder.'"

Andrew snorted. "Dumbo. Of course."

Blaine looked pleased with that response at least. "I figured you'd rather be an elephant than a brownie. Or would you prefer Big-Ears, Big-Ears?"

"No," Andrew said too quickly.

"That's what I thought. Dumbo. Anyway, we could all use some more clothes."

Andrew sighed. *Dumbo, huh?*

"I'll get you some soon."

Blaine's brow raised in surprise. "*You* will?"

"Yeah. A big coat, gloves, a scarf. And that chest holster, for your pistols, like I said I'd get."

"You don't have to get me any more birthday presents, you know. The ones you gave me were more than enough."

Andrew took hold of Blaine's wrist and traced the pattern in the bracelet. "They won't be presents. They'll be just because."

"Yeah? When's your birthday anyway?"

"Not 'til January. Plenty of time to think of a good gift."

Blaine rolled his eyes. "Please. I'll give a better birthday blow job than you ever could."

Andrew gave in. He let himself smile. "Now that I'm eager to see."

Suddenly Blaine looked devious, a mischievous spark lighting his brown eyes in a way Andrew had never seen them look before, a way that made his pulse quicken just a bit. A corner of his mouth pulled up in a wicked grin.

"I admit you're a bit larger than I've tried to take before but I'm sure a bit of practice will help," he purred.

Blaine lowered his hands to the button of Andrew's jeans and occupied his mouth with a kiss. *Oh God, are we doing this right now?* Andrew wondered.

Blaine dropped to his knees, and a bolt of heat went straight to where he was pushing his face against the denim, right over Andrew's dick.

That's a yes.

"It's alright if we take a break from packing, isn't it?" Blaine asked innocently. Andrew nodded before Blaine even finished the question. "Brilliant."

Andrew sank his fingers into Blaine's hair and parted his feet a bit more. For the first time in what felt like a while, he was looking forward to the future, but right now he didn't want the moment to ever end.

If you enjoyed this story, you can sign up for a free membership at
ForbiddenFiction and discuss it with other readers
and the author at the *Love Is for the Living* story page
at http://forbiddenfiction.com/story/NK1-1.000217.

We do our best to proof all our work, but if you spot a text error we missed,
please let us know via our website Contact Form
at http://forbiddenfiction.com/contact.

Author's Notes

This work is the result of many hours spent researching, copious amounts of tea, and the efforts of merciless editors. It's a story that challenged me but that I loved delving into, often with horror movie soundtracks playing in the background.

Like most horror/ sci-fi/ fantasy enthusiasts, one of the types of fiction I greedily consumed growing up was anything with zombies. Luckily for people like me, the zombie theme has been and continues to be on the rise. I remember seeing films like *28 Days Later*, *Dawn of the Dead*, and the *Resident Evil* series in theatres when I was in elementary school. Later there were video games—*Red Dead Redemption*, *Left 4 Dead*, *Dead Island*, *Killing Floor*, and so many more.

Seeing a friend's work of fan art brought to the surface (rather intensely) my old desire to write my own apocalyptic story, complete with zombies. As is usually the case when it comes to creative work, it was an enjoyable struggle to construct the world in which Blaine and Andrew live after the Outbreak. I knew from the beginning that I wanted more than just one type of zombie roaming my wasteland, and took inspiration from my experiences with video games to create the mutations, combining characteristics I'd encountered before with new ones from my imagination.

I also knew I wanted my survivors to find another group to join, a sanctuary to set out for in order to get their happy ending. Therefore Haven is the setting of the next book, *Love in the Ruins*, where Blaine and Andrew's story continues.

—Nick Kinsley

243

Albion Rising

When the Outbreak came to England, things went very badly, very quickly. The virus mutated the infected into violent, twisted cannibals, devoid of all humanity. Those who remained free of the infection became prey, forced to live in hiding from their ravenous, all-but-dead neighbors.

Blaine, a university student, and Andrew, a Royal Marine, would never have met if not for the infected destroying the people they loved and driving them from their homes. After a near-fatal encounter on the motorway, the young men search for family and safety together.

Andrew and Blaine find refuge from the infected with other survivors, but must create refuge from loss and loneliness with each other. Surrounded by death, the two men give themselves a reason to go on living in the love they share.

About the Author

Nicholas Kinsley has been writing since a very young age. After going through school focused on computer science, he discovered that he would rather be a professional author. He grew up with few friends and a love of books, and hopes to create worlds in which others can find enjoyment. Kinsley currently lives in Maryland.

ForbiddenFiction Works by Nicholas Kinsley:

Behind Locked Doors

Driven

Albion Rising 1: Love Is for the Living

About the Publisher

ForbiddenFiction.com is a publisher devoted to writing that breaks the boundaries of original erotic fiction. Our stories combine intense sexuality with quality writing. Stories at ForbiddenFiction.com not only arouse readers through sensations, but also engage them emotionally and mentally through storytelling as well-crafted as the sex is hot.

ForbiddenFiction.com is also designed to be a social reading environment. You'll have fun even if just reading the latest post each day, yet you will have the chance for so much more. Readers and authors can be part of ongoing discussions of specific works and individual authors as well as more general topics.

Sign up for a FREE Membership today at ForbiddenFiction.com